David's pregnant.

He's always wanted to h   g   ...p...ier
for the past two years has been a great adventure. There'd
even been a plan to start looking into adoption and turn
their family of three into four.

But now there's a bump, and David doesn't know what to do.
He's spent years escaping the grip of his own body and
burying the past—but there's no way he can hide from his
history if he lets the bump get any bigger. It's not just his
baby; it's also his breakdown.

He doesn't know if he can do this.

BUMP

Matthew J. Metzger

A NineStar Press Publication

Published by NineStar Press
P.O. Box 91792,
Albuquerque, New Mexico, 87199 USA.
www.ninestarpress.com

Bump

Copyright © 2018 by Matthew J. Metzger
Cover Art by Natasha Snow Copyright © 2018
Edited by Elizabetta McKay

Printed in the USA
First Edition
November, 2018

Print ISBN: 978-1-949909-18-0

Also available in eBook, ISBN: 978-1-949909-10-4

Warning: This book contains homophobic and transphobic language and actions, graphic violence, and some discussion of historical suicide.

With all my thanks to Sophie, Ali, and Omar.

Your advice has been invaluable, and this book simply wouldn't exist without you.

Chapter One

"THANK YOU," DAVID said. "Yes. I'll check my diary and make an appointment. Yes. Thank you. Goodbye."

He hung up and—very calmly—dropped the phone out of the car window. Wound the window back up. Reversed a little to give himself room to wriggle out from behind the BMW in front.

And—just as calmly—made sure to run over the phone with the rear tyre as he drove off.

His palms were sweaty on the steering wheel. His heart was thundering low in his stomach. David hadn't had a panic attack in nearly ten years, but the feeling was as familiar as ever—the creeping darkness at the edges of his vision, the hyperawareness of his own skin, the tightness across his ribs like he was having an asthma attack. He tightened his grip. He needed to get control of himself. He was thirty-two years old. He could—would—handle this like the responsible adult that he was.

He refused to break down screaming at the wheel of a car, for God's sake.

Thankfully, the phone call had happened just around the corner from his usual parking spot. He slid the car into a free space and bent forward to rest his forehead on the wheel. He raked a deep breath in, held it for a count of ten, and let it out slowly.

All right.

So the test result was more or less his worst nightmare. And he'd probably be having nightmares too.

But it could have been worse. Practically speaking. It was a fixable nightmare. He could fix it. It didn't matter right now. He didn't have to deal with it this minute. He could talk to Ryan tonight, make an appointment in the morning—just not the one he'd promised the nurse on the results line—and fix everything.

Slowly, his heart rate started to come down out of the rafters. The tight band around his chest didn't ease, but it got a little easier to breathe.

"Fix it tomorrow," he mumbled.

He straightened, squared his shoulders, and opened the door.

David never bothered trying to park right near the school. It was always a melee of mums and Mitsubishis, and he was terrified of someone's kid running into the road right under his bumper. It was cool outside, threatening rain. The short walk helped clear the rest of the panic out of his head, and refocus. Ava didn't need to know about it. Everything was fine, all happy and normal, no problems whatsoever, nothing.

The school gates were crowded as always, but David had an advantage. In a sea of white mums, he stood out a mile. He leaned against the metal fence, peering through the railings, until he caught sight of two frizzy baubles of hair stuck out either side of a pair of wide, searching eyes.

He waved, and the eyes lit up.

"David!"

"Sorry, excuse me, sorry, thanks, sorry—"

He wrestled his way to the front just in time to stoop and catch Ava as she hurled herself at his thighs. He hoisted her up and turned to carry her through the crowd. She babbled in his ear about finger painting, pizza, and a new gold star on her behaviour chart, and then clung obstinately when he dropped her to the pavement again.

"Only babies need carrying during the daytime," David said. "You're not a baby anymore, are you?"

It had been an infallible obedience tool ever since she started school. She let go with a sulky expression and jammed her sticky hand into his.

"Can we have pizza?" she repeated.

"We'll ask Daddy."

"Daddy never says yes to pizza," Ava said mournfully, in the same tone of voice one might use to say someone had died.

"Daddy doesn't eat pizza," David corrected. "That doesn't mean we can't have pizza sometimes. You had pizza on your birthday, remember?"

She brightened up. "It was Jamie's birthday today!"

"That's nice."

"So we can have pizza for Jamie!"

"I don't think it works like that."

Her buoyant mood was calming, even if Ava was more of a hurricane than anything else. She was five and three-quarters (never just five) and brimming over with energy. She didn't even have the decency to get tired by seven o'clock like normal five-year-olds. She went to bed at the same time as her parents—and usually rocketed back out of it again by six o'clock the next morning.

Still, her effusive enthusiasm helped. There was nothing to panic about. He could fix things, and everything would be back to normal next month anyway.

"Tell me about your new gold star," he said as she scrambled up into the back seat. "Do you need help with your seatbelt?"

"No," she said, giving him a look definitely inherited from her mum. "I'm five. And three-quarters. I can do my own seatbelt."

"Show me," David said.

To be fair, she could. Albeit with a lot of faffing about. Once he heard the click, he promised a new star for her chart at home and closed the door. In the short time it took him to walk around the car and get into the driver's seat, she'd started a whole new deluge of noise masquerading as conversation, all about how rainbows were made.

David's chest slowly unlocked as he drove home to the background noise of a five-year-old on rainbows and a fifty-year-old on the radio. He could hand her off to Ryan once they were back, lock himself in the bathroom, and have a cry in the shower under the pretence of a long, hard day at work. Maybe even have a soak in the bath. He felt bad palming Ava off on her dad, especially on a Thursday, but—

Christ.

He just didn't have the energy. Not after that phone call.

Home was a roomy bungalow with a long, narrow back garden, a decent view over some fields, and the ugliest bay windows in the front David had ever seen. According to the locals, it was in a village near Wakefield. According to everyone else—including David, who wasn't even from Yorkshire and was therefore regarded as an immigrant—it *was* in Wakefield. The rest of the street was occupied by elderly white people called Gerald and Betty whose lives revolved around gardening, *Antiques Roadshow*, and Women's Institute bake sales.

Ryan and Ava had been acceptable when they first moved in. Cute toddlers were tickets to acceptance in these sorts of villages, David suspected. And he'd found out the other week that half of them thought Ryan was ex-army, which meant all the old blokes liked him by default. But when David moved in, that popularity had taken a definite dive.

David didn't really care. He was from Salford. He could think of a lot worse than some tuts and disapproving scowls from ninety-six-year-old Pamela next door. She was there, peering out from behind her lace curtains, as he pulled into the drive. He waved, and the curtain dropped.

"We're going to be nice and quiet," he told Ava as he opened the door to let her out of the car. "Daddy went to see Nathan this morning, so he might still be tired."

Ava nodded, dragging her bag out after her.

"If Daddy's asleep, can we have pizza before he wakes up?" she chirped as David unlocked the front door.

"Nope, Daddy will want dinner too."

"But—"

"Aha!"

Ryan's booming voice bounced down the hall towards them as David opened the door. Ava squealed and shot into the kitchen, jumping up at her dad like she hadn't seen him in a thousand years rather than eight hours.

"Hello, my little star!" He planted a loud kiss on her cheek and grinned up at David. "What's this? Two stars! Well, well, well. What have I done to deserve this, eh?"

Then he smiled, a brilliant flash of white streaking across his face like torchlight. And David—relaxed.

That was all it took sometimes. Just for Ryan to flash him that megawatt grin, and all the fight seemed to drain out of David's body. Even the internal fight. Ryan had that— that air about him. When he smiled, when he laughed, when he was happy, it was like the whole world had to be happy as well. It was like everything faded away and was replaced with a warm contentment, a feeling of security, the sense that no matter what happened, he had Ryan with him.

He hadn't fallen in love with Ryan at first. He'd fallen in love with that smile.

In a lot of ways, Ryan was a ball-ache of a boyfriend. Complete slob. Rap fan. Thought curries every night were compatible with a sex life. David had become a de facto stepdad not three months into their relationship from the sheer number of times Ryan simply forgot which weekend he was supposed to have Ava, and had had to ring David on his way home to swing by the school and pick her up.

But Ryan made him feel—

Warm.

And David could use warm. Unceremoniously, he hoisted Ava up by the armpits, plonked her on the kitchen tiles, and sat in Ryan's lap looping both arms around his shoulders and burrowing his face shamelessly into that thick neck.

"Oh, hello," Ryan said with a chuckle, sliding a hand around David's back. The other landed on his knee and squeezed. "Does this mean Ava's in the naughty corner, or—"

"I'm not!" she objected loudly.

"No," David said, unpeeling himself with a sigh. He pressed his nose briefly to Ryan's cheek. He still smelled faintly of hospital, and it made David's stomach churn uncomfortably. "Just a shi—bad day. Are you feeling all right?"

They didn't usually have Ava during the week, but Marianne had been away at a conference. And Thursdays were Ryan's bad days. Physiotherapy. Usually, a Thursday with Ava meant *David* had a Thursday with Ava, and Ryan beat himself up about it.

Which meant today's phone call had been doubly... inconvenient.

"Yeah, I'm fine," Ryan said, and for once, he looked it. "Wasn't a bad session. Already had a kip. Go and have a bath or something if you're knackered."

David kissed his jaw, and had the back of his neck caught for a proper one—Ryan seemed to think kisses anywhere on his face except his mouth were grossly offensive—before he was let go. He climbed off, hefted Ava back into his spot, and made his way to the bathroom.

He was tempted to—

No. David shook the thought off immediately. It would be possible to fix everything so Ryan would never know, but it would be unfair. Bitterly unfair. It involved him too, much as ultimately it came down to David. He would have to tell Ryan.

But—

He couldn't say anything in front of Ava. She wouldn't understand, and she'd only get upset if they tried to explain it to her. She'd be underfoot all evening, and by the time they got to go to bed and talk in peace, Ryan would be shattered. This sort of thing wasn't for Thursdays—and especially not Thursdays with an added Ava.

David swallowed as he stripped and switched on the water. He looked down and saw nothing. Nothing at all. There was nothing there.

There would be nothing there.

He'd call the clinic tomorrow and book an appointment.

And then he'd tell Ryan.

At...some point.

Chapter Two

DAVID TURNED THE engine off, rolled his head back against the rest, and sighed deeply.

Thank fuck it was Friday.

And thank fuck Marianne had gotten back from her conference this morning. So no Ava. He felt bad for thinking it, but he needed the reprieve.

He'd spent his entire lunch break trying to get hold of someone at the clinic, only to get a belligerent receptionist who clearly thought anyone trying to use their services was scum, and had rudely informed him he needed a GP referral. And getting in to see his GP on a Friday afternoon was never going to happen, so he was stuck until next week. Even then, he was stuck until the referral was passed through and the clinic bothered to issue him an appointment, which could be weeks, and—

David swallowed and inhaled deeply. Held it against the tightening band of fear in his chest.

And exhaled.

The matter would hold for a couple of weeks, he supposed. But he wanted it to be over. He wanted to spend his weekend safe in the knowledge that by the next one, when they'd have Ava back, it would be over, and he could enjoy being a stepdad and feigning ignorance of Ryan's rules.

Appointment, week off to recover, back to life. Like nothing had ever happened. Just like last time.

That had been the plan.

He was disturbed from his study of the backs of his own eyelids by a gentle, familiar creak. When he opened his eyes and lifted his head, Ryan was watching him from the open doorway. Frowning. David mustered up a tired smile and got out of the car.

"C'mere."

He stooped for the offered kiss. Ryan tugged on his belt, locking him close.

"Pamela next door will see."

"Bugger Pamela next door."

"Eurgh, no, thanks."

Ryan snorted with laughter. "Bloody literal-minded, you are. C'mon. I've already called for a curry. Was planning on—well, making some plans with you, but you looked wiped out. Let's stick a film on and have a good cuddle in front of the telly."

David's stomach curled up tight again. The warmth was back. Putting his head in Ryan's lap and dozing off sounded like heaven. Ryan always put his feet up on the footstool, and David would stretch out along the rest of the sofa. He'd eventually fall asleep, and Ryan would switch over to the sports channels once the film was over, and they'd stay like that until some loud ad for a late-night porn channel woke David up again.

It sounded perfect.

But—

"What plans?"

"Doesn't matter, we can hold it until tomorrow," Ryan said. "Get yourself inside."

David sighed, rolling his neck tiredly as he stepped into the house. It was warm and smelled of antibacterial wipes and air freshener. Which, given David did all the cleaning, was unusual at best.

"Spill something?"

"Discovered what Ava's been doing with her broccoli."

"Oh, God." David wrinkled his nose. "Did it walk out of wherever she hid it?"

"Near enough. I think I slaughtered a micro-civilisation behind the TV stand."

David mock-gagged, swallowing hard when a real rush of nausea followed it. He sat on the ottoman to remove his shoes—and blinked when Ryan leaned forward in his chair and tapped David's knee.

"Hey," he said quietly. "What's up?"

David bit his lip.

"You seemed a bit upset yesterday. And you're not yourself tonight. Coming down with something?"

Well, that was one way of putting it.

"I'm fine," David lied. "Just been a really long week. And a lot of talking to arseholes."

"Sure?"

"Yeah. Look, let's not talk about it. Let's—let's talk about whatever plan you wanted to talk about while we wait for that curry, then go for the film?"

Ryan looked sceptical. "I really don't think you're up for it."

David shrugged. "Try me."

"How about I tell you what I wanted to discuss, and then we shelve it for the morning?"

"Deal. After I change and get this lot in the wash."

"Only if you keep those arms on show. I'm liking this new super-vet look. Latest summer trend?"

David rolled his eyes as he pushed himself to his feet and headed back through the bungalow to their bedroom. He was a vet, one of four in the surgery. He'd only been back on the surgery rota since last week, after a long period of time off in the wake of the car accident. So he was back in short-sleeved shirts—and Ryan was liking it a bit too much.

Changing was a welcome relief. He took a long shower, the hot water beating on his neck like it could beat away the stress. He even slumped down on Ryan's shower chair, too tired to stand all of a sudden. It took an age for him to muster up the energy to emerge, and when he did, he shamelessly stole Ryan's pyjama bottoms and didn't bother with a shirt. If Ryan wanted arms, he could have them. For good measure, David stole his hideous orange bedsocks as well—a pair of fluffy obscenities from Ryan's mother that David was sure had been a punishment for having another man move into his house after the divorce.

But they were warm and comfy, and who cared about the colour? David was certainly no fashion aficionado, and if Ryan wanted bare arms to ogle, then he could put up and shut up about the socks.

The curry had arrived by the time he shuffled out into the rest of the house. When he followed the smell into the living room and found a bowl of rice and peas to split, a lump formed in his throat. Ryan didn't even like rice and peas. He thought coconut milk was the devil's work and usually refused to have anything to do with it.

"Thanks," David mumbled, taking the bowl and scraping half of the contents into his foil container of chicken biryani. To hell with what should and shouldn't be eaten together. He was going to have whatever he wanted this week.

"Feet, please?"

David chuckled at the familiar request, putting the bowl down. He heaved the footstool into the right place and lifted Ryan's feet onto it before settling back down.

"Thanks. Feeling better after that marathon shower?"

"Yeah. Might just be coming down with a cold."

"Mm." Ryan didn't sound convinced.

"So, what did you want to make plans about?"

Ryan grunted around a mouthful of curry-slathered naan bread and gestured at the table. Leaflets were stacked under the takeaway bag, and David edged them out carefully.

And stopped.

"Oh."

Oh hell.

Ryan made an unhealthy wrenching noise and said, "I picked them up on Monday from the council offices, but I didn't want Ava to see them until we'd talked properly. They have an information evening coming up that we should go to."

Fostering and Adoption: Information for Potential Parents.

They'd talked about it just before David moved in. Ryan didn't want Ava to be an only child. He'd asked...questions. Questions David hadn't been happy about him asking, and the original conversation turned into a blistering row, but they'd eventually come back around to it from a better angle. Come to agreements. Come to vague plans...that apparently, Ryan now wanted to put into action.

And suddenly, David's decision didn't look so easy.

Because he *did* want kids, when he stripped back all of the mess. If he pretended the world wasn't crap, and he wouldn't be judged for it; if he pretended he hadn't buried the desire under an avalanche of pressure that he couldn't want children because of who he was—he did.

Ryan had one. And wanted more. Being Ava's stepfather, David sort of had one. But she had two parents already. When they'd talked about it, he agreed it would be nice to have one of their own too. And seeing as how having one the way nature intended—as Ryan's mother would undoubtedly have put it—wasn't going to work, they'd jumped straight to adoption.

"It would still be ours, if we adopted a little kid or a baby," Ryan had said. "We'd love them just the same. And it's not like we're going to be the types with conditions on their kids. We're hardly going to go throwing bibles at Ava if she decides she likes girls—"

"Given she said she's marrying Lizzy from her swimming club last week, I think you're onto something."

"—then I think this is the right thing to do. But not Lizzy. I met her dad at that birthday party last month; you've never met a bigger bore in your life..."

Christ, how could David have forgotten that conversation?

He felt sick. Slowly, he leaned over and put his tray of biryani back on the table.

"David?"

He'd—forgotten. Insane as it sounded, his panic had made him forget. Ryan wouldn't feel what David felt. Ryan's reaction would be one hundred percent different. They'd have to talk about it. At length. They'd argue. Probably have a proper row and have to come back to it later. And then they'd have to make a decision together.

Because if David just made the choice for them—if David just told Ryan what was going to happen, then Ryan would never forgive him.

"Hey."

A large hand smoothed up David's back. David hunched forward, burying his head in his hands.

"David? What's wrong?"

"Fuck," he croaked.

"I thought you wanted this," Ryan said, very slowly and very carefully. "We agreed—"

"I do."

The hand paused.

"Then what's—"

"I got the test results."

He just blurted it out. Ryan's stroking stopped. The hand dropped. The arm snaked around his waist and pulled, and David was hauled against a strong shoulder.

"Tell me."

Ryan's voice was brittle. And David knew the sound from his own.

Scared.

Like him.

Only Ryan didn't have anything to be afraid of. Ryan would be happy. Only David had to be scared here, only David had to be unhappy, only David had to tear himself apart. Because—

"I'm pregnant."

Chapter Three

SILENCE.

David ground the heels of his hands into his eyes and tried not to cry. He could hear the cogs turning in Ryan's head. He could feel the pause in the room like a physical thing.

Then Ryan sat forward.

For a brief moment, the arm around David's waist slipped away—then he heard the clink of Ryan setting down his plate, and the arm dragged higher and pulled.

"Come here."

David collapsed against Ryan's side, feeling exhausted. He wasn't much of a cuddler. He wasn't really all that comfortable with being touched at all. They had to compromise pretty heavily—but at that moment, David ached for it. He looped both arms around Ryan's neck and shamelessly clung, pressing his face against the cotton of Ryan's T-shirt and dragging in his scent through a long, choking breath.

"There you go," Ryan murmured, rubbing a hand up and down David's back in heavy swipes. "It's all right. It's— bloody mind-blowing, I mean—Christ. But—yeah. Let's— let's not have any attacks, yeah?"

David coughed a bitter laugh. "Bit late for that."

Ryan squeezed, then twisted his head to kiss David's scalp.

"When did you find out?" he asked softly.

"Yesterday."

"And you're sure?"

"Yes. Blood—blood work confirmed it."

"Right."

David disengaged, scrubbing at his face. "I'm sorry. I should have told you Thursday but—"

"It's all right," Ryan repeated. "I don't think one day is much of a problem. It's—Christ. Pregnant. You're—Jesus."

David snorted wetly.

"Pregnant," Ryan repeated dumbly. His face didn't seem to know what to do with itself. His hand ghosted up to start rubbing David's back again. "A baby. Bloody hell. I thought—I thought you couldn't?"

"Yeah, well, that's obviously how we got here," David said waspishly. "Clearly I can."

"But how? I mean, don't take my head off, but you've not been exactly, uh..."

David shot him a venomous look. "Finish that sentence at your own risk."

"Um. Paying tampon tax?"

David narrowed his eyes. Ryan pointed to the bowl of rice and peas.

"I should get some immunity for that," he said.

"Fine."

"So, how's it happened?"

"Doctor reckons I must have started ovulating again—"

"In English."

David sighed, dropped his head back against the sofa. The three mouthfuls of curry he'd managed were sitting heavy and uncomfortable in his stomach, like they already knew they were sharing space.

"Since they lowered my T dose after the crash, the doctor reckons it must have stopped completely shutting down my—" He paused on the word. "—ovaries."

"But...well, yeah. No tampons."

David shrugged. "Clearly not. But either way, they've obviously spat out an egg. Add you, and...here I am."

The one place he'd never wanted to be again. The one place he'd had nightmares about for years. The one reason he'd kept fighting with the GP for so long to get it all removed.

And he'd kept losing. So, here he was.

"Hey." Ryan's other hand gripped his thigh and squeezed. "Talk to me."

"What's there to say?" David asked. "I'm pregnant."

"I'm a little lost." Ryan's voice was oddly soft. "When Marianne said she was pregnant, it was all joy and phone calls to our parents, and I knew what to say. Right now? I don't. Talk to me. Tell me what's going through your head."

David clenched his jaw.

"When they called with the results," he said, "the first thing I did was throw my phone out of the window and run it over."

Ryan winced.

"And then I got my old handset out of the kitchen drawer and fired it up and started looking at where the nearest abortion clinic was."

Ryan's face seemed to shiver. It half crumbled and then seemed to freeze, like he was trying not to cry.

"Right," he croaked.

"I called them today, and they're insisting on a GP referral," David ground out. "So I was going to book an appointment to see the doctor next week. And then you— you made me rice and peas, and got in a curry, and you've been looking at adoption leaflets, and now I don't know what to do anymore. I don't want to have a baby. But—" He gestured helplessly at the leaflets. "—I want to have a baby."

He wasn't allowed to want children. How many times had he heard that? And not just from other people, from people who called him confused or fucked up or a pervert or a freak, but from professionals. How many well-meaning counsellors had declared that he must be a girl after all, because girls wanted babies and boys didn't? How many times had his own desire to have kids been the thing used to stop him being David?

How long since he'd started lying and saying he'd never wanted them at all?

He did want a kid. He'd always wanted a kid, ever since he was small. He remembered being five and furious with his mum for not having another baby. Ryan having a kid had been a bonus rather than off-putting—and David liked being a stepdad, but there was always that slight distance between him and Ava. He wasn't Daddy; he was David. He was more of an uncle than her father. Maybe that would change as she got older and their relationship evolved, but for the moment? She was a short person who stayed in the same house every other weekend.

He wanted to be someone's dad.

But not like this.

"I want to have a kid, and I want it to be my kid, but I—I don't want to be pregnant. I don't want to be a mum. I don't think I can be pregnant."

Ryan let out a long breath. It shook in the middle, but his face gave nothing away anymore.

"Okay," he said softly. "What do you need from me?"

David blinked. "What?"

"What do you need to hear? Do you need to hear that it'll all be fine and we can sort this out, do you need my opinion, do you want it to rest all in your hands, what?"

David drew his feet up onto the cushions. Ryan tutted, but simply rested a hand on his bent knees and tugged them over into his lap. The twist made David slump more heavily against him. It wasn't exactly comfortable, but he couldn't bring himself to pull away.

"I want to know what you want," David said.

"Sure?"

"Yeah. If—if it were all up to you."

"It's not though."

"But if it were."

Ryan dropped his head, resting his cheek against David's scalp.

"Honestly?" he said. "I don't know. You know I want a kid with you. And the opportunity for the baby to be a part of you and me, just like Ava's part of Marianne and me, that's—yeah. I want that baby. There's a really big part of me wants to order in the champagne."

David closed his eyes

"But at the same time, I love you. I love you more than I love that opportunity. If I didn't, I wouldn't have stayed with you. I never thought this was actually possible. I thought your shots had broken your, um, ability to do this. I wanted you—I still want you—more than I want the possibility of having a baby that belongs to the both of us like that. And if this is going to really fuck you up, then I don't want it. If this is going to destroy you, then I'd swap out the opportunity in a heartbeat. I'd take you to the clinic myself and then drag you to the adoption evening all the same. Still get a kid that way. Still get a kid with you that way."

David took a long, deep breath.

"So I don't know," Ryan whispered, stroking his knee. "If you can do it, I want it. But if it'll break you to try, then I don't."

David grimaced.

"I don't even know what I want," he admitted. "I want it, but the idea of having it makes me want to claw my own skin off."

Ryan huffed. "I'd chop your fingernails off."

David laughed wetly, then the crack in his chest expanded. "Oh, fuck," he ground out as his vision blurred.

"Oh, hey, come on, don't..."

The hug was firm and soothing. Ryan rocked a little, and David was torn between annoyance at himself for getting so irrationally upset, and settling into it and just having a good cry. He was violently opposed to crying if it wasn't in absolute privacy with Ryan. Or perhaps his mum, because he'd been crying on his mum for his whole life anyway, so she'd undoubtedly seen worse.

"Hey," Ryan murmured. "How far along?"

"I don't know," David croaked. "Can't be—can't be more than ten weeks or so." Ten weeks ago had been the first time since the crash. And if it had been before then, it would be months too late to change anything.

"All right," Ryan said. "So the cut-off point is around twenty-four, right?"

"Yeah?"

"You have a bit of time to think about it, then," Ryan pointed out. "We can talk it over a bit more when the shock's worn off, and make a proper decision."

"I want it," David mumbled, "but I don't think I can do it."

"For what it's worth, I think you can."

David slid an arm around Ryan's chest and squeezed.

"You're an explosive." The voice in his ear was warm and solid, firm like a hug in itself. "You've never taken any shit from anyone, and I don't think you're about to start now. You got that nurse sacked last year for being a cow, you didn't let my mum wreck things, and you took Jay all the way to court for his shit. I think you can do this. But if you decide you can't, then our plans don't really change. We go to that information evening anyway, and we just have a kid a different way. Okay?"

David pulled back, nudging his nose against Ryan's briefly for a second. Then he sighed and rolled his shoulders, sitting back and sliding his feet to the floor.

"Okay," he said. "Let's just—have our curry and watch that film. I don't really want to think about it right now."

"Deal," Ryan said, squeezing his arm before leaning forward to pick up their trays again. "We can talk it over a bit more when you're ready."

"Just us," David said. "I don't want anyone else to know."

"I won't tell, but I'm not taking responsibility if your mum finds out."

David cracked a wan smile and said he'd handle Mum.

Chapter Four

THEY DIDN'T TALK about it for the rest of the weekend.

Ryan was actually good at not talking about things without making it weird. David had always avoided cis partners before—the elephants that cis people could pack into a room when it came to gender could bring every related species off the endangered list—but Ryan had proved him wrong. Or at least a little over-sceptical.

He neither talked about it nor reacted to it either. There was no treating David like glass or trying to bring anything up. There were no dropped hints, no indication he'd found anything out at all. They spent the weekend as they usually did when Ava wasn't around—catching up with cleaning and DIY, enjoying being able to sit next to each other without abnormally sharp elbows and knees wedging their owner down between them, and—on Sunday—having a good, long lie in. Ryan snuggled. David put up with being snuggled. It was good.

The weekend bled away like nothing had happened, and so David got up for work on Monday morning in the exact same position he'd been in on Friday morning. No closer to solving the problem and feeling intensely sick.

At least there was no reason to try to hide the nausea. He just shot Ryan a dark look and disappeared into the bathroom to throw up.

"I'll get breakfast on, then, shall I?" Ryan called.

David stayed in the bathroom until the last possible moment. He wasn't sure how much of it was morning sickness and how much was anxiety. He'd had a heavy ball in his gut since getting the phone call, like he'd swallowed lead. And the vomiting didn't really help much.

Still, at least Ryan had dealt with pregnancy before. When David finally emerged, breakfast was just toast and juice. Getting dressed hadn't felt so much like hiding in years, but brushing his teeth took the edge off. By the time he popped back into the kitchen to collect a flask of coffee for the drive over to the surgery, he almost felt like himself again.

"You going to work?" Ryan asked.

"Yeah. Keep my mind off things."

Ryan hummed. "You sure you're all right?"

"Yeah. Won't do me any good to sit around here and worry about things."

"Okay. Drive safe."

He stooped for the customary kiss goodbye and headed out of the door. It was cold out, but the car didn't need de-icing. He set off feeling oddly calm and oddly jittery at the same time.

He'd wanted to have made up his mind by now.

He wanted not to want children. That would be the easiest fix. That would make everything simple. The first—and only—time this had happened, he'd only been sixteen years old, and it had been an easy decision. He'd been little more than a kid, nothing like a thirty-two-year-old man with a reliable partner, a good job, and a slice of the mortgage payments. The logic had been clear, and he'd followed it. He hadn't let himself feel anything else.

So this time felt...harder.

This time, the cold logic was as simple as it had been back then—only working in the opposite direction. This time, he was with someone who wanted a child too. They could afford a baby. And now, he had one, albeit a microscopic and barely formed one. No government hoops for fostering, no endless applications for adoption, no struggling with the social care system, none of it.

Logically, the answer was easy.

But since when did this have anything to do with logic?

He'd have to come out at work. Take time off. Go to hospital appointments and sit in waiting rooms entirely filled with women. Be called a mother, a woman, a wife, over and over and over. Hear the endless echo of misgendering bouncing off the walls like he hadn't for years. Get fat in all the wrong places. Grow. Take on a completely alien shape. Feel all the wrong hormones in his blood. Feel wrong. And that was all before actually giving birth to it.

He'd only felt right, really right, for the last five years or so. Less than a sixth of his life. And he didn't want to go back.

He'd be a mother.

He wanted to be a father, but if he let this run its course, he'd be a mother.

And could he recover from that? David wasn't sure. Ryan might call him explosive, but he didn't see inside David's head. He didn't know about all the times David had struggled just to get out of bed in the morning. He didn't know about the first time this had happened. He knew the statistics for men like David, but he didn't know that David was a part of those statistics.

David didn't like to remember. The last five years had been actual living. And he desperately didn't want to go back into that frame of mind, to revert to being that kind of person.

He arrived at the surgery early and sat drumming his fingers on the steering wheel in the staff parking area for a few minutes, frowning into the middle distance. He was torn. Get rid of something he'd wanted ever since he was a little kid, or keep it and destroy himself in the process?

Slowly, he slid his phone out of its cradle on the front of the stereo, and thumbed through the options for the doctors' surgery.

He took a deep breath.

Then dialled.

DAVID COULD BE a bastard when he wanted something. He knew the law. He knew the right words to say. He'd rubbed shoulders enough times with privileged, pedantic, middle-class students during his degree to know exactly the right mix of snotty attitude, humanity, and threatening undertones to squeeze a letter out of even the most transphobic of doctors.

So he walked out of the doctor's surgery that evening with a referral letter to the clinic in his hand—and walked straight into a familiar face pushing an unfamiliar buggy.

"David!"

"Hi, Vicky," he said, hastily stuffing the letter in his jacket pocket. "How, uh, how are you doing? How's Fred?"

Although David and Vicky Huang went back to university—they'd met at the judo club—he mostly saw her at the surgery these days. Vicky was the hapless owner of an enormous Persian cat called Fred. Confusingly, Fred was a girl. And a master escape artist. No matter what Vicky did to stop Fred from getting outside, it inevitably failed. So, Vicky would bring Fred in to be fixed, and David would immediately send them back home until the next litter of kittens were born. The cycle had been going for three years now, and David was convinced he would never actually be able to fix the damn thing.

"Oh, she's fine," Vicky gushed. "Four kittens! They were born last week."

"Oh, that's lovely."

"It was next door's ginger cat again."

"What a surprise."

"I don't suppose you'd like a kitten for your stepdaughter?"

"I think her mum would kill me," he said diplomatically.

"You should come round and see them sometime," she said.

"You can always call and arrange a home vis—"

"No, *you*. Not the vet!" She laughed at him like he'd said something hilarious. "I haven't seen you in ages. You've not been to judo in weeks! Honestly, pop round whenever you want."

"I'll think about it," he hedged.

"Do, don't think!" She punched him in the arm and then jiggled the buggy. "Sorry, got to run. Billy here needs his jabs. See you soon!"

He lifted a hand to wave as she rushed off into the surgery with her nephew, then slowly removed the letter from his pocket and smoothed it out again.

One more appointment.

And then everything would be back to normal.

Chapter Five

DAVID BOOKED INTO the clinic for Friday afternoon.

The intention was to go to work, leave at two, and spend the weekend and Monday holed up at home recovering. Ryan had pulled a face at the plan but not really said anything. And David's boss, Sonia, was a mother of six and grandmother of six hundred—judging by the pictures on the walls of her office—so bought the line about childcare issues hook, line, and sinker.

Unfortunately, he was woken at five o'clock on Friday morning by the intense need to throw up.

The nausea hadn't been too bad, but that morning was a different story. He barely made it to the toilet before vomiting, and the wrenching feeling of deep, devastating sickness triggered another wave of it. The smell then triggered a third, completing the cycle. The pain caused by not actually having anything in his stomach to reject didn't help.

Pressing his forehead to the cool porcelain, David groaned. Three o'clock couldn't come fast enough.

"Hey," Ryan called, and David heard the soft creak of the chair. "You all right?"

David gagged and spat a mouthful of bile into the bowl to join the rest. "No."

Ryan came into the bathroom, sleepy-eyed and his dreads still loose instead of bundled into their usual bun or ponytail. He rubbed at his eyes, then moved to the sink and wet a washcloth.

"Here."

The cool pressure on the back of David's neck was soothing. He closed his eyes.

"Morning sickness or anxiety?" Ryan murmured.

There was nobody else to know, so David admitted it. "Probably a bit of both."

"Tea and toast?"

"Please."

A hand squeezed his bicep, and then Ryan left him to it. David rubbed away a couple of tears, trying to blame them on the vomiting, even though he knew that wasn't true, and sat back on his heels. Three o'clock. He just had to get to three o'clock.

And yet there was something nagging at the back of his head. Something that told him to go back to bed for the rest of the day and not go out at all. Even to the clinic.

Especially to the clinic.

David flushed the toilet and gingerly stood up. One look in the mirror said that Sonia would kick him out of the surgery even if he did turn up for work. There were deep bags under his eyes, and his skin looked a strange mix of grey and brown. Hell, he looked dead—and David had been practising long enough to know what dead animals looked like.

"Great," he muttered.

He went back into their bedroom to steal Ryan's dressing gown and call Sonia. She was already up, wrestling one of her grandchildren into their school clothes judging by the background noise, and tutted sympathetically when he told her he had a vomiting bug.

"You stay home, dear, get some rest!"

"Thanks, Sonia. See you Tuesday."

Rest. Sure. He'd wanted to go to work just to keep his mind off it.

He found Ryan in the kitchen, tea and toast waiting on the table for David and an obscenely large mug of coffee opposite for Ryan. Their respective pills sat in the middle, laid out in two neat lines. They breakfasted in silence—but that was normal. Ryan wasn't entirely human before the first barrel of caffeine, and David was usually rushing around getting ready for work and too busy for much in the way of conversation anyway.

What wasn't so normal was the sideways hug as Ryan cleared the dishes away, and David sighed.

"Feeling any better?"

"Not really."

"Did you ring in sick at least?"

"Yeah."

"Good," Ryan said. "I know you wanted a distraction, but no offence, you look crap."

"Oh, thanks."

"If you want to keep your mind off it, we could always get started on the garden fence."

David shrugged. "Yeah, all right, then."

The garden was Ryan's haven. He'd gotten into gardening after the accident, desperate for something to do to keep the trauma at bay as best he could. Most of the space was given over to a patio to allow for the chair, but with select outcrops of greenery. A small decking area had been constructed, with a vegetable patch put in on top. Flowers climbed the side of the shed. A bird table at the halfway mark was protected from entrepreneurial cats by a shield of carefully maintained rose bushes in a variety of colours. An area at the very bottom, under a permanent canopy and flanked by solar lights for warm evenings, was surrounded by bushy border plants with pale blue flowers in clusters. There were always bees, and even butterflies in good summers.

David never took any interest in doing any work with the garden, but he liked barbecues on long, hot evenings, or lying in the hammock under the canopy during the always roasting August bank holiday weekend. Pamela next door gave them dirty looks on their anniversary, when the tradition was a home-cooked meal out on the patio. It was a nice garden, and a nice day, and painting the fence would probably help.

Still, he eyed the tins dubiously when Ryan opened the shed.

"If the smell makes me throw up again—" he warned before picking up one of the cans. "You want me to do the bits behind the decking and flowerbeds?"

"Yes, please. I'll come down the side of the patio and meet you halfway."

The paint didn't smell too strong, thankfully. David hunkered down between the peas and the fence and got to work. The new coat was bright and cheerful, bought to match the canopy and the hammock. The rhythm and the quiet helped soothe David's jangled nerves, and time slid by without him really noticing.

Sitting back on his heels, he stared over at Ryan.

Ryan had taken him by surprise. They'd met on a dating site but mutually disregarded each other for the usual reasons. Assumptions and biases. But then they'd bumped into each other at the cinema, both sheltering in the lobby, waiting for the rain to ease off after a film. The same film. They'd swapped criticisms; David had been sarcastic and prickly, and Ryan had smiled.

David bit his lip, lowering a hand to his stomach at the swooping sensation. There still a jolt when he remembered that very first smile. He'd agreed to a coffee the next day simply out of being stunned by it. He'd never intended to actually date this guy.

And now, here he was.

David wasn't exactly prone to great expressions of love, and the idea of calling him a romantic was laughable—but he was happy. He couldn't—wouldn't—deny that. He was happy with Ryan. Happy in the bungalow, with the garden, at the fence.

He clenched his fingers around a fistful of shirt.

They'd talked kids on that very first date. Ryan showed him a picture of Ava and said his biggest regret was not having her sooner. He was still married, but it had already effectively been over. David admitted to wanting kids of his own one day, but said it had never happened, and Ryan had smiled at him again.

It had been there from the beginning. This understanding that someday, they would have a baby too. And the more David had gotten to know Ryan, the more he wanted that with him. Only...not like this.

"You okay?"

He jumped at the call. Ryan was staring back at him, frowning.

"Yeah."

"Sure?"

"Yeah. Just feeling a bit sick."

The frown deepened, but David turned away and got back to work.

It was all academic anyway. In another few hours, it would be over. Then they could go to the information evening and do it the right way.

"CHEERS, MATE," RYAN said and turned from the taxi. "Come on, then."

David didn't move.

Hands in pockets, shoulders hunched, he stood and stared at the main entrance like he'd never seen a building before. Five minutes to go—and suddenly his feet didn't want to move.

"David."

Fingers touched his sleeve so softly David barely registered them.

"Talk to me."

He licked his lips. He couldn't take his eyes off the doors.

"I don't know what to do."

He didn't want to be pregnant. He didn't want to give birth. He didn't want to go back to his own body betraying him. He didn't want to open up the Pandora's box of dysphoria that was lurking in the back of his head, ready and waiting to be used again. He'd not been mistaken for a woman once in years. Long, blissful years. Years of actually living, instead of being merely alive.

It was threatening to crumble around him. And the way to stop it was to just walk forward.

But—

There was a but. There was a reason his legs were frozen.

It would be a baby. And more than any baby, it would be *their* baby. It would look like them. Be like them. Both of them. And for David, blood was important. He was the last Neal standing, the only one out of his mother's three children to actually grow up. The tiny bundle of cells inside him meant it wasn't quite over. Mum would be a grandma. The marks on her soul, on her DNA, on her son, would be passed on.

If he were a woman, David wouldn't hesitate. He would never have booked the appointment at all. The thought would never have occurred to him.

But he wasn't. So it did.

"Ryan."

He would have to walk right back into the hell he'd escaped all those years ago. He'd be that scared, angry, hurting kid all over again, knowing that he was being irrational but having no way to stop it. And maybe he was strong enough to know now—now he'd been through it all, now he was older and wiser—that his wanting to have a child meant nothing more than he was a man who wanted to have kids, just like any other. But David still had to be able to go through it all again if he wanted that bundle of cells to become a baby.

Could he do that?

The fingers circled his wrist and squeezed lightly.

"I don't know if I'm strong enough for this."

The grip tightened

"You are."

"How do you know?"

"Because I know you." Ryan's voice was flat and factual. Firm. He said it with all the arrogant self-assurance David had ever heard from him. "I know you, and I know me. You could do it if you wanted to. You're strong enough. We're strong enough."

A woman by the door was staring at them over a cigarette. A flicker of annoyance sparked in David's chest, and he slid his wrist free—only to clasp Ryan's hand in his own and squeeze back.

"What if I'm not?"

"There's no what if."

"Why?"

"Because you are. And I think you know that, deep down."

David bit his lip.

Then he let go.

And asked Ryan to call another taxi.

Chapter Six

"I DON'T EVEN know where to start."

They'd not discussed it at all after that day outside the clinic. David appreciated the space for the first couple of days—but by Saturday, sitting on their usual park bench beside Ryan and watching Ava on the slide, he found himself wondering.

And bundled up in his heavy jacket against a surprisingly wild wind, it felt all right to wonder.

"How d'you mean?"

"Having a baby."

Ryan quirked a smile. "You don't do anything for another six months, and then—"

"Thank you, Sherlock."

"You asked!"

David snorted.

"What do you mean, then?"

"Telling people. Leave. Work. Where is it going to sleep? I'm not doing classes," David added sharply. A room full of yoga mats and people breathing? No chance. He was going to get stared at enough as it was.

"We tell who we want, when we want," Ryan said. "We can turn the office into a nursery. Mind helping turn the shed into a proper little summerhouse before it gets too difficult for you?"

David shrugged. "Might help. Good distraction."

The timing was awful. The winter would have been better. He'd have just looked fat in the Christmas jumpers the receptionist insisted he wear all holiday season. Just buy several sizes up and pretend he liked beer too much. It would have nixed the misgendering side of the problem. Being correctly taken for a man even when it was blindingly obvious he and Ryan had started out with different letters on their birth certificates would be a huge help.

But he had no hope in the summer. He was always reduced to board shorts and a T-shirt at best by the middle of June. When was this baby even due? He had no idea. The blood test hadn't told him; it had only confirmed its existence. Or at least that his hormonal system thought it existed.

Quietly, David was still hoping for a mistake.

"I think I need a scan."

"Eh?" Ryan said.

"A scan. I don't even know when it's due."

"You don't?"

"No. They just said I was—having one. And then said they'd refer me to a midwife."

"All right," Ryan said. "So, you want to start there? Not make any plans until after the scan?"

David was torn. He didn't want to think about it until after the scan, so not making plans sounded good. But then, David was a planner. That was how he worked. He always relieved stress by making plans, writing out lists, ticking boxes. If he had a huge list of things to do, it meant he wouldn't be able to think about what was going to happen.

But if the list itself made him think about what was going to happen, what was the point?

"Maybe just work on the summerhouse until the scan," he said. "Then think about the rest."

Ryan reached out to briefly squeeze his wrist, then drained the rest of his paper cup of coffee and tossed it in the bin. "Ava! Come on, devilspawn. That's a whole two cups' worth of playing!"

She whined, safe on top of the climbing frame, but sulkily slid down when David stood up. He was her kryptonite when it came to climbing frames, both light enough and lithe enough to get right up after her and wholly willing to do so. And she knew it.

"Can we feed the ducks?" she asked hopefully as she slid a hand into David's and they headed for the gate.

"Not today," Ryan said. "It's too cold."

She stopped dead, stamping her foot. David paused, but Ryan kept going determinedly.

"I was going to say you could have an hour with your new colouring book for being a good girl this morning," he shouted over his shoulder. "But I guess you're not a good girl after all."

She thought twice about having a tantrum at that, letting go of David and running after her father. David stuck his hands in his pockets and watched, gnawing on his lip absent-mindedly. There'd be two of them. Ava and a baby brother or sister. He'd have to push a pram. Get a car seat. Fend off his mum's hideous taste in baby clothes.

Oh hell.

Tell Mum.

David sucked in a breath. Mum would go berserk. She'd cried for hours when he started the hormone therapy. Begged him to reconsider. Got her hands on every leaflet she could find about the lower success rate of IVF using frozen eggs. Pleaded with him not to ask for the hysterectomy. And for what? For his body to go ahead and get knocked up anyway.

And for every minute he didn't tell her, she'd kill him a little bit more.

"Hey! David! You frozen?"

He jumped and started forward. Ryan was waiting at the gate with an amused smirk, one hand fisted around the hood of Ava's coat to stop her running off down the road without them.

"All right?" he asked.

"Yeah. Just thinking."

"About?"

David glanced down at Ava but figured she'd not be too interested. "Mum."

To his surprise, she blinked up at him. "You have a mum?"

"Of course David has a mum," Ryan said. "You met her; she visited for his birthday. Auntie Mary. You liked her."

Her face lit up. "Grater cake! Is she coming to visit? Will she bring more grater cake?"

"You are not having grater cake again," Ryan said.

"I'm sure she'll visit soon," David soothed. He sympathised—grater cake had been his favourite growing up, but it was so sweet it had only been allowed once in a blue moon.

"Thinking you need to call her at some point?" Ryan asked, and David nodded. He raised his eyebrows in silent apprehension.

"Ask her to bring grater cake!" Ava begged, grabbing onto his arm and beginning to swing off it like a demon possessed. "Grater cake!"

"If you don't keep your voice down and ask nicely, I'll tell her not to bring any cake at all."

The scowl was instantaneous, and the grip returned at once to the usual sticky clasp. David rolled his eyes at Ryan's laughing assertion that he was a natural dad and ignored the little jump in his stomach at the words.

Mum was—Mum was just too much for the moment.

So he pushed her aside and ignored the guilty twinge. Summerhouse. He was going to plan for a summerhouse, not a son. And with work, with Ava, with having to do two-thirds of the DIY himself, it would be an age before he had to think of anything else.

"Come on," he said, squeezing Ava's hand. "Why don't you colour, I make a to-do list, and Daddy makes us lunch?"

"Oh, come on—"

"Yes!"

He could do this. Right?

OFFICE WAS A bit of a generous name for it. In truth, it was the remains of the remodelling project Ryan had undertaken with his compensation money. It was a small room at the very back of the house and used to be the kitchen. But it had been too small to comfortably use from a wheelchair, so Ryan had converted the much bigger dining room into a kitchen instead, and the empty space left behind became the office. In theory. It was little more than a tiny, cosy space with a desk, a computer, and a pile of David's books they'd never gotten around to putting away properly.

It would be plenty big enough for a nursery. It was just...in a bit of an odd place.

"Long term, I suppose we can always swap this for the bathroom," Ryan commented as David leaned against the open doorway and eyed the space. "At least then the bedrooms will be all in a row."

"Might it not make sense to do that first?" David suggested.

"Yeah, maybe. But if it's a bathroom refitting—"

"I know."

Refitting a bathroom, there was only one choice round these parts. And that choice happened to be Ryan's younger brother, Jay. He was brilliant at what he did, there was no doubt about it, and he refused to charge Ryan any more than the cost of the actual parts required. Reasonably, it would be stupid to ask anyone else.

Only problem was that Jay was just like Ryan's mother. A piece of shit. The day David moved in, Jay called the social and tried to get Ava taken away on the basis of living with two men at the weekends. Ryan was cut out of his mother's will when he refused to go back on his decision. David had gone to dinner with his partner's family once and only once, and had no desire to repeat the experience.

Especially pregnant.

Because he was one hundred percent certain they didn't know about that particular superpower.

"Easy solution, isn't there?" David said.

"Is there?"

He shrugged, his body feeling easier than his mind. "I'll go and visit Mum and tell her in person. I'll stay out of the way for a week while Jay swaps the two rooms over, and then we never have to lay eyes on one another."

Or anything else.

Ryan pursed his lips. They both knew the argument. David shouldn't feel pushed out of his own home, but there was no way of having them in the same building. At least Ryan's mother just shouted and banged pans. Jay wouldn't think anything of handing out punches. And David wouldn't think anything of handing them back either.

"Fine," Ryan said. "I don't like it, but fine."

"Neither do I, but I like it more than actually seeing him."

"Mm."

"I have some leave left from work," David said. "I'll go next month. Then, by the time I get back, the rooms will be switched, and I can help with the summerhouse to free up that space for the books and things."

"C'mere."

He hesitated, glancing over at the kitchen table. Ava was colouring with furious intensity, ignoring the pair of them in favour of a hideously orange daisy.

"Come here," Ryan insisted.

David stepped away from the door frame and rolled his eyes when Ryan patted his lap. "Nice try."

"I'll hug your legs," Ryan threatened.

David groaned but sat down. They were both too big for this. The chair always looked precariously small under Ryan's frame as it was. Adding David felt like they were asking for it.

"See, that wasn't hard," Ryan said, winding both arms around David's waist. David eyed him sceptically. "Christ, it's like hugging a plank. Relax."

"I'll relax when I want."

"Yeah, yeah." Ryan was smirking though, and the glimmer of his good humour was relaxing, despite the stupidity of their position. "Tell you what. You have a nice time at your mum's. Tell her if you want, or don't; I'm not bothered. And when you come back, we'll sort the summerhouse really quickly, and then it'll be time for that scan."

David swallowed.

"And on the big day," Ryan murmured, "I will make sure to pull out all the stops and make it as easy as I possibly can."

Blowing out a breath, David twisted a hand into the shoulder of Ryan's T-shirt, warping the fabric.

"Even if you don't like what I need to deal with it?"

"Even if."

Chapter Seven

DAVID WENT TO Manchester the following week.

Ryan had arranged everything with Jay while David was at work, the only evidence of his brother the smell of smoke around the back door in the evenings. So on Saturday morning, long before Jay would be up and about and ready to come over, David packed a bag and threw it in the car.

"Drive safe," Ryan said, beckoning him down for the mandatory kiss before David drove anywhere. "Ring us when you get there."

"Will do."

Ryan was still a little twitchy about long car journeys. David had mostly gotten over it—the crash had been a drunk, nothing he could do about that—but given it was Ryan's second brush with what out-of-control vehicles could do, David didn't really object. If a kiss and a text message would pacify him, then it wasn't exactly a hardship.

David was born and raised in Salford. The route home was so familiar he drove entirely on autopilot. The long winding stretches of motorway to cross the Peaks. The rich villages and outskirts as the city began to rise up on the horizon. The grubby interior, the murky skies, the towering blocks of council flats, and the shells of old factories. David remembered every last inch of the place, and despite its ugly memories, despite his desperation in his youth to get out and be something better than a shit kid from a shit estate, there was still a tiny part of him that felt like he'd come home.

But his hands wouldn't relax on the wheel until he pulled up into the tiny parking area outside his mother's flat.

Mum lived on the fifth floor of one of the ugly tower blocks—but she owned that flat, and it was her pride and joy. Even if David hadn't known exactly which windows were hers, they drew the eye anyway, with their colourful charms hanging behind the glass, and the window boxes bolted beneath them, overflowing with jaunty flowers.

The curtain twitched. He smiled.

By the time he'd fetched his bag, locked the car, and walked steadily up the stairs, she was waiting by the front door with a huge smile. Mum hadn't changed in about a million years. She was tall and fat, crushing him into a hug with more power than a pro wrestler, and her smile was forty feet wide. She still wore her crucifix around her neck, though she hadn't been to church since David was thirteen years old, and she still wore her headwrap, even though she'd cropped her hair off when she started working at the school and had never grown it out again.

"You're too thin," she said predictably and shooed him into the flat. "Put that bag down! Let me look at you. Yes, too thin, look at this!" She pinched his arm like it was somehow evidence of malnutrition. "How's Ryan? You'll take some sweets for the little one. How are you?"

It was all said in a barrage. Mum had a harsh voice, her original London accent having wrapped around a hoarse Mancunian one in an unpleasant combination. But she was always warm, always home, and David offered another hug.

"Ooh," she said, clucking her tongue and hugging him back. "This is more like it! Starting to appreciate your mother in your old age, are you?"

"If I'm old, what does that make you?"

"Your elder, so watch your mouth, boy."

He laughed, relaxing. He sank onto the sofa as she bustled around the tiny kitchen, its space too small to hold her plus another human being. Her skinny ginger cat, Thomas, wound around his ankles hopefully, then seemed to detect the smell of vet, and fled into the bedroom.

Mum's flat hadn't changed much either. She'd come to them for Christmas, as it had been Ryan's turn to have Ava for Christmas Day itself, so David hadn't seen the flat in nearly a year. But there wasn't much different about it. It was a clash of bright colours and artwork. The walls were painted a pale, predawn grey, but great oil and canvas paintings were hung over them. A sunset over Saharan sands. A hurricane at sea. Autumn leaves. Mum loved colour, always wearing bright floral clothes and collecting wildly outrageous headwraps—she'd refused to go out without one in all David's life. The hideously pink vase Ryan had bought her last Christmas was in pride of place on the windowsill, supporting an equally pink hyacinth.

But then David raised his eyebrows.

On the bookshelf, there had always been four photographs. His mum's parents at their wedding in Jamestown after the war. One each of his brothers, Sam and Ben. And his official graduation photo, him in his gown and Mum wearing her biggest, proudest smile.

But there was a new one. He remembered her taking it, but he'd assumed it would go in her box of treasures under the bed, the one where she kept his school certificates and his brothers' baby pictures.

Christmas Day, him and Ryan and Ava. Sitting on the sofa together, Ava beaming from her dad's lap, thrilled at having a new auntie who brought grater cake and let her throw wrapping paper everywhere.

They were on the bookshelf, and David swallowed a lump in his throat.

"There!" A cup of sweet tea was banged down in front of him. "Now, what's this all about, eh? Not like you to visit out of the blue! Is something wrong?"

David pulled a face. "No, just avoiding Ryan's brother. He's refitting the bathroom."

"Brother?" She screwed up her face. "What's the matter with the brother?"

"Raging bigot."

Mum snorted. "Can't choose them."

David smirked back. If there was something he and Ryan had in common, it was the eternal frustration of not being able to choose one's family.

"How are you, then? How's work?"

They talked, exchanging stories about feral cats and feral neighbours, and David sank ever lower in the sagging sofa and relaxed as he breathed in the smell of home. He'd never lived in this flat, but it smelled like home anyway. Mum's cooking. Her candles in the bathroom for her Friday night soak after the week at school was over. Thomas. The rug under David's toes was the same one he'd wrestled with Sam on, the same one he'd bawled on when Ben pushed him too hard and he banged his mouth on the coffee table and knocked out a tooth. Mum had thrashed them both—Ben for pushing him, David for getting blood on her nice new rug. He could still see the faint pink stain where she'd tried to scrub it out.

"I'm going to go and see Ben and Sam tomorrow," he said. "Do you want to come?"

She hesitated.

"Yes," she decided eventually. "We'll get some nice flowers. You can help me with—with the rose bush."

"'Course." He licked his lips. "So—anyone about?"

It was the same question he asked every time he saw her since he'd left home. They'd all had different dads, him and his brothers. Ben's dad was Pakistani, a man Mum met at a London market just as she'd left school. He didn't know he had a son, as he'd been violent from the start, and Mum left him before she even knew she was pregnant. Sam's dad was Pakistani, too, a bus driver who chatted Mum up every day on her way to work. He was nice, but it was an extra-marital affair, and in the end, he went back to his wife and faith, but he sent money and presents sometimes, and David remembered him coming to the funeral. And David's dad was a teacher at the first school Mum had worked in, a soft-spoken young man from Chandigarh who taught chemistry and had plenty of it with Mum, by all accounts. He went back to India when David was a year old, and they never heard from him again.

But it had never mattered, really. Mum was the fierce type. She'd fall hard, and there'd be a new man moved in within months. And the minute he didn't like one of them, he was out on his ear again. David remembered fighting with Ben—he must have only been four—and breaking a vase. Mum's boyfriend clipped them both around the ear—and Mum exploded. Never mind that she clipped them too. Never mind that she was a firm believer in the wooden spoon on the backside. A devotee of the spare the rod mentality, she'd think nothing even now of beating David with a spatula if he swore at her. That was her job. One of her boyfriends daring to lift a finger against a boy who wasn't his own? Unforgivable.

When David came out, she stopped dating entirely. Too risky, she said. Too much at stake. *It can all wait.* So when he moved out, he told her to get back to it.

"Have fun," he'd said. "Meet someone. Be happy."

So every time he came back, he asked.

"Ooh, not that serious," she said coyly, and he grinned. "So there is!"

She waved a hand airily.

"Who is he?"

"His name's Jacob. I think you'd like him."

"Where did you meet?"

"Oh, well." She put down her cup. "I've been trying this new church."

David stared.

Mum had quit church after he came out. She was a devout Christian and never missed a Sunday service. But when David came out, the pastor was incensed and immediately recommended camps, counsellors, even an exorcism.

"It's the devil's work," he'd proclaimed.

"I don't think so," Mum had snapped. "He's my son."

And that had been that. She never went again. And as far as David knew, she'd never been to any other church either.

"It's Unitarian," she said. "It had a rainbow flag on its board a couple of months ago. I told the minister about you—"

David groaned. "Mum, you need to stop just telling people about me."

"—and he teaches that God loves all of us, and we ought to follow His example, including for transgendered people."

"Transgender, Mum."

"Yes, that."

"That's—"

He was interrupted by the shrill ringing of his phone. He winced at her withering look as he fished it out of his pocket.

"I'm not on call, I promise," he said. "But I better take this."

She huffed as he ducked into the kitchen, noisily banging her teaspoon as she stirred her cup.

"Hello?" he said, hoping it would be Sonia just asking where he'd left the keys to his drugs cabinet.

"David Neal?"

"Speaking."

"Hi, David, my name's Nadia Akbar, I'm the midwife who's picked up your care plan from Dr Escobar."

Just like that, all the relaxation at coming home drained out of his system.

"Oh," he croaked.

"I'd just like to book in your first appointment with me, if we can? I understand from your test results that we're looking at a dating scan in the next couple of weeks, so if we could put that together with a chat about your ongoing plans, that would be great. Would that suit you?"

One appointment instead of two? "Yes."

"Great!" she enthused. "So we're looking at—"

He swallowed thickly as she began to rattle through dates, carrying on about test results and medications and due dates. He didn't know the answers to any of her questions, and he could feel a creeping darkness around the edges of his vision—yet, her chatty voice was oddly soothing. He blinked away the panic, tamping down on the attack as if he could physically strangle the life out of it, and agreed to the first appointment she offered.

"That's brilliant, I'll send out a letter to confirm. We are a bit strapped for space, I'm afraid, so I do have to warn you that only one extra person is going to fit in the exam rooms with you, but that can be whoever you like—your partner, your mum, a friend, whoever you want."

"It, um—is it step-free access?" he croaked. He'd need Ryan. And he knew better than to think Ryan would be willing to negotiate this part.

"Of course," she trilled.

"My partner will be coming with me, then."

"That's great, I look forward to meeting you both. See you then; have a lovely day!"

"You too."

He hung up and dropped the phone on the counter. His forehead followed, touching the cold laminate lightly.

"Who was that?" Mum called.

He thought quickly. "Lawyer."

"What? What do you need a lawyer for?" she asked sharply.

"Oh, uh, wills. You know. Financial stuff. Gets complicated with step-kids and ex-wives and everything," he said as he passed back into the living room. Mum snorted but didn't argue. "So, Jacob?"

"Oh, yes, Jacob."

"You met him at this new church?"

She nodded, humming pleasantly. "He's a widower. Very sweet. I might bring him to Christmas next year."

David shrugged. "Always room for one more."

Or two.

THEY WENT TO the cemetery on Sunday evening.

Mum in her best church clothes, and David carrying the flowers, they walked from the car deep into the bowels of the sprawling graveyard. It was ancient, spanning from the graves of Victorian babies, through a clutch of white headstones from the two wars, and out the other side of gnarled trees to the shiny black markers with gold lettering, only a few years old and populated with fresh flowers.

And there, two graves lay side by side facing the sunset. Ben and Sam.

The graves were well tended. A rose bush had been planted exactly between them, and David squatted down with the kitchen scissors Mum had given him and began to prune it back into a round shape, chopping off the dead flowers to let new ones grow. Mum laid the bouquets. Sunflowers for Ben, tulips for Sam. Always that way round, though David didn't know why.

They'd both been older than him. He remembered lanky teenage boys, all limbs and loudness. Both just— teenagers. He'd been the same. Angry sometimes. Acting out for lack of anything better to do. Wildly trying to find their places and their souls.

Ben had been angry all the time. David could remember shouting matches, barricading himself in the bathroom to avoid his brother lashing out at him, police in at all hours, therapists, counsellors, medication, never working, never helping, never stopping. He'd had problems. An uncontrollable temper, a violent sense of not belonging in the world, a dark hatred of the father who'd abandoned him. David could find a thousand reasons why Ben had ended up where he was, each more useless than the last.

He'd been nineteen years old. Deep in the wrong crowd. Picked a fight with another group of lads on a Salford street corner. Nobody knew to this day who'd thrown the first punch, who'd produced the first knife, but the result was all the same.

Two dead.

Then three. Ben had died in hospital two days later.

Sam hadn't been long afterwards. It was the grief that had done it to Sam. He'd known the other boys involved. He'd been running with the same crew. And he'd wanted revenge, but knew he'd only get killed as well. David could remember him saying he didn't want to do that to Mum. But he'd been unable to cope. Unable to process the pain. He'd taken more and more of the stuff to cope with it, until one day he just...took too much.

It was David who found him. It had been the routine, back then. He'd walk from school to Sam's flat, and wait there for Mum to pick him up so they could walk home through the estate together. Safer. So, on Wednesday the fourteenth of November, he'd let himself into the flat with his key, and found Sam dead on the sofa, the syringe still in his arm.

It hadn't even been a year since Ben's death, and Mum had been a mess.

And yet, in a strange way, it was all responsible for where David had ended up.

"You're clever," Mum had told him the morning of Sam's funeral as she'd fixed his tie. "You're a clever boy. You always have been. I've lost two sons. I won't lose one more. You hear me? There's a better future for you."

She'd been strict. Almost oppressive at times. He'd been forced into clubs to keep him busy, extra studies to keep him smart, anything to keep him in school and on track and not where his brothers had ended up. His biology teacher, Mrs Olushola, had taken an interest and told Mum he could go to university.

"David's bright," she'd said. "He's very, very bright. They'll be desperate to have him."

His acceptance letters had all come on the same day. He'd applied to five universities, and all five offered him a place. And Mum had dropped her breakfast plate, the ceramic shattering on the floor as she'd burst into tears.

In a way, it was their deaths that had steered him onto this path. That had resulted in his degree in veterinary medicine, in his job vaccinating cats, in his more-than-healthy wage and his living in a town far from Salford, where he met Ryan and formed a new family. The first in his family to finish school, the first in his family to put letters after his name, the first in his family to prove the sneers of the local racists wrong.

David touched his stomach through his jacket and swallowed.

Because of them, he was here.

"Mum."

She looked up from arranging the sunflowers to her satisfaction.

"I need to tell you something, and I need you not to interrupt or say anything at all until I'm done."

She blinked and stood up, brushing off her skirt.

"Is it bad news?"

"No."

He stood with her, shoving his hands into his pockets and staring down at the graves.

"You remember the car accident I had a few months ago?"

Her face tightened, and she nodded.

"My liver was quite fragile afterwards. So my endocrinologist lowered my T dosage. Brought it almost down to nothing—just enough to stop my original system taking over again, but low enough to give my liver the best chance of recovering."

She touched his elbow, but he ignored her.

"It's recovered fine. I was supposed to go back on the hormones last month. But the last round of blood tests showed that he might have lowered the dose a bit too far."

He took a deep breath. His gut was tight. He still didn't know if he'd made the right decision, or if he could see it through—but staring down at his brothers' graves, he knew what to do if he could make it.

"I'm pregnant," he said, "and I'm going to call it Sam."

Chapter Eight

"A BABY," MUM said for the millionth time. "Oh, sweet Lord, a baby!"

She'd been beaming all the way home, and kept repeating it to herself over and over. Her happiness was a little infectious, and David felt the tiniest spark of excitement igniting in his own head as well.

"A baby!" she trilled, and he chuckled.

"Yes, Mum, a baby."

She banged the kettle down, clapping her hands like a child.

"I'm going to be a nana!"

David smiled to himself, drawing his feet up onto the sofa. He swiped open his phone and sent Ryan a text.

David: *Just told Mum the big news.*

The reply was prompt, which probably meant Jay was entertaining Ava for five minutes.

Ryan (& ICE): *And?*

David: *What do you think?*

Ryan (& ICE): *I think she's singing that she's going to be a grandma and rushing out to buy magazines to learn how to knit so she can make booties.*

David: *Yes to the first, not yet to the second.*

"Put that away!" Mum snapped. "Honestly! A baby! You've told Ryan, I take it? When's it due? Do you know what it is yet? Will it be a Neal or a Walsh? How's the little one taking it? What do you want for lunch?"

The non sequitur threw him. "What?"

"Lunch! You're too skinny as it is!"

"Uh, whatever."

She scoffed at him and started to rummage in the freezer.

"Mum, seriously, just put a pie in the oven and sit down."

She huffed, but a steak and ale pie emerged and was shoved in the oven anyway. David rolled his eyes and figured this Jacob was a bit more serious than Mum was letting on. She hated pies.

Still, she was persuaded to sit down with another brew, and David searched the questions for something to tell her.

"I don't really know anything," he said. "I—I initially didn't want to keep it."

"Don't be ridiculous," she retorted. "It's a baby. You can't kill a baby."

David raised an eyebrow. He'd very carefully not let his mother know about the last time this had happened, and had no intention of ever letting it slip.

"Well, Ryan and I have been looking at adoption for a while. So I decided to try and do this."

"Of course you can do it," she said with utmost faith. "Having a baby—pah! It'll all come naturally. You'll be fine. I had three, and you're much smarter than I ever was."

"You aren't a man," he said gently.

She waved a hand again.

"You've always been headstrong. You're just like me. You'll be fine." She leaned forward in her seat with a smile. "Now, tell me everything."

David shrugged. "There's nothing more to tell. I've not even had a scan yet."

"So you don't know when it's due."

"No. I've made an appointment for a scan on the tenth. We'll find out then."

She shot up and rushed for the calendar on the wall, snatched a pen off the kitchen counter and circled the tenth in bold purple. David clearly saw her write the words 'grandbaby scan.'

"You'll be getting married, then."

David coughed on a mouthful of tea. "What?"

"Your Ryan's traditional! He'll be wanting to get married."

"He's not said anything."

"He will," she predicted. "How's Ava taking it?"

"We haven't told her yet. We haven't told anyone yet."

"You'll find out at the second scan if it's a boy or a girl, and then you let me know," Mum said. "A grandbaby! Oh, the boys would have been so excited. I'll tell Jacob, you know I'm terrible at secrets."

"Oh, I know."

David envied other trans men. He'd been in a support group at university. They all championed never telling a soul, the ultimate sanctity of disclosure being entirely in their hands. David had never understood how it was possible. Didn't they have gossipy mums? His mum didn't understand the need to keep certain things quiet. It drove him up the wall and—though he'd never tell her—it was part of the reason he'd not tried to find work in Manchester after he graduated.

Because ultimately, David wasn't a trans man. He was a man. Nothing else. No qualifier. Just that. And Mum's habit of talking about it—like she told people her own name—felt like having a label that he didn't even use sewn onto the back of his neck.

"A grandbaby," she said wistfully once more. "I never thought..."

David cracked a smile, swiping open his phone again.

David: *She's ecstatic.*

Ryan (& ICE): *She's not the only one, let's be honest <3*

The little twinge of doubt was still there, but it seemed somehow unimportant in the face of Mum's happiness. This could be a good thing, David decided. He might have made the right choice after all. Once it was actually here, he would be a father. Mum would be a nana. It would be almost like grounding his odd little family in blood, instead of Christmas cards and grater cake.

"You'll have to tell me the minute you know when it's due," she said. "And you'll have to visit more often. Or I'll have to think about selling up—"

"You can't sell your flat, Mum. You love the flat."

"I'll love my grandbaby more than a flat!" she tutted. "And you'll have to meet Jacob properly, you know."

"Oh, right, it's not that serious, but he's going to be a grandfather too, am I right?"

"Oi! Cheeky."

He snorted with laughter.

"I take it this is why that idiot is refitting the bathroom?"

"Jay?"

"Whatever his name is."

"Yeah. We were going to convert the office into a third bedroom, but it's too far away from our bedroom. And obviously, we can't use the attic space for anything but storage because there's nowhere to get a big enough staircase to fit a lift for Ryan."

"Not thinking of moving?"

"No, we like it where we are." Well, Ryan did. David could do without Pamela next door, but given she was ninety-six, it was probably just a matter of waiting.

"There you are, then, I'll have to move closer," she said. "I'll be retired in a couple of years anyway, and Jacob already is."

"Oh God, it *is* serious."

"Oh, hush. I'm allowed my fun."

He smirked knowingly.

"Wipe that look off your face, boy. You're not too big for the spatula."

"Sure, Mum."

"What do you want?"

"Sorry?" he said. That was the trouble with his mum when she was excited. She veered from subject to subject and just expected him to be psychic and keep up. She huffed irritably at him for his confusion.

"A boy or a girl!" she said, like it was obvious what she'd meant by her vague question.

He shrugged. "A baby?"

"It's all right to have a preference, you know."

"I haven't really thought about it."

That was the beauty of 'Sam,' he realised. It didn't matter if they had a boy or a girl. They could still call it Sam. And he wanted that. He didn't really miss Ben, and a very cruel part of him that he didn't allow much air wondered if Ben hadn't deserved what he'd got. He'd been a bully. He'd had problems, sure, but—well, so had David. David hadn't gone around beating up other people because he was angry. He hadn't gone picking fights and battering his younger brothers and lashing out at everyone else for things they didn't do.

But Sam? Sam had been—nice.

He'd been screwed up the same way Ben was, and the same way David grudgingly admitted he was too. Unable to vent his emotions properly. Unable to turn to other people.

Unable to process, until it was all tangled up in a painful, awful knot that started to hurt just too much to handle.

David could understand the temptation.

David could understand how Sam had died.

And he missed him. Sam had been an addict, he'd been in rehab twice and failed, he'd kept sinking, but he also loved Mum, and stuck by David after he'd come out, and been sorry for messing up when he did. He'd died because he hurt, not because he'd hurt other people.

And their Sam, if David could do this, would have a better chance. They'd have a father who loved them. David was a realist, and accepted that he and Ryan might not work out forever—but if it collapsed between them, Ava was proof Ryan would still be there. He'd not abandon his child the way Sam and David's fathers had. And their Sam would have a grandma who adored them. Another father who'd wanted a child since he'd been a child himself.

They'd have a better chance.

David: *I want to call it Sam.*

He didn't really mean to send it, but it just sort of happened, and he waited with bated breath through Mum's enthusiastic chatter about baby outfits and buggies.

Ryan (& ICE): *Only if it takes my last name.*

David: *Why?*

Ryan (& ICE): *Sam Neal is that actor.*

David snorted with laughter.

David: *Sam Neill but I see your point.*

Ryan (& ICE): *Are you opposed to middle names?*

David: *Depends on the middle name.*

Ryan (& ICE): *Lionel if it's a boy.*

David smiled faintly. Ryan's dad. He'd been killed in the same accident that had given Ryan the chair. They'd been out biking together, along with Jay and a couple of family friends, like they had done almost every month since Ryan was eighteen years old.

Only this time, they'd met a drunk driver on the roads.

And the rest was history. Lionel had been killed, along with two of his buddies. And Ryan had clawed his way back from the brink, fuelled only by the determination not to leave his then-newborn daughter without a father.

It was a bittersweet thing by now. Ryan had been hurt by his family's horror at his new relationship with David. Ryan was openly bisexual and had believed the lip service they'd paid to accepting it. But their revulsion at him putting it into practice and getting together with a man had been painful for him. There was never any doubt that his father would have agreed with the rest of them about it.

But he was already gone, so Ryan had been able to keep that happy relationship, those good memories, without the ugliness overshadowing it.

David knew the feeling. If he had to lose Ben, he oddly wished it had been before anybody had ever known he was David at all.

David: *What if it's a girl?*

Ryan (& ICE): *Mary <3*

Mum.

David smiled. Sam Mary Walsh, or Sam Lionel Walsh. He'd take either one.

David: *Deal x*

Chapter Nine

HE SPENT A week in Salford before heading home.

He left on Sunday, after dropping Mum off at church. He waved to the elderly man who met her at the door, suspecting from the way she slid her arm through his that he had to be Jacob. Then he peeled out into the traffic and headed home.

It was sunny and warm, and he drove with the windows down until he hit the motorway, then rolled them up and put his foot down. The Land Rover jumped, and he surged east with a newfound buoyancy. He really ought to visit Mum more often—she was good for the soul.

It was lunchtime before he pulled up into the driveway of the bungalow. There was a skip waiting for collection, full of debris, but Jay's van was nowhere to be seen, and David let himself in to the blissful sound of silence. No bigots in his kitchen. Perfect.

He found Ryan in the garden, deadheading the rhododendron in the back corner.

"Ah, there you are!" Ryan said cheerfully, grinning up at him. "Come on, get down here and give us a kiss."

David rolled his eyes but did as he was told.

"Love you too," Ryan chuckled. "Everything go all right?"

"Yes. Mum has a new boyfriend."

"Doesn't she always?"

"Looks serious this time. She made noises about moving closer after she retires, and it was specifically mentioned that Jacob's already retired."

"Ahh. He nice?"

"Don't know, didn't meet him, but you know Mum. He'll be gone in a second if she changes her mind."

Ryan chuckled. "True. She gotten over the excitement of our news yet?"

"No. She might when it turns two. Maybe."

Ryan's palm cupped the back of his knee and squeezed. "You look better."

"She's infectious."

"True. You feeling a bit better about it all though?"

"For the moment," David said. "At least, I think I made the right decision."

That wide smile made his heart skip a beat.

"Good," Ryan said. "And we have a name. And a hollowed-out room next to ours, ready for decorating."

"So—summerhouse?"

"If you feel like starting today. I was thinking next weekend. Ava can play in the garden and wear herself out pretending she's helping."

David bit his lip. "What did you tell her about the remodelling?"

"Not much. She wasn't really that interested, to be honest. She just wanted Jay to teach her how to use a drill."

"Please tell me he didn't."

"Nah, he might be a bigot but he's not that thick. Seemed pretty hopeful your absence meant you were on your way out, and I'd find a nice girl."

"Please, nice girls wouldn't put up with you."

"I'm hurt!"

"Truth does hurt, yes."

"Dick," Ryan said, patting his bum affectionately. "Want to go out for lunch?"

"I just drove from Manchester."

"I meant take a nice walk in the sun to that cafe near the playground."

David snorted. "You always want me to push you back from there because of the hill."

"Good exercise."

"Pregnant. You can't make me exercise anymore."

Ryan cackled. "Bloody weaselling out of it already!"

"Eh, take advantage where I can get it. Mum packed us a hamper anyway. We can start on that."

"Cake for Ava?"

"Naturally."

David busied himself with making lunch, leaving Ryan to the flowers, but yielded and joined him out on the patio, dragging a chair out from under the canopy to soak up some sun. Ryan could spend the rest of his life in blazing sunshine and not look remotely different, but David could just about top up in a good summer. He shrugged off his T-shirt and leaned back to soak up a few rays over sandwiches, and was caught up on the latest drama from Ryan's clan over a lazy hour.

Until Ryan said, "I want us to sort some paperwork out."

David opened an eye. "What paperwork?"

"Jay was making his usual comments."

"About us?"

"Yeah. And it occurred to me that if something happens to us..."

"Oh."

David hadn't thought of that. His crash hadn't been so serious as to reshape his life. It had just been a sharp shock and an annoyance at having to breathe with cracked ribs for three months.

But of course for Ryan it had been traumatic.

"Yeah," Ryan said. "I want to make sure that if something happens, the b—Sam ends up somewhere safe. Somewhere unconditional."

"Mum?"

"I was thinking of Mary, yeah," Ryan said. "But also Marianne. If she's agreeable, I haven't mentioned it to her yet. But if your mum's not able to—I mean, we're talking years, there's nearly twenty years to cover, and she'll be nearly seventy by the time Sam's all grown up..."

"You're thinking if Mum can't anymore, you want to keep Ava and Sam together."

"Yeah."

"We'll—we'll talk to her. Not yet though. I'm not ready to be talking to Marianne about our kids yet."

Ryan nodded, squeezing his wrist on the arm of his chair. "There's something else I want to do sooner though."

"What's that?"

"I'm going to write a will."

David bit back the urge to tell Ryan he was being morbid. He knew better—he just didn't have to like it.

"If something happens to me, I want you to keep the house. I don't want you and Sam to lose that. But I don't want Ava to be left out in the—"

"You know I wouldn't—"

"I know," Ryan said, "but I want to make sure. In case it's not you calling the shots, you know?"

David swallowed. "Yeah. Okay."

"So, I'm going to write a will. You get the house, and my money gets split between you and Marianne. You for Sam, and Marianne for Ava."

"Why are you telling me this?" David asked quietly.

"Because I want you to know," Ryan replied.

"Well, now I do. Thank you. But it's a bit—heavy right now."

Ryan nodded. "Yeah, well, best get it ironed out early."

"I suppose."

"Change of subject, the hospital sent a letter," Ryan added.

David groaned.

"Scan next week."

"That was fast. They only called when I got to Mum's."

"I want to come," Ryan said.

"I figured. But I need to not really talk about that," David admitted. "I just—I can't think about all of that yet. Right now, I'm coping by just imagining it once it's all over. Like I can just magic the baby into being."

Ryan laughed. It was gentle and understanding, and David wanted to kiss him for the easiness of it.

"All right," he said. "Can I admit I want it to have my skin and not yours?"

David raised his eyebrows. "Excuse me?"

"Ava was the cutest baby I've ever seen."

"She's yours. Of course you think that."

"She was! Everyone said so."

"What happened?"

"Oi!"

David kicked the chair in retaliation for the swipe thrown his way and smirked. "Just for that, I hope Sam looks like my dad."

"No chance."

"I'll start praying."

"Please, like God is going to listen to a heathen like you..."

"How very dare you," David drawled.

"'He that is wounded in the stones, or hath his privy member cut off, shall not enter into the congregation of the Lord.' Deuteronomy."

"What number?"

"Fuck knows," Ryan said gleefully.

"Call yourself a biblical scholar." David leaned back in his chair. "Anyway, I'm not wounded in the stones. You might be if you keep this up."

"I think not having stones counts as wounded in them, for a man."

David kicked the chair again. "It's only a wound if you lost them."

"You lost them? Careless of you..."

"I hate you," David bitched.

"I win," Ryan said and patted his lap. "Come on. Pamela's curtains are twitching. Let's give her a disgusting display of some other things forbidden in the bible."

"The bible thinks I'm a woman, so it's not forbidden."

"Still adultery, because I'm divorced. So come on."

David laughed, beaten, and decided to hell with it for once. Ryan's good moods were even more infectious than Mum's, so David threw out his own rules and shifted onto Ryan's lap, looping both arms around his neck and kissing him sharply.

"You're awful," he said.

"I know." Ryan beamed at him, full of irrepressible, irreverent glee. He planted a hand firmly on David's arse and squeezed. "Want to see how awful I can be?"

"That's how we got here in the first place," David complained.

"Um, no, that was your fault. I wanted to watch the football."

"I would sleep with anyone to get out of six hours straight of football."

"Who said anything about straight..."

David chuckled, scrunching his shoulder when Ryan buried his face into his neck and bit him.

"Randy bastard."

"Randy, yes, but you're the bastard."

"Thanks."

Ryan's smile dimmed a little. "Eh?"

"For cheering me up and being a stupid sod," David clarified and kissed the end of his nose. "I'm going to need you like this for a long time, you know."

"Yeah, I know." Ryan nudged his damp nose against David's. "We'll manage it. And it'll be worth it in the end."

"Yeah."

"Hey." Ryan squeezed. "I wanted to sound you out about something else too."

"What?"

"Do you want to get married?"

David laughed. "Christ. Mum thought you'd ask."

"I'm not really up for a big wedding or anything. But if you want to sign some papers, go all traditional like..."

David smirked. 'Traditional like.' No chance. He had no interest in being married, and neither did Ryan. He'd only married Marianne because he was supposed to, and that had gone about as well as could be expected from that mindset.

"No," David said, tugging Ryan's earlobe. "I've no urge to get married. We'll both write wills to capture that part of things. But thank you for asking."

"Sure?"

"Sure. If I change my mind, I'll do the asking. How's that?"

Ryan grinned and bit his neck again, short and sharp.

"I look forward to it."

Chapter Ten

THE DAY OF the scan rolled around faster than David would have liked.

Every day was a rollercoaster. He'd start with a wave of terror and dysphoria that rode on the back of his morning sickness. Every heave reminded him what was happening and what he was. Every turn of his stomach felt like a betrayal. But then Ryan would make toast, and talk purposefully brightly about getting a pram, and whether they still made baby swings for door frames, and if Sam would like the hammock in the garden, and it would make David feel better and brighter about everything.

But the day of the scan, he woke up feeling worse than sick.

He just felt bad.

Ryan had suggested taking the day off work, but David didn't want to. Much like the attempt at attending the abortion clinic, he wanted to stay busy. And as he was scheduled for surgery duty on Thursday morning, he'd have absolutely no time to think. So he'd gone into work feeling like shit and had been so short with the nursing assistant that she'd called him waspish and complained.

Usually, that would piss him off. But he just disappeared into the staff toilet to throw up, downed a few mints, and walked back into the little theatre for the second patient.

At half past one, Ryan arrived in a taxi. He didn't come in but texted from the cafe over the road. David heard the beep from the next room but didn't get a chance to look until he was done sewing, so he only saw the message twenty minutes later while drying his freshly scrubbed hands.

Ryan (& ICE): *Shagged out. Nathan was brutal. Getting a toastie and a coffee, just call when you're done and I'll come into the car park.*

David: *Finished. Just got to get changed.*

He changed in the staff toilet, grimacing down at himself as he did. He hoped he was imagining the thickness around his middle. It was probably just last night's extra enchilada, right? Ryan had made too much as usual. That was all.

He waved goodbye to Sonia and stepped out into the car park at exactly two o'clock. Ryan was waiting behind the car, texting someone, but lifted a hand to wave absently. David felt a pang. Perhaps—given there was no way he would be able to hide what was happening from his boss and colleagues—it was time to come out. He'd let them all presume he was dating Ava's mother. Maybe it was time to change that.

He decided to make one positive change out of the day, and stooped for a kiss.

"Hello," Ryan said in surprise. "Something you want to tell me?"

David shrugged. "Just felt like it."

"Uh-huh. Sure you did."

David rolled his eyes as Ryan got in the car, and took the empty chair to fold up and stash in the boot. He was starting to feel sick again, so he paused for a moment to just breathe through his nose. This was definitely the anxiety. Definitely.

He could distract himself on the drive over. The hospital had a crazy maze of parking, the disabled bays no more logically placed than any of the others, and a badly parked Ford next to the only available spot meant a good ten minutes of turning the Land Rover around to squeeze in backwards to give Ryan more space to get out. By the time they were done, it was only ten minutes to go, and David wanted to vomit.

He put his hands on the back of the chair and said, "Can I?"

Ryan stilled. They joked, but in reality David never pushed. The chair wasn't even designed to be pushed—it had no handles, and the back was smaller than the back it supported. Ryan usually only let David push him if Ava wanted to sit in his lap, like when they'd gone to the aquarium and she'd been scared by the octopus exhibit. Otherwise, he regarded it as insulting and patronising. And to be fair, David usually didn't want to do it either. Who the hell wanted to try pushing a fourteen stone man around? Never mind bending nearly double to do it, and having no handles to help.

But Ryan slowly put his hands in his lap and said, "If you want."

David did want. The effort was distracting. Nobody stared as they headed into the main entrance. He could pretend it wasn't about him, it wasn't about this, it wasn't about Sam, all the way up to the gynaecology unit—until he was faced with the wide desk, with a sign on one side saying gynaecology, and one on the other saying maternity.

His stomach clenched.

"How can I help?" the receptionist asked, giving them both a funny look. "Are you lost?"

"Does that say maternity?" Ryan asked.

"Er, yes."

"So this is where the ultrasounds are done?"

"Well, yes—"

"Then no, we're not lost. We have an appointment at two forty-five. David Neal."

She blinked—then pinked. "Oh! Yes. Um—let's see—"

David felt a little numb. He simply stood as Ryan rattled off their address and his date of birth as if he were the pregnant one, and not David. Selfishly, David wished it were that way around after all. Perhaps Ryan would cope better than he could. Perhaps Ryan could have done it, when David still wasn't sure.

They were directed to sit and wait. David perched on a chair, his chest tightening as he felt every eye in the room on him. The hairs on the back of his neck were standing on end. That strange, strained feeling of his skin being too small for him was beginning to inch its way up his spine. He shouldn't be here. He shouldn't be—

"David Neal?"

Ryan had to tug on his wrist to make him stand up. David stepped forward with the feeling he was wading through water. He only realised Ryan was following him when he heard the soft *thunk* of the chair going over the rubber seal at the bottom of the door frame.

"David, is it?" The sonographer held out a hand, smiling. "I'm Grace. I'll be doing your scan today. Is this your partner?"

David said nothing, perching on the edge of the bed with trepidation as Ryan introduced himself. There'd be nothing to see, surely? He wasn't even showing. What on earth could she possibly see?

"All right, David, let's pop you up on the bed here. I need you to just unbutton your trousers and push them down to your hips, and lift your shirt up for me so I can get at your abdomen."

David grimaced as he lay down. He heard Ryan come a little closer and reached out a hand as he lifted his shirt and closed his eyes. He didn't want to see her fuzzy screen, he didn't want to watch that probe on his skin, and he didn't want to see his own gut, starting to swell already.

"Just try and relax for me, David," she said gently. "I appreciate this is probably very difficult for you."

David wasn't in the mood to appreciate the sentiment.

"Hmm. How far along did your consultant estimate you were?"

"Anywhere between five and ten weeks," David mumbled.

She hummed again. The cold shock of the gel made David flinch, and she apologised quietly as she smoothed it over his stomach.

"Now, I'm just going to press lightly with this wand, and it's going to use sound waves to give me a picture of what's inside you. I'll then use that picture to give you an estimated due date, see how many babies we're talking about, and so on."

The idea of more than one baby made him grip Ryan's hand even harder. One would be hard enough. Two? He couldn't even stand the thought.

He felt Ryan lean forward in his chair as the pressure moved over his stomach. They talked in low tones—not much to see, second child but first with David, small talk that David would ordinarily join in with so as not to appear rude. But he had to focus on not being sick and squeezing Ryan's hand tightly.

"Does it hurt?" Ryan asked, and David shook his head.

"Just—don't want to be here."

"I'll be done very soon," the sonographer said. Christ, he couldn't remember her name.

Ryan's thumb rubbed along the back of David's hand. "Try your breathing exercises," he murmured, and David tried to obey, but felt the telltale catch around his ribs.

"Everything all right?" the woman asked.

"Yeah," Ryan said. "Panic attack. Best just get it over with."

David nodded. He could feel the sweat on his temples.

"Here we go," said the sonographer. "Do you want to see?"

"I do," Ryan said. The chair creaked as he presumably leaned forward again.

"See that round curve just here? That's the head. It's very small at the moment—judging by these measurements, I'd say you're only eight weeks along. That would put your due date at the fifth of November."

"Bonfire Night baby," Ryan said.

"There's only one—"

David breathed a sigh of relief.

"—and everything looks good at the moment. I can't tell the sex at this stage, but the second scan should tell us if you'd like to know."

"We haven't really talked about that yet."

"Okay. Now, I see from your notes you have an appointment next with Mrs Akbar?"

"Yeah."

"Well, that's at quarter past three, so I'll pop out now and book you a second scan with the receptionist and give you a minute to get settled. When you're ready, just head back into the waiting room, and Mrs Akbar will call you from there."

David jumped when he felt tissue on his stomach. It was Ryan. The door clicked shut behind the sonographer, and David immediately pulled his T-shirt down, not caring if the gel smeared on it.

"I want to go home," he muttered.

"Okay. You all right?"

"No."

"No, I know." Ryan was calm and gripped his knees when David sat up, preventing him from getting down. "Hey. Look at me. You did fine."

"I had a panic attack just at the first scan."

"Doesn't matter. You got through it. And there's a perfectly fine little life in there."

David swallowed. He could still turn back, and said so.

"I know," Ryan said. "And I wouldn't argue if you decided to. You know that. But you also know I think you're perfectly capable of this."

David swallowed, sliding off the bed, and pulled his trousers up an inch or two.

"Sam," he said. "It'll—it'll be Sam. If I do this."

"Yes."

He took a deep breath. "Right. Let's go. Let's just see this midwife, and then it'll be over."

Only it wasn't over, and David knew it.

It was only just beginning.

Chapter Eleven

MRS AKBAR THE midwife had conjured up mental images of a plump, plain, middle-aged Muslim lady in sensible shoes. But the woman who called David's name in a loud, cheerful voice didn't quite fit the bill.

She was tall and willowy, with long black hair in a neat ponytail. A name was tattooed on the inside of her left wrist in a flowery font—Angie—and a stamped date underneath, underscored by an EEG line punctuated with a strong heartbeat. She had a large nose, wide smile and firm handshake, and she walked with an authoritative stride as if she were a senior consultant, not a midwife in her late twenties at most.

And it was the swagger that did it. David relaxed as she showed them into a little consultation room, sat, and flipped open his notes with an airy hand like she'd delivered thousands of babies from men before.

"Is this your first child, Mr Neal?"

"David. And yes."

"And you are—?"

"Ryan Walsh." Ryan reached out a hand to shake hers. "I'm the father. So I'm told." Mrs Akbar laughed; David didn't.

"None of my concern," the midwife said. "I'm Nadia. I'll be your assigned midwife throughout your care. Now, obviously babies come whenever they want to, so I can't guarantee I'll be the midwife assisting at the birth, but I'll be with you all the way up to that point. If there's anything you need, any questions, any concerns, you just give me a ring. Here's my card..."

Ryan tucked it into his jacket and said, "Sorry, this might be totally out of order, and I'm sure you have a schedule..."

"No, go right ahead."

"I have HIV," he said. "It's undetectable and David's been taking prevention drugs for our whole relationship, but—yeah. Obviously, the baby needs a test."

Nadia didn't bat an eyelash, and David relaxed further.

"Of course," she said. "That's standard. We'll be doing a test today, but I'll make a note to repeat it at the second scan as well."

"And David can still take his drugs?"

"We'll go through lists of medications in a moment, but yes, there's PrEP drugs that pregnant w—people can take," she said. "I really would recommend keeping a close eye, maybe increase the frequency of your tests."

David nodded. At least that part he was used to.

"Right, here's a schedule of appointments you'll need, but you let me know if there's any worries you've got or anything I can do to make it all easier on you, and I'll try my best," she said. "Grace says you're due on the fifth of November, and it was a good, clear scan, so we'll work to that date. So, I'll start with your health information..."

She went at full speed. It was both reassuring and overwhelming at the same time. David had never known there were so many tests and appointments—though he was equally surprised at only having two scans. She took blood, she listened to the bump, she talked diets and supplements, she even breezed through safe sex without a hint of embarrassment. David wished she'd gone to medical school and become a GP so he could have a doctor who was so understanding.

"Is there some way we do all of this without coming to a hospital?" he asked. "I just—this is…"

"It's a waiting room full of pregnant women," Ryan finished quietly.

"Ah, I see." She chewed on her lip. "Let me think. Well. Yes and no. There's nothing I can do about the next scan, I'm afraid. That really does have to be here, although we can try and book you for first thing so it's quieter if you like. But if you could attend the walk-in clinic on South Street, I do a midwifery clinic there every Friday. The waiting area is a joint one, so it's a bit more like going to your GP."

"Can we try that?" David asked.

"Of course." She scribbled on his notes. "It'll throw your schedule slightly off, but it's not an exact science and babies are just as different as all the other human beings in the world, so by the end of it, we'll be all over the place anyway."

"How many babies have you actually delivered?" Ryan asked.

"Jesus, Ryan—"

But she laughed. "I'm older than I look. I qualified twelve years ago, and I rotate between antenatal care and deliveries. Honestly, I've lost count. You're in perfectly capable hands, and you will be on the big day as well. Are you planning for a home birth, or a hospital delivery?"

"Hospital," Ryan said.

David opened his mouth.

"If it goes wrong, I want you in a hospital," Ryan said. "Both of you. Where there's doctors and things."

"Actually," David said, "I wanted to ask if I can have a caesarean."

"I'd have to talk to one of the consultants," Nadia said. "We prefer to try a natural birth if—"

"I can't."

"—that's a safe thing to do," Nadia continued. "However. If a natural birth would cause excessive stress or harm to either of you, we would move to a caesarean. I will make mention of it, but ultimately, we make that decision later down the line."

"I want a caesarean."

"Then I will make that known to the consultant and arrange a session with them when we're further along the road. In any case—" She gestured at Ryan. "—if your little one takes after its father, it may be that a caesarean is the only way forward, irrespective of everything else."

Ryan chuckled.

"Do you have other children, Ryan?"

"I have a daughter with my ex-wife."

"Was she a big baby?"

"Er." Ryan made a gesture along his right forearm from wrist to elbow. "She was about this long when I first got to hold her?"

Nadia chuckled. "That's a pretty big baby. For your sake, David, I hope this one takes after you."

David winced at the idea of delivering some ten-pound monster.

"I'm going to give you these—" She handed over a stack of leaflets, all about mental health. "Pregnancy is tough when there're no other factors. But I appreciate you might struggle more than most expectant m—parents, so please use these resources the minute you have to. It doesn't have to be me if you're not comfortable talking to your midwife, or your doctor if there're issues with the GP, but if you're struggling, talk to someone. It can be quite literally anyone, just don't bottle it up and don't feel ashamed. I've had expectant parents who've been trying for years to get pregnant, then go into shock when it happens and have huge emotional swings, get depression, trigger anxiety, the works. It's nothing unusual, it's nothing to be ashamed of, and it's nothing to worry about as long as you don't try keeping it to yourself."

David nodded numbly, crushing his fingers around the leaflets.

"Do you have a name?" she asked as she rattled away on her keyboard.

"Sam," Ryan said, but his voice echoed in David's ears as he stared at the leaflets.

Suddenly, everything seemed that little bit too real.

Chapter Twelve

DAVID WENT BACK to work on Friday like nothing had happened. He ignored the leaflets. He didn't bother to call the GP. He just went off to work, then worked through his lunch break and went home late.

Late enough that he'd only just pulled up outside the house when he saw lights in his rear view mirror, and Marianne's BMW pulled up alongside.

"Hi, Marianne," he said as he fished for his keys and unlocked the front door.

Marianne nodded politely. She was Ryan's ex, and they never really had a lot to say to one another. She was small and slim, with long dark hair meticulously straightened out of its natural frizz. She was a QC, poised to be a judge before she was forty, ridiculously clever and ridiculously successful. Quietly, David agreed with the rest of the universe: Ryan was mad to let her go.

"Hi, David!" Ava shouted as she slid down out of the back seat. She went tearing off into the house the minute David opened the door. "Daddy, Daddy, look at what I made at school today!"

"I see someone's in high spirits," he said.

Marianne shrugged, hefting Ava's bag out of the boot of her car. "Yes."

"Anything we ought to know about?"

"No."

"Good. Um. You doing all right?"

"Yep."

She plonked the bag on the doorstep.

"Say hello to Ryan for me."

And that was that. She got back in her car and drove off without a backward glance. David shrugged, used to it, and put the bag by the hall table before closing the front door.

"Oh, you've decided to come home, have you?" Ryan said as he walked into the kitchen, but he was wearing a smile and most of a clamouring five-year-old, so David didn't bother to take offence. "I was thinking of calling you-know-where for you-know-what."

"What-what-what?" Ava demanded.

"Go for it," David said. It was their code for pizza. The minute Ava found out, she'd blow a gasket, and it was more fun to hold off on the surprise.

"Who are you calling? Daddy! Who are you calling?"

"Why don't I call?" David suggested.

"Good idea. Usual, please."

David rolled his eyes. Great. Bed was going to be like sleeping in a war zone after a biochemical attack. He could hardly wait.

He shut Ava in the kitchen with her dad while he made the call to their usual pizza place—mostly because they could get burritos at the same joint for Ryan, who was clearly some kind of alien creature and didn't like pizza—then went to shower and change. By the time he came back, in jogging bottoms and a sleep vest and not much else, Ryan had successfully attached Ava to the TV and a Star Trek film, and had put Coke in fancy wine glasses.

"May as well pretend to be posh," he said.

"Thanks—I think."

"You feeling a bit better today?"

"Yeah, I think so."

"Good." Ryan squeezed his knee. "Feet, please?"

David chuckled, lifting Ryan's feet onto the footstool as usual before settling back and sinking into the arm that hooked around his waist.

"When do you want to spread the news?" Ryan asked.

"Don't know," David admitted as he watched some random side characters burst into what he thought was supposed to be a fight scene, but was so obviously choreographed it looked more like a dance number. "What is this?"

"No idea. Her new favourite—Marianne put it in her bag."

"Mummy doesn't like it," Ava proclaimed loudly from her spot on the rug.

At a blinding flash from an exploding starship, David winced.

"I'm not surprised."

"Marianne say much?"

"About as much as she usually says to me."

"I didn't marry her because she was chatty. Doubt a divorce was going to make her more talkative."

"Yes, but after the way you decided to break it off, it's no wonder she doesn't talk to you. It wasn't my fault."

"Eh." Ryan waved a hand. "Kind of was."

"Was not."

"Didn't want to get a divorce until I met you."

"You were already separated."

"Yeah, but I didn't want to get a divorce."

"Semantics."

"What's semantics?"

David raised his eyebrows at Ryan's not entirely accurate definition but said nothing. Marianne would put her right again by the end of Monday.

"We are going to have to tell Marianne though," Ryan said, when Ava had resumed staring at the magical babysitting box. "Monster is going to have questions. A lot of them."

"And I'm not answering them."

"Means you'll be out to Marianne."

"By the seven-month mark, I'm going to be out to everyone who sees me," David said waspishly. "Your ex-wife is hardly going to make a difference."

Ava shoved up from the rug and clambered into her dad's lap. "Look!" she crowed, pointing at the screen. "She's my favourite. Mummy says she's an astronaut. I'm gonna be an astronaut like her. Look, Daddy!"

"I'm looking, I'm looking—"

Then the doorbell rang, and David resigned himself to an evening of excitable five-year-old, cheese on the carpet, and absolutely no room to think, breathe, or relax.

Which, actually, was probably the perfect remedy for his ills.

HE WAS UP at six o'clock on Saturday morning to throw up again.

At least it was getting less intense. And when he heard the shuffle of slippers as he was putting bread in the toaster, he was grateful at least Ava was manageable in the early morning.

"Hello," he said. "Do you want some toast with me, or do you want to wait for Daddy to get up and have a big fry-up down the cafe with him later?"

She rubbed a sleepy fist across bleary eyes. "Can I have both?"

"You can have one slice of toast if you're going to have a fry-up later."

"Yes, please." Then, to his surprise, she lifted both arms.

"Everything all right?" he asked as he picked her up and popped her on the counter. Ava usually wasn't too bothered about getting a cuddle off him. She hugged him by proxy occasionally—wriggling between him and Ryan on the sofa or in bed if she'd gotten up first—but she rarely wanted him to hold her independently.

"Yeah." She kicked her heels off the cabinet door.

"Stop that or you get down again."

It stopped. He regarded her quiet demeanour with a frown.

"What's up, kiddo?"

"Nothing."

"What if I promise not to tell Daddy?"

She eyed him sceptically. Then she hunched her shoulders briefly, pursing up her mouth just like her mum did.

"Mummy has a boyfriend."

"Oh."

"He's called Jack."

"Is he nice?"

Another exaggerated shrug.

"He works with Mummy."

"Are you sure he's her boyfriend, then? He might just be a friend."

"I saw them kissing."

"Ah." He squinted at her, not entirely sure what the problem actually was. "Is he nice to you?"

"I guess."

"Is he nice to Mummy?"

"Yeah."

"Then what's wrong?"

"Nothing."

"You obviously don't think much of this," David opined as the toast popped. He had to put Ava's back in for a second go. She liked it incinerated.

"If Mummy gets a new boyfriend then she'll get a new baby."

With a jolt, David suddenly realised where she was going.

"And then she won't want me anymore."

"Ava," he said carefully. "That's not true."

"It is. Katie at school, her daddy got married and they had a baby and now Katie never sees him anymore."

"That's because Katie's dad clearly isn't a very good dad," David said. "It doesn't matter how many children you have. You still love them all just as much."

"You can't; you have to spread it out."

"Nope. Love's infinite. My mum had three sons, and she loved us all just as much as Daddy loves you."

Her toast popped. David plonked it on a plate and offered jam, but she shook her head and prodded it with a stubby finger.

"If Daddy and I had a baby, we'd still love you just as much."

"You can't though. Teacher said only women can have babies."

"Some men can too. And some women can't. And everybody can adopt one."

"Like a kitten?"

"Yeah, kind of."

"Are you gonna?"

"Maybe," he hedged. "But if we do, it doesn't mean Daddy's going to love you any less."

She picked up the toast and jammed a corner in her mouth.

"Promise?" she mumbled, spewing crumbs everywhere.

"Promise," he said. "Now get that down you, and go and wake Daddy up and ask him."

She brightened up at the prospect of getting to jump on Ryan before he was even awake, and David mentally apologised for the hurricane he was about to unleash.

"Is Daddy being lazy?" she asked gleefully as she ripped the toast in half and began to chow down on it.

"Very lazy. He needs a little monster to go and get him out of bed."

"Yes!"

The rest of the toast vanished, and he slid her down off the counter. She shot out of his hands to go and shriek in her father's ear, and he rubbed a hand over his bare scalp, blowing out his cheeks. Shit.

He'd thought telling Ava would be relatively easy. Kids were generally easier than adults. She wouldn't really care what he was or what bits he had.

But he hadn't seen this snag coming.

Chapter Thirteen

IN THE END, David actually told his boss first.

The surgery and the shelter formed two halves of the same small company. Sonia's father had set it up, way back in the 1950s, and she'd taken it over when Frank had started on the downward slide of dementia. He died a couple of years ago, and the black-and-white photograph of him and his wife, Lizzie, opening the place in the summer of 1953, was still hung in pride of place over the reception desk.

Sonia wasn't a vet, and never had been. She'd been the fundraising manager for the shelter for most of her adult life and had taken over as practice manager after Frank. Luckily, the senior vet, Paul, absolutely hated budget and business management and had been more than happy to let her. And while David had senior partner ambitions some day, that wasn't for a good ten years or more yet.

The only downside of the matter was that Sonia was difficult to pin down. In a typical partnership surgery, it was easy enough to collar the senior vet—just look at the surgery rota, and hang around ready for their break. But Sonia had a far more unpredictable schedule, and for weeks at a time could be up and down the country with funding matters, equipment resourcing, and countless other tasks.

So David picked the one day she was certain to be there: the annual inspection of the shelter.

He left her alone in the morning to have her pointless meltdown, and then for the early afternoon to show the clearly satisfied inspectors around the joint. He even let one of them sit in on his examinations, something he usually staunchly refused. Thankfully, Mungo was one of his regulars due to a nasty habit of eating quite literally anything put in front of him, and old Mr Masters wasn't bothered by the suit and clipboard in the corner.

"He sicked it up again," he said in a hoarse voice, handing over the plastic bag containing one well-chewed battery and a lot of slobber. "But I thought best be safe."

Mr Masters was eighty-seven, and Mungo the only soul he had left in the world. David was certain when Mungo died, Mr Masters wouldn't be far behind.

Thankfully, Mungo was only four, and—even though he was dumb as a sack of soup—was one of the friendliest and healthiest dogs David had ever seen. Somehow.

"He looks fine to me, Mr Masters," he said, petting Mungo and offering a treat for sitting still all the way through his tests. "Keep an eye on him for the next couple of days, and keep batteries firmly locked away in the cupboards. Give us a call if you're worried at all."

It was his last appointment of the day, and he showed both Mr Masters and the suit out before packing up his kit and nipping into the staff toilet to change. He had to get up his nerves for the conversation he was about to have.

David didn't make a habit of coming out. It was an endless, exhausting process, and never ended well. Once he'd started to consistently pass, he simply stopped. The only people he'd told in the last ten years were his partners. Work had never known. The neighbours didn't know. The pub quiz team didn't know. The gym certainly didn't know. Nobody else knew, and that was exactly the way David liked it.

Telling Sonia was going to be against everything he'd worked for.

And being outed by his own body was going to be something he hadn't experienced in nearly a decade.

Still, he'd chosen his clothes carefully that morning. A tight T-shirt he usually wore at home to wind Ryan up with a bit of a show. Low-slung jeans that gave the impression of narrower hips that he really had, and a bigger cock than he'd ever get. Workman's boots. He oozed masculinity, and he oozed it on purpose.

It helped, all right? It just helped.

Once the inspectors' car had pulled out of the car park, he crossed it to the shelter, ducking through the door and heading to the little office off to the side. Sure enough, he found Sonia buried in papers, her glasses almost falling off the end of her nose, looking flustered but pleased.

"Go okay?"

She jumped. "David! Good gracious, I thought you'd already left. Yes, yes, they seemed—well, we'll see."

"It'll have gone fine," he said. "Can I take a seat?"

"Of course, dear!"

He closed the door, and Sonia paused in her scribbling. "Is something the matter?"

"I need to discuss something with you. Confidentially."

Her smile dropped. "Nothing serious, I hope?"

He shrugged, sinking into the chair in front of her desk. "I'm going to need to take parental leave from the beginning of November."

Her face lit up. "Oh! Oh, that's exciting!"

"My partner and I are expecting a baby."

"Congratulations!" she gushed. "Is she due in November, then?"

"He's not," David said carefully. "I am."

Silence.

"I'm—sorry, what?"

"I'm due in November."

"You—"

"I'm transgender," David said, his chest starting to tighten. He so rarely said those words. So rarely even thought them—because for so long, he hadn't called himself anything but a man. It felt so strange. "And I recently found out that I'm pregnant."

"Oh my goodness," Sonia said, jaw sagging. "You're—really?"

He winced at the incredulity in her tone.

"I would never have guessed!"

He bit back on the urge to say that had rather been the point.

"And your—he? I thought you had a stepdaughter?"

"I do. His daughter."

She stammered something completely incomprehensible, then put down her pen and waved both hands in front of her face, going pink.

"I'm so sorry; I must sound like a blithering bigot," she said in a rush. "You know me, David. It's totally fine with me, you know, people are people and—"

"Please don't give me a lecture about love is love and you're an ally and how you saw a gay couple holding hands that one time and thought it was sweet," David said, a little too harshly. "I don't need to hear how my lifestyle is acceptable."

The pink deepened to red.

"Well—I—yes—"

"I don't want anyone else to know for as long as possible."

"It's nothing to be asham—"

"Sonia."

He snapped her name. She fell quiet.

"I am not ashamed of who I am," he said. "But I am a private man, and I have no interest in all and sundry asking about the state of my genitals and what name was written on my birth certificate for the rest of my working life. I do not. Want people. To know."

She nodded dumbly.

"I'm well aware my own body will give everything away before I go on leave, but when the time comes, I will handle that. I don't want you to tell anyone."

"Of course. This is all confidential."

"Except for gossip. We all knew when Paul was getting divorced, but he never told a soul."

She coughed awkwardly. They both knew how bad the place was for gossip, and David had no illusions he'd be spared.

"I'll put in the leave request form a bit closer to the time," David said. "I've not decided yet how long I'll take off." In truth, he wanted to not return to work before he was put back on his HRT, but the endocrinologist hadn't exactly been helpful about when that would be after the birth.

"Take all the time you need—"

"I will."

He knew he was being rude, but he didn't particularly care. It wasn't like he didn't already have a reputation for being sharp. His colleagues were persistently bewildered by all the customers liking him, and couldn't imagine him being nice and fluffy with them when he was such a git with the staff.

Honestly, David thought it was easily explained. His colleagues were nosy. His clients didn't give a shit who he was as long as he had a certificate on the wall and gave the impression that he, too, thought their precious Fluffles was the most important creature in the universe.

"I'll keep you informed if anything changes," he said and pushed up from the chair. "Thanks."

"Um. Yes. Con—congratulations again."

"Thank you."

He closed the door behind him and had to take a fortifying breath before he could release the handle.

If anything, that had been the easy one.

Ryan's family were going to be much, much harder.

Chapter Fourteen

"YOU DON'T HAVE to hide that from me, you know," David said.

It was a Tuesday evening. He'd won the argument for the remote and was watching the news with one eye and a WhatsApp argument unfolding between Vicky and Andi with the other. Ryan was sprawled out in his usual spot, pretending to absent-mindedly check his phone now and then.

Unfortunately for his conniving plans, David could see the screen.

Ryan coughed awkwardly. "I, uh. I thought you'd not be happy."

"You're allowed to be excited about the baby."

"I know. I just didn't want to wind you up with it. You've been pretty clear that you don't want to think about it too much."

"Yeah, well, enjoying the last few weeks before it becomes inevitable every time I look down."

He was already swelling. Two pairs of jeans were too tight. He'd started wearing his actual scrubs at work instead of suit trousers, given the clasps dug uncomfortably into his skin.

It could still easily be overeating, or what at Christmas his mum would call 'festively plump' but David knew better, and that preyed on him.

Ryan sighed and stopped trying to hide his browsing.

"It's a development app," he said. "Tells you how big the baby is and what's forming."

"So?"

"Twelve weeks, right?"

"Yeah."

"Umm—" Ryan swiped. "It's developing reflexes. Curling fingers and toes. I don't know what those are."

David looked. "Nerve cells."

"Oh, okay. Um. It looks like a little human being now. And it's about the size of a lime." He frowned and then glanced at David's stomach. "No offence, but you've eaten lime-sized things and not, er..."

"Most of a bump is fluid; you do realise that?"

"Oh. Oh, right, yeah..."

David rolled his eyes. "You'd think you'd never had kids before."

"Marianne didn't know she was pregnant at all until six months."

"How?" David asked incredulously.

"She stress eats, and she'd just qualified as a QC, so she'd put on a lot of weight really fast and thought that was what had stopped her periods. It was only when she was struggling to lose the weight again that she went to the GP, and he said there was no way she should have lost her periods. She wasn't nearly overweight enough for that."

David smirked.

"What?"

"You."

"What about me?"

"You like fat women, don't you?"

"Yep," Ryan said. "Don't even need to be fat, curvy does very nicely too. I want the Marilyn Monroe figure to come back into style. Got to have something to hug. Marianne was gorgeous back then. If I hugged her now, I'd snap her in half."

David could believe that. Ryan's answer to his loss of mobility had been shifting his training from marathon running to weightlifting. He could probably bench press a car.

"Quite frankly, you could do with a few cheeseburgers yourself," Ryan said.

"I'll bear that in mind."

Ryan grinned and David groaned.

"You're going to be insatiable when I start to show, aren't you?"

"Pretty much."

"I'll get a cattle prod for the bedside table..."

"You'll love it."

David snorted.

"Ooh, a challenge."

"Come near me in the mornings before this nausea wears off, and I'll gut you like a fish."

"Duly noted," Ryan said, stealing the remote and starting to channel-surf for a film. "So, I can keep the baby app?"

"You can tell me what's going on in there if you like. I don't want to know how big it is though."

"Why?"

"I have to get that out, you know."

"Ooh, shit, yeah, good point."

"And on that day, you are going to regret ever putting it in me," he said, then kicked his feet up on the stool beside Ryan's and sank back with his phone.

If he could just about rest it on the small jut of gut sticking up above his waistband, so what? He'd had bigger beer bellies after a hard night on the tiles at university.

It'd be fine.

DAVID WALKED OUT of the GP's office feeling—for the first time ever—relieved.

He hated seeing the GP. He'd tried every single one of them in the practice, and they were all equally ignorant. The minute they saw the word 'trans' on the screen in front of them, every single ailment could boil down to that. And if the ailment was related to that? Not their problem, off to a specialist. Who had a waiting list measured in years.

But at least they could handle pregnant people.

"Well?" Ryan asked when he got back into the car.

"She took Google's word for it that I can keep taking PrEP. She's prescribed some safe antianxiety drugs to help with the panic attacks. Endocrinologist is going to call the shots about the shots, which I already knew. Gave me a diet sheet and said get some over-the-counter folic acid pills because I'm always a bit low. Didn't give me a straight answer when I asked about a caesarean."

"So, I guess you push Nadia for that."

"Yeah. Also wanted to sign me up to an antenatal class, but I said no. I'm not going to any of that shit. Whatever I don't know about handling a baby, you can cover."

"'Course I can."

David dropped his head back against the rest.

"So, two more pills in the morning, and everything else the same?"

"Yeah. Basically."

"Want to go and get those now?"

David wrinkled his nose.

"Lunch in town? My treat."

"Yeah, all right."

"By the way," Ryan said as David put the car in gear and began to squeeze back out of the absurdly small parking space. "Your mum rang while you were in there."

"What'd she want?"

"Due date. When I said November, she decided she's going to retire at the end of the next school year and move over to Wakefield in time for Sam turning six months old."

"Did you tell her about the scan?"

"Nah, only the due date. Figured she might cry; you know I can't handle your mum crying."

"You should try her when she's shouting, then."

"She also said she wants a picture from the second scan."

David grimaced.

"Hey, I want one too."

"Why? You can take a better picture when it's born. And for the next eighteen years."

"Doesn't matter," Ryan said. "I want one."

"You know, you're more like my mother than either of you care to admit, and I don't know what that says about me."

"Says you recognise a good thing, congratulations."

David pulled a face.

"Also, I've been thinking about when to tell Ava."

"Uh, yeah, about that. She's worried about Marianne's new boyfriend. Thinks that if they have a baby, Marianne won't want her anymore."

"Oh, Christ."

"Yep."

"Shit. Right. So we need to handle this carefully."

"Well, when Mum had Sam and then me, she made a big fuss of Ben—and Sam, I guess—becoming older brothers. Like they had an important role to play. We could try that."

"How do you mean?"

"Things like—*use your fucking indicator, you goddamned son of a fucking whore! Jesus*—taking her to help buy baby things, helping pack the baby bag for hospital, making a big deal out of stories of brothers and sisters and how they had to look after each other. Framing it like it's her baby too."

Ryan simply said, "Sometimes I forget you're from Salford, and then you get behind the wheel."

"Oh, please, he deserved it. Prick."

"You can take the man out of Salford, but..."

"Yeah, yeah. Like you can talk."

"It's a good idea though," Ryan said. "I don't think she'll get especially jealous of it, but if she's upset about Marianne's new boyfriend, then she might."

"She should be all right. It's you she'll get upset about. She's not bothered about me."

"You what?" Ryan said. "She threw a right strop when you were in Manchester."

"Really?"

"Yeah. She's dead attached to you. It was really pissing Jay off—it was David this and David that and that isn't what David says."

David tightened his grip on the steering wheel as a warm flush filled his body. He smiled goofily at the traffic lights.

Ryan chuckled. "Christ, you're oblivious."

"I just—I just figured if she were that attached to me, she'd call me Dad or something."

"I think that's my fault. I call you David, I tell her you're David, so she follows my lead."

"Huh."

"Can try it, if you want."

"No, no, I don't—I don't mind or anything. I just...really didn't think she was all that bothered about me."

"Well, she is. And how you make toast. God forbid you put bread in the right way up, apparently."

"It's the only way to get the top bit done right!" David said.

"Oh, sure..."

David snorted with laughter, then sobered slowly as they took the curve in the road down towards the shopping centre and its car park, well stocked with disabled bays and the magic free parking for blue badge holders.

"In all seriousness," he said. "We need to tell Marianne before we tell Ava."

"Yeah—"

"But we also need to tell her that *we'll* tell Ava. Not her. I want that to be in our hands."

"All right," Ryan said. "Next weekend?"

"Yeah. Next weekend."

Chapter Fifteen

THE MORNING SICKNESS wore off. But the bump got bigger.

David wasn't entirely sure which was worse. The vomiting had been skirting cruelly close to panic every time, but at least it wasn't exactly a gendered thing. Everybody did the technicolour yawn. The bump? Even if it was still small enough to pass for porkiness rather than pregnancy, it was only a matter of time.

Time that David hadn't realised would slip by so quickly.

Ryan called Marianne to come early on Sunday and have dinner with them, to talk about something. It was a warm, sunny day—a blazing May well underway—and Ava was happy to have her dinner on a picnic blanket on the patio with her dolls, ignoring the adults completely as they ate over an awkwardly quiet dinner.

And Marianne, unfashionably forthright for a lawyer, cut straight to the chase when she put down her fork.

"What did you want to discuss?"

Her voice was cool. David suspected deliberately so.

"Wanted to give you a heads up," Ryan said quietly. "We haven't told Ava yet but when we do, she's going to have a lot of questions, and she's probably going to ask you some of them. So we wanted you to be prepared."

She watched the pair of them, saying nothing.

"David and I are having a baby."

She didn't miss a beat. "Oh, you're adopting?"

"No."

A tiny frown line appeared between her eyebrows.

"David's pregnant," Ryan said.

She did miss that beat. Then she raised an eyebrow.

"Very funny. There better be a point to this, Ryan."

"I'm not joking."

The frown line reappeared, and deepened.

"I'm transgender," David said, very quietly and not looking her quite in the eye. "I was taken off my hormone therapy after my car accident last winter, and I got pregnant."

She started.

For the first time since David had met her, she looked surprised. She hadn't batted an eyelash when they were introduced. She hadn't flickered when he moved in. She was always permanently calm and collected, as if nothing in the world could so much as surprise her, never mind shock her.

But for a split second, the facade cracked, and her eyes widened.

"It's due around Bonfire Night."

"You're serious," she said.

"Yes."

There was a very long pause.

Then, slowly, she nodded.

"All right. I—appreciate the..." Long silence. "...forewarning."

The silence yawned once more. David usually felt a little awkward around Marianne, but his skin was prickling uncomfortably at the unblinking stare. He stood up and began to gather plates.

"Coffee, anyone?"

"Please," she said, still staring at his chair like he hadn't moved.

"Ryan?"

"Irish it up for me?"

"Okay."

On the way to the kitchen, he passed by Ava but was refused permission to take her plate as Barbie was still eating. He took his time, loading the dishwasher before switching the kettle on, and leaning back against the washing machine to watch them out of the window. They were talking quietly. Ava had disappeared—though not for long, as the kitchen door opened and she came traipsing in with her plate.

"We're finished too."

"You haven't finished your cabbage."

"Barbie doesn't like cabbage."

"Well, Barbie needs to eat her cabbage. She'll never get to go to space if she doesn't eat her cabbage."

Ava wrinkled her nose. "Really? But she doesn't like it!"

"Well, you need to set a good example for Barbie, don't you?"

He managed to persuade two more mouthfuls of cabbage down her—which she did like, she just liked trying her luck even more—then took the plate and scraped the remnants into the bin.

"Can I have an ice cream?"

"No. You only get ice cream if you cleaned your plate."

"Not even a little one?"

"No. You can have two buttons from the bowl. What colour?"

"White!"

"You're weird," he informed her, very seriously, as he popped the lid off the treats bowl and passed down two giant chocolate buttons, both white.

"Am not," she said with all the pompous arrogance of a five-year-old self-declared princess. "*You're* weird."

"What a cutting riposte," he drawled.

She stuck the two buttons in her mouth and stared up at him with wide, curious eyes. "What are Mummy and Daddy talking about?"

"I don't know."

"Are they going to get married again?"

"No."

"Are you and Daddy going to get married?"

He bit back a smile. "Probably not."

"If you do, can I be a flower girl?"

"Yes."

She beamed, teeth covered in melted chocolate, then turned and tramped back outside. David followed her to the door and rolled his eyes as he watched her start to pull flowers off the plants into a clumsy, very colour-uncoordinated bouquet.

Then Marianne got to her feet.

"Come on, Ava!" she called. "Time to go home."

The usual war began—no matter which parent was taking her where, Ava kicked up a fuss at being shuttled between the two homes. David stood back and watched dispassionately as she was wrestled up into her mother's arms, the flowers abandoned on the patio, and wailed all the way to the car.

Only when the door had closed behind them, and the rumble of Marianne's car was long gone, did he turn to look at Ryan.

"How did that go?"

Ryan shrugged.

"You think she's going to have a problem?" David asked.

"With you? I doubt it."

David raised his eyebrows. "There was an implication there."

Ryan blew out his cheeks. "Yeah, well. I...might have raised the custody agreement."

"Why?"

Ryan jerked his head at the kitchen, and David followed him back to the table. He sat while Ryan made fresh coffee, and stared expectantly when a steaming mug was delivered without a word.

"I might have mentioned changing the custody arrangement."

David frowned. "Oh."

Ryan shrugged helplessly. "Things have changed. I was a mess when we separated. I could barely handle Ava every other weekend, and you were still so new in my life that I couldn't trust you'd be there in the long term."

"And now things are different?"

"Yeah." Ryan waved a hand at his stomach. "We're more than capable of handling a baby. And we'll have Sam full-time. Things aren't the same."

"So, what do you want?"

"A proper split. Fifty-fifty."

"I take it Marianne wasn't too receptive to the idea?"

Ryan made a so-so gesture. "She wasn't—argumentative."

"But?"

"But she was wary," he admitted.

David pulled a face. "Let's hope you don't need to get the solicitors involved again."

"I think I might anyway. Just to make sure, you know? Get some stuff signed."

David nodded.

"Would you support me?"

"You know I would," he said quietly.

"It's just..." Ryan trailed off a long minute, then sat back in his chair, frowning at his coffee mug. "I can be a dad now. I couldn't really do it after the accident. I couldn't look after myself, never mind Ava, and I get why Marianne wanted me to have limited responsibility for her. I do. I'd have made the same call. But—it's not true now. And how am I supposed to reassure Ava that I'm gonna love her just as much as I'm gonna love Sam if I have Sam all of the time, and her only two weekends a month?"

Put like that, David thought it made sense. He could see how Ava might interpret it—and he could see how Ryan was starting to rankle against the prolonged agreement that had, ultimately, outlived its reason for being.

Chapter Sixteen

IT STARTED AT the end of July.

The first twenty weeks had been manageable. No more scans. His eighteen-week appointment with Nadia in the clinic had been far easier to handle, and the HIV test had been negative. The bump seemed to just stop growing in June and stayed where it was, hard but hidable. Loose T-shirts kept the secret a secret, and the worst David felt was the inevitable, telltale rise of his own hormone levels. It was like HRT in reverse. He felt shakier, felt less assertive, felt more inclined to pull back from conflict and shrink away. He could feel his mind changing, like something was leaking away and the foundations of stone were crumbling to sand. He felt like he had twenty years ago when he first realised who he was: shy.

But then at the end of the July, it began to grow again. Whether Sam was going for a growth spurt or David's body was just packaging the baby up in more fluid, David didn't know or care. All he knew was that the indigestion-sized bump suddenly doubled, and Paul said, "Married life suiting you, mate?" when David got out of his car at work.

Shit.

"Guess so," he mumbled and ducked past Paul to his exam room. "Sorry, got an early one..."

His hands were shaking as he unpacked his things and checked his schedule. It had begun. All right, so Paul hadn't misgendered him or anything—but the bump was noticeable now. He probably only had a couple of weeks left, maybe even just days, before the first "Can I help you, miss?" Before the first "That bird looks like a bloke." Before the first "You're David Neal?" and a long, awkward pause.

He planted both hands flat on the exam room table and sucked a deep, desperate breath through his nose.

He'd have to change his parental leave plans. Bring it back. If it meant leaving Ryan with a three-month-old instead of a six-month-old, then so be it. But he couldn't cope with that here. He'd worked so hard at not being out, at not being anything but a man and a vet and David, that he wasn't about to risk that now.

A jaunty knock on the door disturbed him from his reverie, and when it cracked open, Vicky was beaming at him over the top of Fred's carry cage.

"Morning, David!"

"Ah, here we are." He plastered a smile on his face. "And how is Fred feeling?"

"I've got a nasty feeling she's done it again. And I brought all the kittens for their shots."

"Well, let's have a look, shall we?"

Fred was an enormous round ball of grey. She looked like something swept out from under the bed. The only indication she was a cat at all were two huge orange eyes that peered out of the back of the carrier with righteous indignation.

David opted to leave her to it until he'd sorted the kittens. They had no such qualms—fluffy orange lumps that squeaked and bounced around, and off, the exam table. He and Vicky were beyond used to this, though, and simply scooped them back up after every shot, passing them back and forth to keep track with ease.

"When are you coming back to judo?" Vicky asked as they swapped kittens. "James is grousing about not having a good heavy sparring partner, you know."

"Gee, thanks."

"You were going to grade together! You can't let James get the brown belt on his own. He'll be a right insufferable git."

David smiled thinly. Of all people, he could tell Vicky. She knew. They all knew—he'd not passed when he was at university, and that was where he'd met every last one of them. At least he didn't have to come out to them.

But he said nothing, handing off the last vaccinated kitten. "Third round in a few weeks, you know the drill. Still got enough worming tablets?"

She huffed. "Yes, but I need to get more flea treatment."

"Okay. Ask Susan at reception. I'm pretty sure we've had a restock since you saw Paul." He stooped to peer into the carrier. "All right, Fred. Let's have a feel, shall we?"

Fred hated him. Even if he paid a house visit, or just went round for a brew with Vicky and her boyfriend, Fred could be out of the house and over the back fence before David had put so much as a foot inside the front door. She spat and hissed and clung. But first-year veterinary college taught the basics of removing cats from carriers above all else, and David had her out on the table and pinned down without further ado.

"I knooow, baby, he's so mean!" Vicky crooned, and David rolled his eyes.

"Well, I hate to tell you this, Vicky—"

"Oh, no—"

"But I don't even need to give her a scan. There's definitely more growth here."

She sighed, intent on stuffing kittens back in the carrier. "Short of just putting her in a cattery, I don't know what else to do."

"In my experience, that's the last thing you should do."

"Oh, God."

"Keep her somewhere really contained. A single room, if you can."

"She's just so fast," Vicky complained. "Do you reckon I could put her on a lead like a dog? That's the only way I'm going to manage to keep her contained."

David sympathised as he smoothed the ruffled fur. She hissed but settled grumpily onto the surface.

"She's upset enough I'm not going to try for a scan, but I'm sure that she's managed it again and she's pretty far along," he said. "Next couple of weeks, you'll probably have a new litter."

Vicky grumbled sourly.

"We can try a hormone implant next time you bring her in, try and give her body some time to recover before getting her fixed."

"I'll try anything at this point," Vicky said, coaxing Fred back into the carrier with her noisy brood. David stripped off his gloves and turned to type up his thoughts into Fred's file. "How are you anyway, David? Paul said you were off sick when I came in last time."

"Oh, stomach bug. Nothing serious."

"It's going around, isn't it?" she said. "Still, you're looking better. You've gained some weight! You really needed to, you know."

David's fingers clattered on the keyboard. He had to clench his teeth against the rush of nausea.

"David?"

"Sorry."

"No, I'm sorry. That was rude of me."

"No. It's fine."

"It's obviously not, by your face." She clicked the carrier shut. "I am sorry. Is—is there anything you want to talk about?"

She was a friend. He usually wound her up by being almost too professional in the exam room. She was his friend first, and his client last. He could tell her. He could.

But the words stuck in his throat. The sickness was too great to share.

"No," he said. "It's fine. See—see you next time."

RYAN HAD PLANNED on taking Ava to the scan with them and telling her about the new baby then.

David nixed the idea three days before.

"I just can't," he said. "I can't do it. I'm—this is bad enough as it is."

If he'd thought his nerves before the first scan were bad, it was nothing compared to his dysphoria before the second. To David, the bump was the most obvious thing he'd ever seen. It screamed what he was. It didn't matter that nobody seemed to have noticed it yet—the paranoia was still there. It was like when he'd started transitioning, when he'd been thirteen years old and wearing his very first binders. He'd be out shopping with Mum in some new place, and be totally and utterly convinced that everyone could tell, no matter how many times the shop assistants would say, "The boys' section is over there, love."

He'd forgotten what that paranoia felt like. And he wanted to forget again.

The scan was on a Monday. He booked the day off work completely, but when he got up in the morning, his chest was so tight that it took three tries just to rake in a proper breath, and a good twenty minutes of breathing exercises before he could get out of bed. The prospect of taking his now undeniably feminine figure into a waiting room full of women and having that blank, uncomprehending stare from the receptionist again—

He wasn't sure he could handle it.

"Taxi," Ryan said, taking one look at him. "You're not getting behind the wheel like that."

"I can—"

"No. You can't."

He knew better than to argue with Ryan about driving, and listened dispassionately to the call to their usual taxi firm, watching his fingers trembling on the tabletop. He was wearing a heavy jumper despite the hot weather, and baggy jeans. They were Ryan's jeans, not his own—but he didn't need a belt. The bump could hold them up.

"I don't want to go," he said.

"We have to go."

"We don't. The leaflet said the scans are optional."

Ryan squeezed his knee. "Hey. Look. I know you're—struggling right now. But we need to make sure Sam's okay. And we can find out if it's Samuel or Samantha today, can't we?"

David closed his eyes and shook his head.

"David?"

"I don't want to know."

He ought to not care. He of all people ought to not care. Yet his brain had latched onto this insane need for Sam to be a boy. For something masculine to come out of all of this. To get a son, rather than a daughter.

It was a hideous thought, and he felt guilty as hell about it, but it was still there all the same. Somehow, he'd struggle even more if he knew he was having a daughter. Somehow, it would make this worse.

He didn't want to say it out loud. He didn't want to make it real. He didn't want to really ask himself if it meant he'd not love a girl as much as a boy, or what it said about him as a parent. He knew better, yet he felt that way anyway—so he didn't want to admit it.

So he said, "I want a surprise."

"Yeah?"

"Yeah. I want—something to look forward to."

"Oh, I see."

He felt sick at Ryan's tone of understanding.

"Okay," Ryan continued. "I guess I can wait too." He chuckled. "Marianne wouldn't let me find out either. Maybe it's a pregnant thing."

"Yeah. Yeah, maybe." He doubted Marianne had been virulently opposed to having a girl—or a boy, for that matter. Marianne wouldn't have cared. She probably just genuinely wanted the surprise.

The taxi came at half eight. David said nothing, shivering in his jumper like he was cold, and the cabbie simply clucked sympathetically when Ryan asked for the hospital.

"You all right, pal?" he asked.

David nodded jerkily.

"He's fine," Ryan said. "Doesn't get carsick or anything."

David wanted to tell him not to jinx things, but couldn't unlock his throat long enough. He spent the ride in silence, hunched over the bump in an effort to hide it. He insisted on pushing Ryan up to the maternity unit again—and more tellingly, Ryan let him.

And took his hand, lacing their fingers together in full view of everyone else, while they waited.

"It'll be fine," he said gently. "You'll be fine. Promise."

David nodded shakily. People were staring. He could feel their eyes on the back of his neck. He hadn't shaved in a week, he was wearing winkle-pickers, his jeans were clearly cut for a man—but here he was. *They must be able to see the bump. They must.*

"David Neal?"

Heads actually turned. He lurched to his feet, trying not to stand entirely straight and have the bump jut out too obviously. Once again, he sensed Ryan following him rather than really knew he was there.

The closed door between him and the waiting room was a blessing.

"How have you been, David?"

It was the same woman. Grace, he faintly recalled. He nodded jerkily.

"It's been a bit of a struggle, the last couple of weeks," Ryan said as David climbed up onto the bed.

"You're really not showing too much yet," Grace said as he wordlessly exposed his belly. "Hopefully things will get a little easier soon."

David just grunted as the gel was smoothed onto his skin. He stared resolutely at the ceiling, not wanting to see the bump looking so blatant.

"Any movement yet?"

"No," he croaked.

"Okay. That's fine. You'll start feeling that any day now, but some babies are a bit slow to get going. I'm sure your little one will make up for it."

The pressure was more deeply uncomfortable than last time, though still not painful. He felt oddly sick for entirely different reasons as the weight shifted lightly in response to her probe, and the odd, building pressure on his organs moved.

"Has the morning sickness worn off?" she asked in an almost conversational manner.

"Yes."

"Any unusual cravings?"

"Not really."

"Night sweats? Restlessness?"

"No."

"Sleeps a lot more, actually," Ryan chimed in.

"Well, your body is doing a lot right now. More good food, more sleep, it all helps."

David grunted again.

"Ahh, there you are, little one. Have a look."

Ryan leaned forward, but David kept staring at the ceiling.

"Here's the head. And that little ball there is a fist. Looks like he or she has already learned to suck their thumb!"

Ryan made a cooing noise, and David called him soft, scrambling for something to take his mind off the prickling disgust under his own skin. It shouldn't be there. This was all wrong.

"And there's—do you want to know the sex?"

"No," Ryan said. "We agreed we'd like it to be a surprise."

"Ah, well, I won't tell you what that bit means, then. This all looks fine though. The growth rate has been very good. The placenta is in a good position and looks healthy. Now, let's see—do you want to hear the baby's heartbeat?"

"Oh my God, yes," Ryan said.

She fiddled with something. A couple of clicks.

And then a soft rushing sound, like water, filled the little exam room. Drained away. Quieted.

Bu-bmp.

Bu-bmp.

Bu-bmp.

"Oh my God," Ryan breathed reverently. "You hear that, David? It's Sam."

It was inside him. It was something inside of him, a heart hammering away inside of him, like—like—

David covered his face in both hands, and burst into tears.

Chapter Seventeen

THE HEARTBEAT ECHOED in his head.

David could hear it at night. Not literally, but it thumped away in the background all the time, like something out of Edgar Allen Poe. It kept him awake at night, touching the growing bump under his vest, like he could feel Sam getting bigger, getting worse, getting more and more undeniable. And always to the tune of that heartbeat.

He'd never known he could hear his own dysphoria.

Sleeping was getting harder and easier at the same time. The sight of the bump when he lay down was awful, but if he turned on his side and kept it pressed between him and Ryan, it just felt like a cushion, and he could sleep easier again. Plus, it kept Ryan happy. Octopus.

But no matter how much he slept, he always felt tired. No matter how many hours he lost in the dark, he woke up feeling like he'd only had a quick nap. And he knew—the tangled sheets around his ankles, Ryan putting the rail back up on his own side of the bed, the mornings he woke up shirtless when he'd gone to bed dressed—that he was tossing and turning too much.

The violent swinging between happiness and horror continued without pause over the two weeks after the scan. One minute, he would be downright excited, browsing cribs online or catching Ryan buying baby toys on their joint Amazon account, and the next, he'd get a glimpse of the bump in the bedroom mirror or find a new pair of jeans that didn't fit, and it was like his heart would dissolve in a pool of bile, and he'd have a panic attack or worse.

And every night, David found himself counting down. There were only three weeks left to change his mind.

And then two.

And then one.

The bump didn't grow all that much. Nothing moved that he could tell. But he could feel its weight when he walked now, and couldn't brush it off as indigestion or bloating with the heartbeat echoing in his memory all the time. And worse, people were starting to notice. Paul cracked jokes about who ate all the pies. Ryan would come home with bags of new jogging bottoms and hand them over—wisely—without a word.

And then, one Sunday morning over breakfast, Ava said, "David, why's your tummy gone all round?" and the world pitched under his feet.

"Steady," Ryan murmured, reaching out an arm. His voice was low and calm, but he frowned.

David swallowed. "It's—it's nothing, sweetie."

"You look like Holly's mummy," she opined, chewing on a corner of toast and staring at his T-shirt.

"Which—" His voice squeaked and gave out, and he had to start again. "Which one's Holly's mummy?"

"Holly's mummy," she repeated, as though not instantly being able to picture Holly's mother was akin to not instantly being able to picture Queen Elizabeth II. "Holly says she has a baby brother in her tummy, and you look like that."

Ryan glanced up at him.

"Oh Christ," David said. "Yeah. Okay. I guess—"

He stared helplessly back at Ryan. Maybe it was time to have that conversation after all. He nodded and sat with a thump.

"Would you like a baby brother?" Ryan asked.

Ava shrugged, sucking on the toast like a lolly. After a long pause, she said, "No."

Oh.

They exchanged slightly panicked looks. David had anticipated that telling Ava might be awkward, even awful for a little while, but...he had expected her to be excited. She liked babies. She was always tugging on their hands when she saw a pram in public and wanting to go back and look at the baby. Ryan said she'd even put a baby brother on her very first Christmas list.

"Why not?" Ryan asked.

"'Cause I don't."

"You used to ask for a baby brother."

"Yeah, but I don't want one now."

"What about a baby sister?"

"No."

David coughed awkwardly. "Um. Well—you might be getting one anyway."

She screwed up her face. "No. If Santa brings one, we have to take it back."

"Santa doesn't bring babies," David said automatically before his brain even caught up with her.

"Doesn't matter who brings them 'cause I don't want one," she said. Her voice was taking on a warning tone.

"Ava, honey, you realise we're talking about me and David? Mummy's not having another baby."

"It doesn't matter!" she snapped. Her fists were shaking on the table. She knew better than to shout at her dad—hell, even David tried to avoid shouting when he and Ryan argued. If anyone shouted, Ryan shouted right back. And

Ryan shouting was a deafening bellow that scared full-grown men, never mind five-year-old girls.

"There's no need for that," David said, hoping to mediate a little.

"It doesn't matter!" she repeated and dragged her plate—toast and all—off the table. It smashed on the floor in pieces. "You can't have another baby!" Her glass of orange juice followed the plate. "You can't!"

"Corner!"

She burst into tears at Ryan's bellowed command and fled into the hall. David sighed, pushing back from the table.

"You go and sort her," he murmured. "She needs her dad right now."

He cleaned up slowly. Ava could throw a decent tantrum now and then, but she wasn't usually so angry about it. She almost always knocked it off after one sharp word from Ryan. David grimaced and tuned out the argument about the naughty corner, putting a hand on the bump after he'd finished cleaning.

"She'll come around," he said to Sam but wasn't too convinced.

After all, if Sam's own father hadn't quite come around to the idea just yet, what right did he have to demand that Ava did?

THE FRONT DOOR closed, and David dropped his head back against the cushions.

He was lying on his side on the sofa, watching a TV marathon. He'd been there most of the day, largely staying out of Ava's way. She'd been enormously upset and kicked off three more times at the slightest provocation. In the end, Ryan had called Marianne to come and collect her early.

"Hey."

A hand squeezed his bare ankle, and David blinked muzzily.

"Sorry." Ryan was smiling. "Didn't realise you were taking a nap."

"Wasn't."

"Room for one more?"

"Mm."

He shifted enough to let Ryan into his usual spot and lay back down with his head in Ryan's lap. The scratch of blunt nails over his scalp was soothing.

"Going to need to shave this again soon."

"Mm."

"I had a word with Marianne. She's going to see if she can get what's upsetting Ava out of her."

"I didn't think she'd be upset in the first place," David mumbled.

"Neither did I," Ryan admitted. "I thought she'd be confused as all hell, but not upset. Also, Marianne sends her apologies."

"For what?"

"For being so awkward when we told her. She's realised she came off a bit...not good."

"That's one way of putting it," David grumbled.

"She says she still has Ava's baby clothes if we want them, and the highchair in the garage. And if you need to talk at all..."

Ryan trailed off. David snorted with amusement.

"I'm good," he said. "Marianne's not exactly the soft and squishy type."

"You'd be surprised," Ryan said. "Anyway, she's not going to kick up a fuss. And she's agreed that we need to revisit the custody arrangements, but only after the baby's born. She said you'd probably struggle to cope with Ava in the last couple of months, especially on a Thursday."

"She's not wrong," David said. "What do you reckon is Ava's problem?"

"Honestly? No idea," Ryan admitted. "She used to love the idea of a baby brother or sister. She was mostly upset when I moved out because she realised she wasn't going to get one."

David turned on his back and stared up at Ryan's face, absent-mindedly stroking the bump.

"You reckon she thinks Sam will replace her?"

Ryan blinked. "Replace her? How?"

"Well, it's a new baby. Kids get jealous. Maybe it's all a bit...worse somehow."

"Huh."

"She did tell me a while ago that she doesn't like Jack because she's worried Marianne might have a baby with him." David grimaced as the conversation came back in full force. "She seemed to think if you have two kids, you only love them half as much as you would one kid."

"Why are kids so dumb sometimes?" Ryan complained.

David chuckled. "You were never a dumb kid?"

"No way. I was a genius. Protégé, that was me."

"Prodigy. And you're a dumb adult, so I refuse to believe that."

"Hey!"

"Oh, excuse me. It must have been someone else who was insisting Spain was on the equator last time we played Trivial Pursuit with Ava."

Ryan rapped his knuckles on David's forehead. "Twat. Not all of us have a degree."

"Nothing in my degree included where Spain was. That was school. Primary school."

Ryan shrugged. "I spent all of primary school giving daisies to everyone, so I guess I missed that lesson about the equator."

"What about secondary school?"

"Upgraded to shagging everyone."

David smirked. "Is that where you met Marianne?"

Ryan snorted. "She's class. Three thousand pounds a term for her secondary school. No, I met Marianne the same way I met you. Chatted her up on a dating site."

"You didn't chat me up. We ignored each other, and then you recognised me at the Vue."

"I may have written several messages but never sent them."

"Why? Thought I was too snobby for you."

"Yeah, but you were hot as hell."

David laughed. He reached up and knocked his fist lightly against Ryan's head in echoing retaliation before grasping one of the long dreads and beginning to toy with it. "Well, you were all right yourself."

"Gee, thanks."

"Back on track, if you don't mind? What are we going to do about Ava?"

Ryan blew out his cheeks. "I don't know. I'll talk to Marianne next week if she doesn't cheer up. You never know. She might just get over it."

But he didn't look convinced.

Chapter Eighteen

WHEN THE DOORBELL rang, David shot Ryan a filthy look.

"Don't you dare make me get up and get that."

It turned out that neither he nor the baby liked cheese any more. He'd spent most of last night throwing up after lasagne for dinner, and today hadn't been too much better. He was contemplating calling in sick on Monday morning if things didn't significantly improve.

"Sorry," Ryan said, pulling a face and gesturing at his feet. "My back's playing up again. I'll make it up to you?"

David grunted and heaved himself off the sofa. The swoop of vertigo was sudden, and he froze for a long minute, bracing himself on the back.

"Hey. You all right?"

"Yeah. Yeah, just—give me a minute."

The doorbell rang again, and he grimaced before easing his eyes open and shuffling for the living room door. Blood rushed back to his feet as he reached the front door. It was probably just the postman, or even Mum turning up unannounced, but he tugged the hoodie a little lower anyway, self-conscious of his shape.

He didn't expect Marianne though.

"Oh," he said and opened the door wider. "You coming in, or—"

"Please. Is Ryan home? We need to talk."

"All right. I'll go and—"

"All of us."

David raised his eyebrows. "Er. Right. I'll go and put the kettle on, shall I?"

"I'll help."

She walked in like she owned the place—although to be honest, Marianne walked everywhere like she owned the place—and kicked off her shoes by the mat.

"How's everything going?" she asked as he closed the front door.

"Be glad when it's over," David admitted.

"Yes, it gets old, doesn't it?"

"Mm. Ryan! You want some tea?"

"Eh?"

"Marianne's come over!"

"Why? Maz! Everything all right?"

"My name is not Maz," she said, stalking off to the kitchen. David rolled his eyes but followed.

"What's this about?" he asked as she began to dig through cupboards, rattling about as though he was the visitor and not her.

"Ava."

"Everything okay?"

"Well, no, but I think we can sort things out." She didn't look especially anxious, but then Marianne never did, so David wasn't sure what to make of it.

"Where is she?"

"A birthday party at Xscape. I don't have to pick her up until four. How's Ryan?"

"Pain flare-up today, but he's managing all right. Think he overdid it at physio on Thursday; it's been playing up all week."

"Not on a load of drugs?"

"Er, not really, why?"

She opened her handbag. A thick folder of papers was squeezed into the available space, threatening to burst the seams.

"What's that?"

"Our custody agreement."

Custody? David physically took a step back. She'd been resistant to the idea of sharing more of Ava with Ryan. She'd completely stood her ground against changing things until well after Sam's birth. Surely she didn't mean to take her away even more?

"Marianne, you can't—"

She shook her head. "It's not what you think."

"Promise me it's not what I think," he said in a low, urgent voice. "If you take Ava from him, it'll destroy him."

"It's not," she said. "What you. Think."

They stared at one another in silence until the kettle clicked. Then David backed down—a bit. Marianne could be vicious when provoked, could be cold, could be harsh. She'd insisted on a legal arrangement. She'd vetoed Ryan moving over to Salford with David last year on the grounds that it was too far to see Ava, and if he wasn't going to be there enough, then their daughter would be better off if he weren't there at all.

But at the same time, she wasn't cruel. And she did things for Ava rather than herself. David decided to trust her with that, and backed off.

Ryan was looking worried when they walked into the living room together. David sank back onto his spot on the sofa, grimacing when the change of position drove the baby up into the base of his lungs and knocked the breath out of him. Marianne perched on the armchair usually made up to look like a princess throne for Ava, and there was a brief silence as mugs were distributed.

But Ryan couldn't keep it for long.

"What's this about?" he demanded, not touching his tea.

"Ava."

"I guessed that."

Marianne wrestled the papers out and dumped the file on the table. The cups jumped. Tea sloshed. And Ryan's jaw tightened.

"That's—our custody agreement."

"Yes."

"I thought you didn't want to change it."

"I didn't," Marianne said. "I thought—well, you know what I thought. I was wrong."

"You were wrong?" David echoed.

"Ava burst into tears last night at bedtime and...things were said," Marianne said.

"Like what?"

"She wanted a bedtime story from Daddy, and when I tried to compromise and offered to ring you so she could say goodnight, she had a meltdown and didn't want to."

"Why on earth not?" Ryan demanded. He looked wounded, and David's heart wrenched in his chest at the stunned, hurt expression.

"Because—she said—you didn't want her anymore because of the new baby."

"What?"

Marianne held up a hand. "We both know it's not true."

"Shit," Ryan muttered, dragging a hand down his face.

"I managed to get out of her that she thinks it's true because—well, you were right. Because you're going to have the baby all the time and not her. And I tried to tell her that you share the baby with David, and he just happens to live in the same house, so it's not that different to the way we share her. But she came back with the weekend thing."

"So she thinks because we only have her at weekends, she's not as important as Sam," Ryan concluded in a dull voice.

"And that eventually you won't want her for weekends anymore either."

"Fuck. *Fuck.*"

"Yeah."

"So—"

"So I brought the agreement. I was just thinking of her. And honestly, of you, David. I didn't want you to be overwhelmed with Ava and a new baby. I know she can be a handful, and I know you must be struggling with this as it is, and I thought it might make her more jealous of the baby, to be around you so much and seeing your focus on it. I didn't think she'd get this idea instead. Obviously it's backfired, and I'm sorry. So I thought maybe we could sort a verbal agreement today, take down some notes, and get them formalised through the solicitors over the next couple of weeks."

"But start with Ava sooner."

"Ideally."

Ryan glanced at David, squeezing his thigh. "What do you think?"

David shrugged. "She's your daughter. She deserves to know there's no first and second place with her and Sam. We can work it out."

Marianne looked openly relieved, and David felt a twinge in his chest that was nothing to do with where the baby's feet were.

"You'll have to start taking that hill to the school to pick her up, though," he told Ryan. "I can only collect her on Fridays usually, and it won't be long before I can't drive at all anymore."

Ryan nodded thoughtfully and looked to Marianne. "Is she still not adjusting well to Jack?"

"She's coming around," Marianne said. "I just think the timing is poor. She's already worried about losing you to Sam. I think she's scared of Jack and me having another baby and shouldering her out there as well."

"Bloody kids," Ryan muttered. "Right. So—what's the new arrangement?"

"Well, I was just thinking she spends one week with me and the next one with you. And so on and so on. So, what if I drop her off at school on Monday, and you pick her up and keep her until Sunday evening?"

"This Monday?"

"Yes?" she said in a questioning tone, glancing between them.

Ryan nodded. "Okay. Yeah. Shit. So—I have her Monday to Sunday, then we swap her over like normal on Sunday evening, and you have her the whole of next week?"

"Yes."

"I'll need to ring work and sort out my shifts. And I'm going to need more of her clothes and things, then. She never really leaves much here. And you're going to tell her, right?"

"Yes. She might be a bit clingy," Marianne warned, giving David an apologetic grimace. "It might be best if you collect her from school for the first couple of days, Ryan."

David shrugged. "I'm not exactly into crowds right now anyway."

That earned him a frown. But when Ryan shook his head minutely, Marianne seemed to decide to leave it.

"You want me to sign anything?"

"I wrote down my idea—"

David levered himself up off the sofa and went out to the kitchen to leave them to sign their things and book appointments with lawyers. For once, the conflicted feelings were soothed. If Ava wanted to see more of her dad, then bring it on. She might be a good distraction in the last few days, and she'd have to get used to Sam sooner or later.

Plus, if they managed to get her excited about having a baby brother or sister, then maybe David would catch it too. Right now, he just wanted it to be over.

As he tipped the rest of his tea down the sink and rinsed the cup out, he glanced up at the framed photos on the wall by the back door. The top one—him and Ryan at a friend's wedding last year. The middle—Ava's first school photo, her hair brushed out into a fluffy halo, grinning proudly and showing off the gap in her teeth where the tooth fairy had struck the previous weekend.

And the bottom one—an empty frame, added by Ryan only the day before.

Ready for Sam.

David put a hand on the bump, and wished he could be ready too.

Chapter Nineteen

THE FIRST MONDAY that David came home to find Ava still there was a bit of a shock.

He didn't realise how he could tell the days of the week by Ava's comings and goings. He felt off all week, uncertain what date it was or what he ought to be doing. He almost missed his appointment with Nadia at the clinic because he forgot it was Friday. And Ryan's adjusted shift pattern didn't help.

That first week, Ava was quiet and sulky. She didn't want the slightest thing to do with him, kept glaring at the bump, and clung obstinately to her dad at all times. But the second week they had her, school was out for the summer, and whole days to herself with Ryan while David was at work seemed to mellow her mood. At least she stopped kicking up a fuss at dinner if he was the one to cook.

For the most part, David ignored Ava in return. The pressure was getting worse. Not only on his skin—and his clothes—but on his mind. He took to touching his chest repeatedly, like he had right after the top surgery, as if he'd forgotten that they'd been removed. He expected to find them again all of a sudden. Going to work was getting harder and harder. He kept waking up in the night, dreaming of the so-called miracle of childbirth. Quite frankly, Ava was the least of his problems.

At the weekends, he worked on converting the shed into a summerhouse. A sweltering summer was rolling in thick and fast, and the only way he could be comfortable was to take off his shirt and wear nothing but board shorts when he was home. And the only way he could avoid a violent swell of dysphoria at the sight of himself and his swollen belly was to be busy.

Very busy.

So the conversion—which had only been to put a window into the side, throw up some shelves, insulate the roof and run out an electric cable for the computer and desk lamp—turned into a much more artistic job. The roof insulation turned into fitting a fancy overhang to shelter the doorway. The window earned itself a window box to match, filled with overspilling spider plants. The floor was torn up and replaced with tiles in a soft yellow colour like sand. The walls were stripped and sanded, and then tubs of pale blue paint arrived from the DIY place to turn the room into something airy and light. Putting the summer into summerhouse.

Ryan just watched in amusement and said nothing.

On their third week of having Ava for seven days in a row, though, the sulkiness seemed to abate, and she started to gravitate towards the garden and David's weekend work. He came home from the surgery several times to find one of his screwdrivers included in her tea parties, or suspicious blue paint daubs on her dresses for the wash. And on the first Saturday in August, he went back to the shed-cum-summerhouse after lunch to find her loitering on the threshold, staring up at the green vines he was carefully painting up the corners of the walls.

"Is this where the baby's going to go?" she asked.

"No, this is a nice new office for Daddy."

"So where's the baby going to go?"

"In the new room next to yours."

She fidgeted with the hem of her top, staring at the new blue walls. It stank of paint, and there was sawdust all over the floor. Usually, she'd be in her chaotic, destructive element—but David waited, seeing the cogs turning in her head, rather than asking what was wrong.

Then: "Daddy says me and the new baby are the same."

"You are. You're Daddy's children, and he loves you both the same."

"Really?"

"Really."

"But Daddy is with you now. Not Mummy. So—"

"So that just means he loves me and Mummy different now. Not you and Sam."

"Sam," she echoed and wrinkled her nose. "Is it a girl?"

"We don't know yet."

"I don't want a baby sister."

"We don't get to pick."

"I'm not sharing my dolls," she said. "And she can't be a fighter pilot like me."

"I thought you were going to be an astronaut."

"I'm gonna be both."

"Sam can be whatever Sam wants too. And Sam might not like dolls, even if Sam's a girl."

She screwed up her face. "Sam has to be a boy."

"We'll find out when they're born," David said.

She regarded him suspiciously for so long he heaved himself back up on the stepladder and returned to his vines. After a little while, she disappeared—only to come back with an armload of dolls and set up a school for them under the ladder. A school for defeating Klingons, apparently, but a school was a school.

David shrugged, and left her to it.

THAT EVENING, AVA climbed up onto David's lap instead of Ryan's.

"Er," David said.

She didn't answer, just dragged her blanket up too and jammed a thumb in her mouth. They'd put one of the *Jurassic Park* films on, because—in David's opinion—Ava had inherited Marianne's nerves of steel and was far more disturbed by bland acting than by dinosaurs ripping people and each other apart as noisily as possible. Usually, she'd sit on Ryan's lap, get bored halfway through when the killing lost its thrill, and fall asleep in time to be put to bed at the end.

She'd never sat on David before.

"You want David to give you a cuddle tonight?" Ryan asked.

She nodded wordlessly and burrowed into his chest a little harder. David shrugged and tucked his arms around her. Her weight against the bump wasn't unpleasant, although it was a little uncomfortable. He doubted he could last the whole film before turfing her off again so he could go to the bathroom.

Still, he'd take the thaw in relations.

It was the third film. Inexplicably, Ryan's favourite. David half watched and half dozed, idly wondering why he had the poor taste to be in love with someone who thought the third film was superior to almost anything out there, never mind the masterpiece that was the first film. Ava seemed to share his opinion, and before the second act was over, took to prodding the bump curiously.

"Stop it, sweetie," David mumbled.

"It's all round."

"Yes."

"Babies aren't round. Maybe you're not having a baby."

"Sorry. Definitely a baby. We checked."

She pouted and poked it again.

"It's in a big ball of water, to keep it safe from being prodded," David chided.

Her finger touched his T-shirt...then she flattened her hand out and pressed instead.

And—

David jolted as something fluttered inside him. It was like his stomach turning, his heart skipping a beat, and the throbbing pulse of a severe headache. It was like water running down his throat, vomit coming back up, and the rush of adrenalin in his own blood. All at once. All in the same spot.

And Ava squealed.

"It moved! Daddy, Daddy, it moved! The baby moved!"

Ryan's jaw dropped. He lunged across the sofa to clap a hand over the bump, completely hiding Ava's. David gripped his hand tight around his jaw and mouth as the lurching feeling rippled outwards again, and Sam—kicked? Punched? He couldn't tell.

But then his stomach really did turn.

"Off," he said brusquely.

Ava had barely slid off his knees before he staggered to his feet and fled for the bathroom. The punch of a violent upchuck hit him like a freight train, and he threw up in the sink instead of the loo. Sweat broke out on his forehead as Sam moved, and his stomach lurched once more.

"Hey."

Ryan's hand snaked past and turned the tap on. David groaned, resting his forehead on the ceramic as Ryan wet a washcloth and rested it on the back of his neck, cool and soothing.

"You all right?"

"No."

"Is it—something wrong as in you need me to call a doctor or the midwife, or something wrong as in you shouldn't be pregnant?"

"The latter," David mumbled. "It just feels so wrong when it moves..."

Ryan made a hushing noise. An arm slid around David's thighs and hugged his hips, stroking the side of the bump. Sam answered with a ripple of movement and then stilled. David swallowed back another surge of bile.

Then Ryan's hands slid up under his T-shirt.

"Ryan—"

"Ssh."

He cupped the bump between his palms, turning David gently from the sink. He leaned back against it, frowning as Ryan lifted his T-shirt and pressed a kiss to the straining skin.

"You need to knock it off," he told the bump in a serious tone, and David found a hysterical giggle rising from his chest. "Dad doesn't feel well when you do that. So while we're glad you've figured out your arms and legs, keep the flailing to a minimum until you're born, yeah? Then you can kick away to your heart's content. Deal?"

A flicker of movement stirred. Ryan didn't seem to register it, but David retched and clapped a hand over his mouth again.

"No," Ryan said, rapping the bump lightly with his fingertips. "We know you're awake. No need to prove it. Just settle down and listen to the film with us, eh?"

Nothing. David gritted his teeth and pushed off from the sink.

"I need a drink. Where's Ava?"

"On the sofa. Probably stealing my ginger beer."

"I might steal the rest."

"Have the whole bottle if it'll help," Ryan offered. David raised his eyebrows. "What? Don't get me wrong, if you steal it after Sam's born, I'll break both your legs."

"Sure, whatever, hard man," David muttered and pulled his T-shirt down. "I'm good. I'm going to get a drink, and then I'll join you again."

"No offence, I'd rather not just leave you."

David nearly snapped at him for that, but rubbed both hands over his face and shoved it away.

"Sorry."

Ryan squeezed his knees. "Sorry, you just—really don't look very well right now. You look a bit...faint."

"I'm not."

"Well, you can prove it by getting your drink and coming back with me."

David nodded. In truth, he wanted a little space. Everyone got excited when the baby started to kick. It was a big moment—and he'd been sick. He'd been so horrified by his own baby moving that he'd thrown up. He wanted a little space to process exactly what that meant.

But he also didn't, because he didn't think he'd like the answer all that much.

Chapter Twenty

RYAN'S BACK FLARED up on Sunday morning. So he spent the rest of the day on the sofa, doped up on his strong-enough-to-kill-an-elephant painkillers that he'd been taking on and off ever since the accident, and in no condition to handle Ava.

"I'll drop her back off at Marianne's," David said. "You get some sleep. Call me if you need anything."

There was sweat standing out on Ryan's forehead, but he nodded and squeezed David's hand wordlessly before he got up.

"Come on, Ava! Let's get you home to Mummy. Be a good girl and give Daddy a kiss goodbye."

For once, she didn't kick up a storm. She offered a get-better kiss, then took David's hand and followed him out to the car obediently, scrambling up into the back seat without a protest. She might be a monster, but at least she knew when it really wasn't a good idea to go mad.

"Will the baby have a wheelchair like Daddy?" she asked as David backed the car out of the driveway.

"No, honey."

"Why?"

"Because Daddy had an accident; that's why he has the chair."

"Why?"

Oh God, the why game. David sighed.

"Daddy needs the chair because he broke his back. If you break your back, your legs don't work anymore. But the baby hasn't got a broken back, so it won't need a chair."

"Will his back get better?"

"No, sweetie."

"Why?"

"Because the doctor doesn't know how to make it better."

"Why?"

David sighed. "Doctors know lots and lots, but they don't know everything."

"Why?"

"Because they're still learning."

"But if they learn everything, then they can fix Daddy's back?"

"Yes, perhaps," he said with no small amount of relief.

"They need to go back to school," she said, and he snorted with laughter.

"They go to school for a very long time."

"Longer than me?"

"Much longer than you."

"I don't wanna be a doctor," she decided. "I'm gonna be a vet like you."

David's stomach flooded with warmth.

"I thought you were going to be a fighter pilot astronaut?"

"And a vet."

"You have to go to school for a long time to be a vet too," he said.

"Oh." There was a long pause. "What about Mummy?"

"Yes, she went to school."

"Daddy?"

"Daddy didn't, no."

"Okay. I'll do what Daddy does. And be a fighter pilot astronaut."

David smirked, waiting for the next question.

"David?"

"Yes, Ava?"

"What does Daddy do?"

He grinned. "He answers telephones for policemen."

"Is that good?"

"It's very good. It means he can tell the policemen to come and help you when you need them."

"I'm gonna do that!" she cheered.

David privately thought Marianne would have his guts. She was determined that Ava was going to have three PhDs and run a multimillion-pound business by the time she was thirty. Ryan's ambitions for his daughter started and ended at getting all her swimming certificates.

"What's the baby gonna do?"

"I don't know," David said. "We'll have to ask it when it's all grown up."

"It's going to be a boy, right?"

"I don't know. Why?"

"You can't have two girls."

"Of course we can," David said. "I had two brothers."

"Did you?" she demanded with keen interest, and when he glanced in the wing mirror, she was sitting forward, staring intently at the back of his head. "Why didn't they come and visit with Auntie Mary at Christmas?"

He swallowed. "Uh. They're—they're gone, love."

"Gone?"

"They passed away. They died. Like your grandpapa."

She fidgeted. "Just like grandpapa?"

She'd only been told that it had been a car accident, and that was why she mustn't kick the back of the seats when anyone was driving. The detail—rightly, in David's opinion—had been left out. So although it was a blatant lie, he didn't feel bad about agreeing.

"Oh," she said and made a huffing noise. "Cars are stupid."

"They're very useful, but they're big and heavy, and if you don't respect them and be careful, they can be very dangerous. Just like water. Remember all your safety lessons about water when we go to the lake or you go swimming with Mummy?"

"Respect the water and it'll respect you," she recited.

"That's right. Cars are just the same."

To prove his point, he didn't swing up onto Marianne's drive like he usually did, but pulled over carefully to the side of the road, tucking Ava's door alongside the pavement. She didn't so much as take her seatbelt off before he came around to open her door, and he promised a gold star for her chart on the fridge as a reward.

"That's you nearly up to a full ice cream," he added. "How many's that?"

She counted to ten, holding his hand firmly through the garden gate then letting go, forgetting his existence on the face of the earth, and running ahead to pound on the front door.

"Mummy, Mummy, Mummy!"

Marianne opened the door wearing a woolly jumper over a suit skirt and heels. David raised his eyebrows, and she pulled a face.

"I had to take some papers over to Leeds in time for a hearing on Monday morning," she said. "Hello, darling! Have a nice time at Daddy's?"

"Yeah, I got another star, can we have chicken, I didn't have any dinner, where's Jack, where's Molly, can I have my colouring book?"

"She did have dinner," David said. "Spaghetti bolognese. Two helpings."

"She didn't get that appetite from me," Marianne said and then jerked her head at the kitchen. "Come in. Have a cuppa. I have some things for you."

David blinked, but obediently stepped into the hall and toed his shoes off on the mat.

"I'm sorry about the other week," she said as she set Ava up at the kitchen table with an apple and a colouring book. "You took me completely by surprise. I didn't mean anything by it."

David shrugged.

"Are you excited?"

"Apprehensive."

"Mm, I was the same. Ryan was like a tweenager at a boy band concert the whole time, just constant loud excitement, but I spent three months wondering if I'd done the right thing."

"Only three?"

"Well, I didn't know about her for the first six." She chuckled.

David smiled. She flicked the kettle on and leaned back against the counter, appraising him.

"But then, I imagine it's harder for you," she said quietly.

"Yeah."

"It'll pass."

"What?"

"All the—mess you're feeling right now. It does pass." She nodded at Ava, who was merrily ignoring the pair of them. "By the time she was six months old, I'd have murdered anyone who dared even hint I'd not made the best choice or I regretted it. For a long time, I denied even having thought those things myself. But at the time, it is hard. It is messy. But it does go away."

David shook his head. "No offence, but—it's not the same."

"No," she agreed.

"Please don't lecture me about how I'll be fine. At the end of the day, women get pregnant every day and have spent their whole lives with the knowledge that it's just something natural they do. But me? I didn't. I didn't have that."

"You didn't think you could?" she asked in surprise.

"No, I didn't."

She winced. The kettle clicked, and she turned away to pour out tea.

"So to say I'm surprised is an understatement. I thought I was ill. I was convinced I was ill. And honestly? I was placing cancer higher on the list of preferable results than this."

Cups rattled, and Marianne gestured for him to sit at the table with her. She looked thoughtful as they sank into their chairs.

"I wanted a kid, but not like this," David admitted.

"At least you wanted one. That's half the argument right there, isn't it? You'll love it when it gets here."

"I hope so."

"You will. You love Ava, and she's not even yours. You're going to adore—what's its name?"

"Sam."

"Sam. Sam Walsh, I take it?"

"Er, yeah. How did you—"

"Ryan was very firm about that when we divorced," she muttered, and David snorted with unexpected laughter. "I think he's trying to outweigh any awful kids that Jay produces. I take it Jay isn't happy about this?"

David coughed. "Er."

Marianne laughed. It was a sharp peal of high sound, somehow sadistic and sunny at the same time. "You haven't told him, have you?"

"Nope."

"What about Aggie?"

"Also nope."

"Do they know you're—uh—capable?"

David shook his head mutely.

"Christ," Marianne said, still smirking. "She won't like that."

"Take it she liked you?"

"Oh my God, no. Aggie's from the Dark Ages. I was studying to be a lawyer, I was going to have a job and earn more than Ryan, I was going to emasculate him, I was probably a lesbian, the works. You know, at our wedding, she actually told Ryan right in front of me that he ought to take the belt to me for dancing with his best man?"

David's jaw sagged. "Seriously?"

She nodded.

"Fu—" He glanced at Ava, who was still devoted to her colouring book. "Er. Christ."

"Ryan's only turned out the way he has because he hates Jay so much. It took him a long time to come to terms with being bisexual, and I thought the HIV might kill him for a while. He took that really badly."

David made a face.

"What are you going to do when Aggie and Jay find out?"

"I don't know. We haven't really talked about it."

Marianne bit her lip. "What do you want to do?"

Although they'd never discussed Ryan's family before—in fact, David had discussed very little with Marianne on a one-to-one basis—some shared experience hung in the air between them. A shared disgust and loathing. Ryan's mother was the bigoted evangelical type, like David had feared his own mum might be when he was a kid. And Jay was violent about it. Ryan had turned out normal, in David's opinion, because he'd fallen for such a smart girl when he met Marianne and had most of his own vile learning smashed out of him in exchange for getting to be anywhere near her.

And in the back of his mind, David wondered if he wasn't unconsciously continuing Marianne's work. Ryan had asked many stupid and offensive questions when they first met. The idea of actually having a baby with this man had been, back then, a laughably bad idea. Now? Now, not so much.

"I'd like Sam to believe Ryan was just left by the stork thirty-five years ago," he said, and Marianne chuckled.

"Mm. Me too."

"If it were up to me, Aggie wouldn't be allowed within a hundred miles of my kid. And I am banning Jay from the house if Sam or me are around. After the last time we met—"

Marianne's eyebrows nearly flew off the top of her head. "You've actually met him?"

"Yeah. He came over the week after I moved in."

"What happened?"

"He decked me."

David hadn't even known who he was. He'd just walked in from the back garden on hearing Ryan's raised voice, and saw him rowing with a lad in his late twenties wearing jogging bottoms hung suspiciously low. He knew then and there it had to be Jay. Ryan and his younger brother looked very alike.

But he'd only said, "You must be—" before Jay turned and punched him in the mouth.

"Oh my God," Marianne said. "What did you do? I hope you called the police."

"Er. Well. Later."

"Later?"

David coughed.

"What happened before later?"

"I...punched him back."

Marianne narrowed her eyes. "David."

"Fine. I hit him. Technically."

"With what?"

He chuckled. *Busted.* "Remember Ryan told you he'd broken that lamp your mum had bought the pair of you at your wedding?"

"Ye-es?"

"He didn't. I did. On Jay."

He hadn't even thought about it. It had been sitting on top of its box, ready to be packed away and given to Marianne next time she came over to drop off or collect Ava. David had just seized it round the ugly pink middle and swung it into Jay's face with all the force of a novice on the golf course.

"He left after that. Then he sent me death threats, so I took him to court."

Marianne started to laugh again. "Oh my God!"

David shrugged.

"Well, send my apologies to Ryan for getting mad at him about that lamp," she said, chuckling. "That seems like a good use of it."

"That's what I figured. I don't really know what to do about Aggie, but Jay is easy. I'm not letting him near Sam."

"Good idea." Marianne drained her tea. "I know I didn't react as best as I could, but—I'm happy for you. For both of you. Ryan needed someone like you, and you're so good with Ava. I think this is going to be great for the both of you."

"Maybe. Eventually."

"It will," she promised and squeezed his elbow. He jumped at her touch. "And if you need anything, you know where to find me."

He blinked. "I—yeah. Thanks. Thank you."

She squeezed again and stood up. "Come on. I still have some of Ava's baby clothes. May as well start getting prepared for Sam, right?"

Chapter Twenty-One

HIS BACK HURT.

David spent most of his day standing up at work. He preferred standing to sitting now he was unquestionably showing, but eight hours was taking a toll on his back. And his thighs. And everything else.

Plus, Sam thought standing up was the best thing ever and had taken to punching every organ within reach.

So when half past four arrived, and his last appointment opened the door, David could have cried to see Vicky.

Just Vicky, holding a blatantly empty carrier. No Fred, no kittens. Just Vicky.

"I'm not a doctor," he said, and she laughed at him.

"You've not been answering our texts or calls, you've been skipping judo for months now without a word, and this is the only way I get to see you," she said. "So I'm going to sit here for half an hour, and you're going to talk to me until the surgery closes, and then we're going to get a drink."

David rolled his eyes. "You know, we could fine you for this."

"We both know you won't," she said. "So, come on. What's going on? Are you okay?"

"Yes?"

She eyed the straining lab coat pointedly. "You've been off sick, you've gained a lot of weight, and you're not coming to judo. You're obviously not all right. So I can start guessing or—"

She knew. They all knew, his judo friends. They were all his university friends. But David had found that a strange thing happened over the years, once the passing had kicked in.

People forgot.

They just—forgot. In the beginning, there was a sharp tinge of awareness about everything, like everyone saw that he was trans before they saw that he was David. Like they'd remember his identity prior to his name. But after his first surgery, when he'd jumped from obviously trans to obviously a man, the people around him just seemed to forget. There had been...moments. Incidents where it became obvious they no longer quite remembered. The night out after he and James had passed their blue belt, where James told him to hurry up and stop waiting for the cubicle and just use the urinal. The day Vicky had rummaged through his bathroom cabinet in search of condoms to steal for her own use, and had a go at him.

"You could get someone pregnant!" she'd raged, and David just stared in stupefaction at her.

He looked obvious—but people forgot. People saw what they wanted to see. And so he knew—knew—Vicky wouldn't guess right.

"I'm not ill," he said.

"So explain—"

"I'm pregnant."

She stopped mid-flow. Her jaw sagged. She'd lifted a finger to point accusingly at him, but it hung in mid-air like she'd forgotten she had hands at all.

"Pregnant?"

There was a long pause.

Then, "Oh my God!"

She squealed and jumped forward. The carrier clattered to the floor. She hugged him tightly, and he was smothered in the smell of perfume and paint.

"That's amazing!" she enthused. "Oh my God, why didn't you say anything! No, wait, I know why, you never say anything anyway! Oh my God, David! You have to come over now. Right now. Come on, we're going for drinks—no, dinner, *dinner*, you can't drink—and I'll call the others, and—"

"No."

She let go, sliding back with a frown.

"David?"

"I'm—this isn't—it wasn't exactly planned," he admitted. "And I'm—we wanted a kid, so I kept it, but I'm..."

He trailed off. Vicky's face softened, and she rubbed his arm.

"You're struggling," she said.

"Yes." He hesitated, chewing on his lip. Then all in a rush: "I don't know that I made the right choice to keep it."

It felt like a weight was lifted off his shoulders. To just say it. He couldn't tell Ryan—it would crush him. He couldn't tell Mum, because she'd flat out kill him. But he could tell Vicky, because Vicky had no stakes in this. Vicky was just Vicky. She wasn't going to be a grandmum, she wasn't a father. She was—

His friend, and his heart clenched when she reached up and hugged him again, tight and warm, despite the bump in the way.

She was his friend, and he'd forgotten about the others that might gather round when he needed them.

"You've always wanted children," she said gently. "I think you're finding it really hard right now, but that'll get better after it's over and you have your little baby in your arms. Just like—just like nobody would ever volunteer to do it again when they're in the middle of labour, because it hurts and it's awful, but afterwards, it all feels better."

"I hope so," he admitted.

"So—boy? Girl? When's it due?"

"Baby," he said with a shrug. "Bonfire Night."

"Oh, that's not too long to go," she said.

He snorted. It wasn't even August yet.

"Are you all ready for it?"

"God, no. We haven't even got a crib. I have a box of baby clothes from Ryan's ex-wife, but that's about it."

"You've got time," she said and beamed up at him. "You know what we need to do, don't you?"

"If you say baby shower, I'm going to punch you."

"Uh, no. Exported tat. Nooooo, we need to get together! Have a big meal out, and you can tell the others!"

David raised his eyebrows. "Kind of assumed you would."

"Uh, you do not remember the betting pool, do you?"

"No?"

"Third year? When James and Andi graduated? We all took bets on who'd be first to have a baby, and James picked you. And it's going to be you! He'll win!"

David snorted with laughter. "I thought you didn't want me to give James an ego."

"For the look on his face, it'll be worth it. Come on. Come out to dinner with us. This weekend! This Saturday, I'll sort it all out. We'll have a big get-together and you can spring your news, and James will shit himself."

As always, Vicky—tiny, pretty, posh Vicky—swearing made David grin.

"All right," he said. "Organise something."

"It'll be good for you," she promised. "And talk to us, David. You're obviously finding it hard. Just talk to us. Talk to me."

"I know. I'm sorry. It's just—"

He trailed off, fighting for a word, and she pulled a face. "Force of habit?"

"Yeah. I guess it is."

"Unforce it," she said and picked up the abandoned carrier. "Come on. It's five o'clock. Walk me out, and go home to your Ryan, and tell him all about how James's going to brick it."

"Ryan's never met James."

"Just as well, they'd hate each other. You know James had a crush on you in first year?"

"Oh, I know, and that fact never fails to creep me out," David drawled as he retrieved his coat and mashed some details into the appointment log. "All right, Saturday. But not too late—we've got Ava this weekend again."

They made plans as he walked her out to her car, waving to Sonia but not stopping. He'd forgotten just how good for him Vicky was. She was always so unfailingly positive that it became infectious. She'd twist even miserable situations around into something funny or something pragmatic, and had talked him out of much darker days than this in university.

Christ, why hadn't he called Vicky up right from the beginning?

"Talk to me," she said once she'd closed the empty carrier in the boot of her car. "And I'll call you about Saturday."

"Will do. Promise."

"And let me know when the baby arrives!"

"Sam," he said.

She beamed widely at the name, though David couldn't remember ever telling her who Sam had been, and hugged him hard around the middle as though hugging the baby too. Sam didn't kick for once, but David felt a flicker of movement anyway, and—for once—didn't feel nauseated by it.

"Saturday," she said, and then she shut the door and left him standing behind his car in the warm evening.

And David simply...smiled.

His back still hurt. His ankles did, too, come to think of it. He felt conspicuous in his light jacket and thin trousers, everything bulging out of everywhere. He still felt raw and jagged—in an odd way, more so after her hug and happiness—but less like he might cry.

He got into his car, and put a reminder for Saturday into his phone. Then he smiled faintly at the wheel, before finally turning the key in the ignition. Ryan accused him fairly frequently of being closed-off and forgetting to actually reach out to the people who cared about him. And David couldn't really argue. He did. And he'd done it again with Vicky and the others.

A meal out with the lot of them was a good idea. Maybe he could relax. Put all the bad parts of having a baby out of his mind, and focus on the good ones. Time off work, cute Babygros, getting to use lifts all the time with the pram—Vicky was right. It would be good for him.

Mood buoyed, he drove home with the radio on loud and a smile on his face. Sam kicked away, and it didn't feel revolting, for once. It felt—nice. Hopeful. He just had to last until early November, and then he'd have the baby he'd never been allowed to admit he wanted.

He'd be first in their group to do so, and apparently win James a load of money from the others.

He couldn't wait to turn up and break the news to them. James's face was going to be a—

The thought came screeching to a halt, along with the car, not ten feet from the end of their driveway. There was a van in his spot. A white transit van, with a plumbing company's logo on the side.

A very familiar logo.

Jay Walsh was in his house.

And usually, David would turn the car right around and leave. Find something else to do until Jay left. Not put himself anywhere near that ignorant, bigoted waste of air and resources.

But his fists tightened around the steering wheel.

To hell with that.

His house, his rules. And if Jay didn't like them, *he* could leave.

And if he didn't want to, then David was going to make him.

Chapter Twenty-Two

HE FOUND THEM in the kitchen.

Six eyes stared back at him, two of them apologetic and four cold and hard. David's lip curled in response to their sneers.

"Aggie. Jay." He stepped around them delicately and bent to kiss Ryan. A hand caught at the back of his head and deepened it, Ryan apparently no more impressed by their presence than David was.

"Good day?" Ryan asked.

"It was going all right," David said. There was a heat in his chest like a furnace. It was familiar like Mum's flat was familiar—he thought he'd forgotten how to be so angry and defensive, but now it was back, he could remember every single aspect of the sensation. "Yours?"

Ryan snorted. "Yeah. Same."

"So, it's true," Aggie interrupted.

Aggie was Ryan's mother. She was short and solid, and built like a pear. She had a habit of squeezing into tight skirts, like the mother of the bride at a wedding. She always walked around in a heavy cloud of perfume, and wore nails as long as the fingers they sprouted off. She lived out in Huddersfield with Jay, and worked as a receptionist somewhere. Privately, David couldn't imagine a less welcoming woman to front a business.

He rarely saw Aggie, and it was regarded by all parties involved as the best possible deal. She had hated Marianne, but at least Marianne was a woman. Aggie hated David even more, and in the last two years, had cut Ryan out of her will, threatened to disown him from the family, and attempted to have Ava taken away from him. If her son was going to be a pervert, the least he could do was keep it on the down-low like anyone with a shred of decency ought to.

So if David wasn't pleased to see Jay at his kitchen table, he was even less delighted to see Aggie. Hence the snort that he let out at her question and the sharp, "What's that, then?"

She eyed his bump, obvious through the shirt, and pursed her lips.

"I've put on a few pounds?" he asked. "Or my shirts don't fit like they used to? Wouldn't have thought it'd bother you, Aggie. Lord knows you haven't worn an outfit that fits in years."

"Wind your fucking neck in," Jay snarled.

"Watch your fucking mouth in *my* fucking house," David replied casually as he leaned against the counter, folding his arms over his chest. "I take it you two are here for a reason?"

Aggie threw him a look that would have set fire to lesser men. "I came to talk to Ryan about seeing my grandchild. Jay was kind enough to offer me a lift. It's more than you've ever done for us."

"Wouldn't have thought you'd want to get in my car," David sneered. "There's gay all over it; it's disgusting."

"Yeah, except you're not gay, are you?" Jay interrupted, jabbing a finger at the bump. "You're not a bloke at all, you're just pretending to be one."

David narrowed his eyes. The hairs on his arms were rising. He clenched his jaw and his teeth ground together.

"Jay, knock it o—"

"No, Ryan, let him talk. I've never seen slime talk before. I'm interested to hear what it has to say," David hissed.

"Jay, stop it," Aggie snapped. "And you!" She clicked her fingers imperiously at David. "Go out or something, go on. We're here to see my son, not you."

"Oh, he's your son again, is he? That's funny, at his birthday he was the disgrace of the family and wasn't fit to be near you."

"David," Ryan murmured. "They were just leaving."

Aggie swelled like a bullfrog. "We were not!"

"You are now," Ryan said. "I'm not having you upset David, not in his—"

"I swear to God, Ryan, if you say the word 'condition' I am going to murder you," David snapped. His temper was fraying around the edges. "Come on, Jay, you were winding up for a good rant there. Out with it."

The snarl turned into something feral, and Jay stood up, pulling away from his mother's restraining hand.

"You should have had an abortion," he spat. "You're not a man, you're just a girl who's fucked in the head, and that proves it. Men can't get fucking pregnant, and retards like you shouldn't be allowed to have kids. You should have had it aborted, and then been put down."

It wasn't anything David hadn't heard before, but then he felt the cotton of his shirtsleeves straining under his own fingers. Almost distantly, he realised he was about to lose his temper. When Ryan started forward from the table, David shook his head sharply.

He wanted to lose it.

He wanted to give Jay exactly what he deserved.

And he wanted to make sure Jay would never forget who was in charge here.

"Should've come round," Jay sneered. He held up a balled fist and smiled grimly. "I'd have done it for you. Free of charge. Family rates, right?"

"Get out of my house."

Jay's lip curled. "*Your* house?"

"Yes," David said. "*My* house. My name is on the mortgage. Yours isn't. So you're in my house, and now I'm telling you to get out. And stay out."

An ugly steeliness lit behind Jay's eyes, and he puffed his chest out.

"And what's a bitch like you going to do to make me?"

How fucking dare he. How dare that useless, worthless piece of lazy shit walk into his house and start sounding off about who he was, like he had the first clue about what David had gone through to get where he was, like he had the first idea of how hard David had worked to make something of himself. And how dare Jay—Jay, the man with four kids by four women and who never paid a penny towards any of them—start passing remarks about fitness to be parents.

"Get out," he said, "or I'll make you."

The disgust was just like Ben's. Just like school's. Just like hundreds of people before, of every colour and every background, when they'd seen what David was.

Or what they thought he was.

"Then make me."

And just like that—David let go.

University disappeared. Education vanished. Sense and composure evaporated. His temper exploded into red all around the edges of his vision, and the adrenalin jumped in his system like he'd been plugged in to the mains.

Before he knew he'd even moved, David had cool metal in his hand. The extendable arm he'd been using on the rollers to repaint the summerhouse. Heavy. Solid. The crack when he swung it into the side of Jay's head shivered up his arm like raw energy, and history flooded back.

Every sneer. Every punch. Ben's horror. Mum's tears. Every beating behind the school bins. Every chase through school corridors. Every burn, every slap, every scar, every humiliation.

How. Fucking. Dare. They.

"Get the fuck out of my house!"

He swung it again. And again, and again, and again. He wasn't a vet, he wasn't a graduate, he had no letters after his name. He was a Salford boy, he was Mary's stray one, he was Davey Neal, and he was fucking angry.

Jay was a big lad, but he was a bigot and David was done. And Salford wasn't for pistols at dawn, it was for cracks on kneecaps and knees in balls. As Jay doubled with the pain, David simply went for the back of his head instead, and drove all six foot of him down the hall and out of the door in a furious barrage of unleashed, unbottled, unstoppable fury.

"You think I'm a fucking bitch now, you just step back in here and try me!" he roared, until Jay hit the van and the metal bar smashed the window. The alarm went off. Curtains started to twitch. "Get out! Get out of here! You set one foot on my property again, and I'll have you fucking shot, you waste of your father's cum!"

Knees hit brick. The final blow cracked the stick, a great shard of metal flying off and embedding itself in the flowers like a knife. Jay spat—and backed down. Backed off. Retreated to the end of the driveway with loose teeth and a broken nose.

And David turned on the evil cow of a mother who'd started the whole damn thing.

"And you!"

He pointed the splintered bar like a shotgun.

"You can fuck off an' all!" he bellowed. "You're no fucking mother, and you're no fucking grandmother neither! If you even think about coming near our kid, you'll wish you'd never been fucking born!"

He sounded like his mother. He felt like his brothers. As Mrs Walsh edged around him to join Jay at the end of the drive, wide-eyed and silent for the first time since he'd met her, David turned and smashed the remnants of the bar into smithereens against the side of the wailing van.

Then he dropped the splinters and walked inside.

Shut the front door.

Locked it.

And reached for his mobile on the side to call the police.

Ryan's hand caught his wrist. And then he smiled.

Just—smiled.

The rage simmered. The heat dropped. Slowly, David's heart calmed, and the thundering rush of adrenalin ebbed into a low, warm tide. The Caribbean sea on sunlit sand.

"That was hot as hell and well overdue," Ryan said. "You might have just turned Sam into a professional boxer or something, but to hell with it. Jay's had that coming for a long time."

David smiled back a little hesitantly.

"Jay's going to smash up the front door, you realise that?"

"Not for a bit. Mum'll kill him if he tries. You might have kicked the shit out of him, but you've spooked her."

"What do you mean?"

"My mother only gives you shit because she thinks it'll never come back to bite her," Ryan said. "But you just threatened to block her from seeing her grandchild. Spawn of sin or not, Sam's her grandkid."

David shook his head. "She's having nothing to do with them."

"Oh, after that little display and the bollocks they were coming out with before you got home? I agree," Ryan said, and David relaxed. "We just—don't tell Mum that."

Realisation dawned. David began to smile.

"So you think as long as she thinks there's a chance we'll let her into Sam's life, she'll keep Jay on a lead?"

"Yep."

David nodded. "Okay. We don't—ever—but okay."

"And by the time she figures that out and lets him loose again—" Ryan reached out and patted the bump affectionately. Sam patted back, plainly exhilarated by the whole saga. "—you'll be fighting fit and do a lot more than break a window."

David coughed.

"What?"

"Pretty sure I broke his nose. And a couple of teeth. Not just the window."

Ryan grinned.

"Oh, that is—not fair." The next pat aimed lower, and David laughed shakily. "Bed with you. For—you know. A chat."

"A chat. I'm sure."

The grin widened. "Hey. We can talk during. Multitasking."

"I can talk during. You? You'll be busy."

Ryan tapped his lap, grinning, and turned the chair towards their bedroom door.

"Deal."

Chapter Twenty-Three

DAVID HADN'T LOST his temper quite like that in a long time. And he certainly hadn't been pregnant the last time he'd done it.

They didn't even get around to the anticipated sex. Ryan had cosied up to him in their bed, lavished lazy kisses on him, and then—David woke up to the sound of crashing pots in the kitchen.

Levering himself up on his elbows, he patted the bump when Sam kicked. The usual rush of horror wasn't there for once, and he wondered if Jay's bigotry and his own explosion had triggered some kind of parental override. Maybe his instincts had fired up at last, and he wouldn't feel so crap for the next three months.

"You going to behave for dinner?" he asked the bump, and Sam squirmed. That was a little less delightful, and he tensed his chest against the urge to retch.

When it subsided, he heaved himself out of bed, wrapped himself in Ryan's dressing gown, and went hunting for why Ryan was making dinner quite that noisily.

He found Ava standing on her stool, enthusiastically doling out three-quarters of a pan of rice and peas onto plates, and the last quarter all over the floor. With a guilty pang, David realised she must have been playing in the garden when he'd had his fight with Jay. Christ, he hoped she hadn't seen that. Ryan was watching with an expression torn between horror and amusement, and David could distinctly smell fish. Taking a deep breath, he plastered a smile on his face and asked if he could help.

"No," Ava said, smacking him with the draining spoon when he got too close. "Daddy says you're tired, so you have to sit down and wait."

"Yes, ma'am. What are we having?"

"Salt fish and rice and peas and dumplings!"

He raised his eyebrows at Ryan, who shrugged. "Apparently we can't have Auntie Mary food without Auntie Mary dumplings," he explained. "I'm not totally convinced I've done them right, but we'll see."

"Why that combination?"

"I made the mistake of googling, and she picked the first three things that looked nice."

David chuckled. "I'm not totally sure I've ever eaten salt fish and dumplings at the same time, but all right, let's try it."

"Oh, and there's fried plantains for dessert, because it was that or grater cake, and Madam here doesn't need grater cake."

"Not sure the plantains won't have her bouncing off the ceiling either, you know."

In the interest of harmony, David firmly told himself to act like it was the best meal he'd ever had, but it was surprisingly good, despite the haphazard way it had been thrown together by a five-year-old who was even less Jamaican than he was. Ryan had even made proper cornmeal dumplings instead of the usual heavy tat David found in the supermarkets around here. He took a picture on his phone and sent it to Mum.

"You feeling better?" Ryan asked.

"Yeah. Slept all right."

"Ava has a question for you."

David grimaced. "Oh."

"Ava? Why don't you ask David what you asked me earlier?"

She fidgeted, stabbing her fish repeatedly with her fork, before finally saying: "I don't like Uncle Jay and Grandma anymore."

"Oh?"

"They were really mean."

"Oh, you heard that..."

"They were saying mean things like—like you and Daddy shouldn't have a baby and I shouldn't live here with you and—and you're not gonna get rid of Sam, are you? You're not gonna get rid of me?"

"Of course we're not going to get rid of you. Or Sam," David said gently.

She nodded. Ryan didn't move a muscle, and David figured they must have already had this talk. In depth.

"Daddy says I don't have to see them anymore if I don't want."

"That's right."

"And he says they won't be allowed to come over anymore."

"Yep."

"Ava, get to the point, honey. Your food's getting cold."

"Can Auntie Mary be my grandma now?"

David raised his eyebrows—then smirked and reached for his phone. "How about you ring her and ask?"

He didn't quite trust her with his phone—less Ava, more the things that James liked to text him—so pulled up his mother's number and dialled before switching to speakerphone.

"David! Everything all right?"

"Hi, Mum. You get my picture?"

"I did. Did Ryan do that?"

"Ryan and Ava," David said. "It's pretty good, actually. Ava might give you a run for your money in a few years."

"Cheeky!"

"Ava wants to ask you a question." David pushed the phone towards Ava on the table. "Go on."

"Hi, Auntie Mary!"

"Hello, baby girl. What's this question, then?"

"Are you gonna be Sam's grandma?"

"Yes—"

"My grandma was really mean to Sam and David today, so will you be my grandma instead?"

Mum—squeaked.

The sharp little noise, a single intake of stunned breath, was one that David instantly knew he'd remember for the rest of his life. His heart jerked violently in his chest, and he reached blindly for Ryan's hand. It was caught and squeezed tightly.

"Sweetie, I already think of you as my grandbaby. You're on my little shelf of family pictures, both you and your dad. If you want to call me Nana, then you go right ahead, honey."

"Thank you!" Ava trilled, clearly completely missing the emotion in Mum's voice, and David picked up the phone, switching the speaker off.

"You all right?" he asked.

"What's happened?" Mum snapped, the softness vanishing like it had never existed. "What does she mean her grandmother was mean? Ryan's mother?"

David pushed back from the table and took himself out into the garden. It was warm and still light, and he padded barefoot along the hot paving slabs to the canopy at the end, where he sank into a chair, grunting as Sam was pushed up against his organs again.

"I came home from work to Aggie and Jay on a visit."

"Oh, good Lord..."

"I didn't realise Ava was in the garden, or I'd have not done it—but I might have lost my temper a bit."

"What was said?"

"From them or from me?"

"Both."

"Basically that I'm f—messed in the head, and I shouldn't be allowed to have children or be around them." He hadn't found that particular remark the most offensive himself, but knew Mum would go ballistic. "Said that I ought to have aborted it. Jay even offered to do it for free."

She sucked in a breath. "That—!"

"I know," he interrupted. "I lost my temper."

She snorted. "Oh, I see. Good Lord, you're more like Ben than you care to admit."

David shrugged. "He threatened me and Sam, and called me a—yeah, well. Words were used."

"And I imagine a bit more."

"Possibly."

She chuckled. "As long as the police don't get involved, you don't need that nonsense."

"Doubt Jay will bother calling them, given what he likes to get up to," David said, pulling a face. He leaned back in his chair. "At least Ava seems to have come down on my side."

"Rightly so," Mum said. "They didn't say anything to her, did they?"

"I don't know," David admitted. "I know she at least overheard something about them wanting us to get rid of Sam and not being fit to have children at all. She was asking if we're going to get rid of her."

Mum said something incredibly rude. David smirked.

"Language," he chided.

"You're not too old for the spoon, boy!"

"Sure, Mum. Hundred-mile-long spoon, I'm shaking."

"You watch your tongue," she snapped. "Jacob and I are going to come over and visit soon, and after that little mess, I'm going to make it sooner. What does Ryan think?"

"He was as pissed as I was."

She harrumphed. David could imagine her expression.

"Evil lot," she muttered. "You make a big fuss of that little girl for her nana, you hear me?"

"Yes, Mum."

They said their goodbyes and David stretched out his feet in the dying sunlight and stared thoughtfully off into the distance. Ryan's family wouldn't like this turn at all. If Ryan banned Aggie and Jay from seeing Ava, they'd likely have to get the family courts involved.

But then—

David smiled as he thought of the box of baby clothes in the spare room.

So what? They had contacts.

Chapter Twenty-Four

THERE WAS A crib in Sam's room on Saturday morning.

David had slept in late. He'd had nightmares all night, a constant loop of sweat on his skin and Ryan's voice and hand trying to soothe him, and then flashes of pain, someone screaming, the ripple of dysphoria and disjoint under his skin, the sensation of his soul peeling away from his bones, anger—

At five in the morning, Ryan had gotten up, fetched the nail scissors from the bathroom, and trimmed David's nails right down to the quick.

"You're scratching," he murmured softly. "No more scratching, all right?"

Somewhere about six, David had finally managed to fall asleep, and had woken up at noon with a brutal headache. On shuffling out into the hall in his pyjama bottoms and a tank top, bump jutting out like a coastal shelf over the waistband, he smelled sawdust and fresh paint, and wondered for a wild moment if he wasn't having a stroke.

But no. There was a crib in Sam's room.

"What the—?"

He edged inside carefully. Jay had painted the room a pale lemon yellow when he'd done the fitting, apparently buying Ryan's bullshit about wanting a neutral spare room for visitors. But they hadn't done much decorating otherwise.

Someone apparently had been.

An IKEA dresser was tucked up against the wall, and the box of clothes Marianne had given him had disappeared. When David cracked open the top drawer, a pile of neatly folded Babygros were stacked inside. The scent of spring fresh fabric softener floated free.

The dresser and crib were in matching pale wood, and David shuffled across the carpet to touch the bars. He felt a twinge. He'd long imagined having a child, but never quite a crib. He'd always assumed they'd adopt, and there were a lot more toddlers and small kids to adopt than babies. His fantasy life had jumped from no kids at all to a bed and school uniforms.

The crib seemed—odd.

And yet sweet too. He could imagine stooping over the bar to pick up a heavy little baby. The bars dropped deliberately low, so Ryan could do it too without hurting his back or tipping the chair. There'd be mornings, in a year or so, when he'd open the door to find big dark eyes staring at him, and chubby fists banging a toy off the bars, demanding the morning fun to begin. And it would be four o'clock and still pitch black outside.

The crib was made up as if Sam had already arrived. The only thing missing was a mobile to entertain them. Even the blanket was folded back as if the baby had been there just last night. And the ragdoll propped up in the corner was—

David narrowed his eyes.

His ragdoll.

"Mum!" he shouted.

"Kitchen, dear!"

Tugging his tank top a little looser around his swollen belly, he shut the door to the new nursery as he headed for the kitchen. The back doors were open. He could see Ryan out on the patio, watching Ava doing handstands on the deck by the vegetable patch. Someone else was out there too, and Mum was up to her wrists in the washing up.

"I can do that."

"Don't be silly," she said. "Sit down. Ryan said you had a bad night. Let's get some breakfast down you. A proper breakfast too, none of this yoghurt and muesli nonsense."

He shrugged and pushed his feet into the flip-flops he kept by the back door. The sun was blazing. Even Ryan, who could be happy in the Sahara, had retreated into the shade of the canopy. He smiled at David and pulled out the chair next to him.

"You feeling better? Get some proper sleep?"

"Yeah."

David hesitated, given the presence of the old man at the table with Ryan, but then decided to hell with it. He had to be Jacob. So David leaned over and gave Ryan a morning kiss that tasted of death, and threw caution to the wind.

"Mm, hello."

"What's with the crib?"

"Your mum brought it," Ryan said. "Jake here helped me set it up."

David glanced at his mum's new boyfriend, sizing him up. He was like Mum, tall and fat. He was almost completely bald, except for a pure white frizz ringing his head like Friar Tuck. He had gnarled hands folded over the top of a walking stick, and sat low in his chair like his frame couldn't quite support him anymore. He could have been anything from a decrepit sixty to a fighting fit ninety.

But he smiled, holding out one of those twisted up hands, and shook David's with firm confidence.

"Just call me Jake, boy," he said in a thick accent that was some mix of Mancunian, Liverpudlian, and possibly Trinidadian. "Your mother's told me all about you."

Usually, people calling him boy riled David up. It was infantilising and insulting. But it sounded oddly affectionate and confirming in Jacob's deep, slow voice, and he found himself smiling back.

"Nice to meet you at last. Mum's actually not told me anything about you."

Jacob chuckled, and they swapped life stories in the shade. He didn't ask about the bump, and David didn't mention it, yet it felt easy and comfortable. Jacob was from Chaguanas originally, but moved to Liverpool in his thirties and had been a school caretaker ever since. He'd moved to Manchester to be closer to his wife when she had to go to a specialist hospice. She died two years ago, and he'd started going back to church for some company.

"Guess you found it," Ryan said a little crudely as Mum came down the path with a plate for David.

Jacob coughed a hoarse laugh, and they both got scolded by Mum as she banged the plate down.

"Honestly!" she said and sat on the only chair left. "Eat up, dear, then get yourself ready. We're going shopping."

"We are?" David asked.

"Of course! That room is far too bare. And you haven't even got the essentials. I saw a lovely pram at the Trafford Centre when I was there with Ellie—you remember Ellie, don't you? Nathan's mother—"

Ryan smirked but said nothing. David tuned her out as he tucked into his breakfast. Truth be told, he didn't want to go anywhere, especially not a hot, busy shopping centre on a Saturday afternoon in this heat, where he couldn't hide and couldn't ignore what was going on. But when Mum decided they were going shopping, they were going shopping. He had thirty-two years of experience to tell him that.

Ryan attempted to tell her it might be better to go tomorrow morning, when the shops first opened, but was met with a dismissive snort.

"Ryan. This is my first grandbaby. If you think this is just going to take one day, then really, dear."

David sighed and resigned himself to a weekend of absolute torture.

AVA WAS A godsend, and David had never thought he'd say that.

Mum was used to huge shopping centres like the Arndale or the Trafford Centre. The White Rose just didn't cut it as far as she was concerned, so she'd bullied David into driving them all the way down to Meadowhall in Sheffield, almost an hour away in Saturday traffic.

But the minute Ava saw the play area by the entrance, she hauled on David's arm and gave him the biggest, roundest, wettest eyes she possibly could.

"Pleeeease?"

"Look, you and Jake go on ahead," David said. "We both know you're going to go straight to that Build-A-Bear place anyway. Go and get the baby a teddy, and we'll catch up to you when Ava's done."

Then he let go of Ava's hand, and she shot off into the soft play set-up, pausing only long enough to take off her shoes when Ryan uttered her name in a warning tone.

"Oh, go on, then," Mum said, torn between scolding David for not playing along and indulging her new granddaughter. "I'll ring you when we're done."

She and Jacob vanished arm-in-arm, and Ryan snorted as David levered himself gingerly down onto a bench.

"So, when are they getting married?"

"Eh?"

"Your mum and your new stepdad. I've never seen your mum so loved up."

David waved a hand. "That's just Mum with a new bloke."

Ryan chuckled. "Ava called her nana when they arrived this morning. I thought she was going to cry."

"Who was going to cry?"

"Mary."

David smiled faintly. "She already had a picture of the three of us on her bookshelf at the flat. After the other day, I guess she is Ava's nana now. Speaking of which. I've been meaning to talk to you about your family."

"Oh, hell."

"I don't want Jay near Sam. Ever. I don't mind going to visit my mum when he's coming round to help refit the bathroom, but I'm not having Sam driven out too."

Ryan blew out his cheeks. "I, uh. I rang Marianne while Jake and I were putting the crib together."

David raised his eyebrows.

"I asked her to sound out a good family lawyer for us."

"You're going the legal route?"

"After what they said on Wednesday, I'm not having them near Ava or Sam. Jay won't give two shits, but Mum will push things. So, yeah, I'm going the legal route. I'm not having my kids exposed to that."

"Did you explain it to her?"

"Yeah."

"And she's—"

He pulled a face. "She issued a told you so, actually. She used to fight like hell not to have Mum come over and see Ava even when we were married. If I didn't have any custody rights, she'd have already locked Mum out."

David swallowed. "Ryan, I don't—I don't mean to block you from seeing your mum."

Ryan grimaced, shaking his head.

"She might be a bitch, but—"

"But she's not my mum."

"What?"

"She's my mother," Ryan said, "but she's not been my mum for years. The way she's been even since you came along..."

He trailed off. David bit his lip, wishing he could hold Ryan's hand. He didn't dare, not in the middle of a heaving shopping centre, so he tucked his hands between his knees.

"Were your family all like your mum? You know. Accepting?"

"No," David said. "My oldest brother used to try and beat it out of me. And for a long time, Mum would cry a lot and ask what she'd done wrong. She only really came to terms with it after I—"

He stopped. Christ, he hadn't meant to get that close to the truth.

"David?"

He coughed. "After I, uh..."

There was a long pause and then Ryan suddenly jolted with realisation.

"Oh, Christ," he said. "Oh. I didn't—I didn't realise it had got that bad."

"It was years ago."

"Was it—was it just—the one—"

"No," David admitted. "But it's been a long time. A very long time."

Ryan chewed on his lip, dropping his head. Ava shrieked in the play area, and he lifted it again with a painfully false smile and a wave.

"You'd tell me if it got that bad again, right?"

"Yes."

"Promise me."

"I promise." David nudged the chair. "Anyway, this wasn't about me. It was about you and your mum."

Ryan shook his head. "I never got that bad, but there were some—dark moments. I'd only just unpicked it in my own head and realised I wasn't a dirty pervert for liking blokes too. And Marianne was the first one to know about you, because we'd agreed to be totally open about new potential step-parents for Ava. And when she asked if you were nice and wanted to meet you herself so she could trust you with Ava, I—assumed my mum would be the same."

"Not so much."

"Yeah. Not so much," he drawled. "She's made her position clear. If she can't accept you, if she can't accept where Sam's come from, then she's not seeing them. And I'll take it to the courts to stop her. Both the kids will have a great grandma in your mum, and Ava's got Lily on Marianne's side. They'll be better off without."

David nodded. "Okay, but—remember, that's to protect me and the kids. If you want to see her, I'm not going to stand in your way or argue."

"Maybe in time I'll take you up on that, but right now—" Ryan shook his head. "No. She said some disgusting things about you, about me, about us, and I'm not giving her any more second chances."

"If Jay comes back around and smashes up our door or something, I'll take him to court again," David said. "I didn't buy all that household security for little old Pamela next door."

Ryan snorted with laughter and clapped his knees. "Ava! Come on, sweetheart! We have to go catch up to Nana!"

She cajoled for one more go on the slide, which was granted, then let David put her shoes back on and stretched up to be carried.

"Please?" she whined. "Just this once?"

David rolled his eyes, but—given Wednesday—stooped and let her scramble up to ride on his shoulders.

"Remember to duck in the lift," he said, and Ryan chuckled as he led the way through the throngs of people.

"David," Ava whispered in his ear. "When's Nana coming to live with us?"

David cracked a smile.

"I don't know," he said, "but I'm sure it'll be soon."

Chapter Twenty-Five

DAVID WENT OUT on Saturday evening as planned.

He'd tried to call it off, citing Mum's unexpected visit and having a proper sit-down dinner all together and discussing the baby.

"Don't be silly," Mum had trilled. "We can finish decorating that nursery without you. And we're staying until Monday morning, so I can whip up a curry chicken on Sunday night, and we can have your talk then. Go and have a nice time with your friends!"

Somehow when she put it like that, David felt about ten years old and like he was being told to go out and play. But when Ryan had simply smirked at him and said, "Say hi to them all for me," he knew he'd lost the battle.

So David gave in and called a taxi.

Thanks to the direct correlation between the size of the bump and the weight of David's dysphoria, he'd called off having dinner in public. Thankfully, James wasn't much one for going out, either, and immediately volunteered to cook.

"Housewarming," he'd said. "We're finally moved in. You can all come over to us."

They lived in Pontefract. The posh side. Neither of them liked city living, and James often worked from home when he didn't have lectures or seminars to deliver on a given day. Andi's car was paid for by the company—a vast Land Rover on the latest plates—so she didn't mind the commute. David didn't see much of them outside of the judo club, and he hadn't gone there for months.

Last time he'd seen them, they'd still been living in Leeds. And last time they'd seen him, he'd most definitely not been pregnant.

On the other hand—they knew he could be. David and James had been in the same first year flat in the halls of residence. Vicky and James had been on several of the same history modules, and then Vicky and Andi had both been devotees of the university judo club. But ironically, James and Andi had met in the university cafe completely independently of their mutual association with Vicky, and closed the four of them into a circle. Square. Whatever.

James was a lecturer now and writing books on Ancient Mesopotamia or something like that. His hair was always sticking up all over the place, his glasses fell off his face a dozen times a day, and he looked perpetually startled if anyone asked him a question. David had bought him a tweed jacket with elbow patches as a joke when he got his first lecturing position, and James actually wore it, the odd sod.

Andi was both completely the opposite, and completely the same. She was always pretty and composed, with her short pixie cut and big blue eyes. Where James was a stocky, awkward-looking man, as if he'd been stitched together out of spare parts, Andi was crafted. She could have been a model if she wanted—but underneath the perfect smile and photogenic cheekbones, she was just as much an oddball as James. God forbid anyone use bad science in front of Andi.

They'd officially got together last year, and bought a new house together. David had never seen it before, and the taxi pulled up into a quiet cul-de-sac with rows of identical front doors. Their neighbours were celebrating an eighth birthday party, going by the banner on the door, and the ones on the other side either owned or were being held hostage by the biggest cat he'd ever seen, stretched out across their doorstep in the evening sun and eyeballing him like it was considering wandering over and eating him.

"Thanks," David said. "Keep the change."

"Bloody hell, cheers, mate!"

He climbed out, eyeing the house for clues. He was still getting his head around James and Andi being a thing. It hadn't exactly been a surprise—they lived in each other's pockets, and more than a few times James had brought Andi to formal functions as his plus one—but at the same time, it sort of was.

David smiled to himself as he knocked. Maybe it wasn't so surprising after all. Maybe he and James had that in common too—if they didn't overthink things, the perfect person was where they hadn't bothered looking before.

"David!"

Andi hugged him, and Andi was smart. She had a PhD in genetics, and was fighting not to be promoted out of being able to do the research herself. The moment she made contact, she jumped back and gawped down at his stomach.

"Is that—"

He raised his eyebrows.

"David! Are you—"

She paused. He waited.

"Don't make me say it," she said.

If it were someone else, he might have been angry. But standing in the hall with Andi, closing her front door behind him and hearing James bashing around the kitchen like he was trying to build a working space shuttle rather than cook a dinner, David felt oddly warm and relaxed. Maybe Vicky was right. This would be good for him.

So he whispered, "Pregnant," in a conspiratorial tone, and Andi beamed.

"Oh my God!" she whispered back.

He put his fingers on his lips, and she giggled. Then she leaned forward to throw her arms around his neck and brush up her lips against his ear.

"Me too."

He squeezed silently, grinning.

"Don't tell. Nobody knows yet," she hissed and backed up. "Okay. Let me give you the tour! We're all properly moved in now—you would not believe the fuss James kicked up on moving day when the van man tried to put all his books in an ordinary box..."

David believed it. He toed off his shoes and followed her around the little house. Her ginger cat, Arthur, purred appreciatively when they paused in the master bedroom to make a fuss of him. The tortoiseshell, Ford, eyed him imperiously from the windowsill but then turned back to keep watching the birds in the tree in the neighbours' garden.

"Where's Zaphod?"

"Probably in the living room. We put up a cat tree, but she's the only one who uses it. So—" Andi leaned in to whisper. "—when's the baby due?"

"The fifth of November."

She held up crossed fingers, grinning. "I take it James and Vicky don't know?"

"Vicky does. Not James."

"You want to tell him?"

"I'll tell him tonight, yeah."

"Okay. I'll not say a word, then."

"What about you?" David asked. "I didn't think you two were trying."

"We weren't," Andi said, shrugging. "I only did the test a couple of days ago. I haven't told him yet. Like I said, we've got news."

"Fine, keep your secrets until dessert," David said, heaving himself up from the bed. "I won't tell you the baby's name if you don't tell me your news."

Andi pulled a face, whining that it wasn't fair as she followed him down the stairs.

James had clearly been at the university during the day. He was cooking with his shirt sleeves rolled up and an apron over suit trousers. He smiled, offered a drink, and asked if David was coming to judo next week with his usual airy obliviousness. David smirked.

"Not really in a fit state for it at the moment," he said.

"Oh? You not well?" James asked, frowning down at the pan. "Andi. Is it supposed to look like this?"

"Try stirring it occasionally, then you get more food and less pan-glue," she chided as the doorbell rang. "Oh, it'll be Vicky—"

David lurked at the kitchen counter and let the warm bustle sink into his bones. He and James talked politics, while Andi and Vicky stayed in the next room and tried to noisily persuade Zaphod down from the cat tree to play. The house was cosy, but littered with evidence as to what James and Andi were like. There was a collection of Marvel magnets on the fridge door, and Andi had painted the kitchen walls with chemical symbols, hiding in pale blue amongst the warm aqua colour scheme like secrets. They finally migrated into the dining room to eat, where James's books were lovingly encased in a glass-fronted bookcase, the top shelf given over to his pottery collection.

And the salt shaker was a Dalek. Go figure.

Dinner was the usual mix of insulting new films, loud arguing about the government that somehow never quite turned nasty, and identifying something in the meal James had added which he really ought not to have done but somehow worked anyway. The cats circled their feet, meowing hopefully, and when the cake was broken out and slabs of triple chocolate goodness piled high in front of everyone, Andi said, "Let's swap news. You first, David."

He rolled his eyes. James looked up at him, blinking owlishly.

"You have news?"

"Well, it's only news to *you* now," David said. "I'm pregnant."

It just fell out. It almost felt natural to say. The unpleasantness of the word still curled around his tongue and tasted sour, but it didn't feel like he had to spit it out or grind it past his lips. In these surroundings, with these people, it felt strangely okay to say.

And then James did exactly what David thought he would do.

"Pregnant?" he echoed, as if David had spoken in Swedish. He adjusted his glasses with a frown. "Pregnant?"

"It's that thing when people have babies," Vicky said.

"I know what it is!" James said. "But how can you be—"

Then he stopped, and David started to laugh.

He ought to have been insulted. And yet James's absent-minded nature made it impossible. He'd forgotten. He'd genuinely forgotten what David had looked like when they first met. Hell, he'd probably forgotten what David had been called. And whereas the idea of having to explain it usually made his heart sink, and usually his cynicism was too thick to believe anyone could just forget, James's genuine look of surprise felt...nice.

"Usual way," he said.

"Sorry," James said, going red. "Wow. That was—sorry. And congratulations. Um. Yeah!"

He lifted his glass awkwardly, and the women fell about laughing before lifting their own, still giggling.

"Congratulations," they echoed.

"Does it have a name, then?" Andi asked.

"Your news first," he said, waving a hand. "Come on, what is it?"

He was expecting the pregnant news. But to his surprise, James went a funny shade of pink and started grinning like an idiot. Andi beamed right back at him, the pair of them looking ridiculously loved up, and David smiled as he realised before James managed to say it what had happened.

"We, uh. Well. We're engaged."

Vicky shrieked and nearly dropped her glass.

"We thought it was about time," James said, looking horribly embarrassed and yet incredibly pleased at the same time. "We've decided on the fourteenth of May next year."

"That doesn't leave you long to sort everything!"

David mentally did the maths and winced. If Andi was only a couple of weeks pregnant—and knowing Andi's tendency to tell James absolutely everything, David assumed it was a very new situation if he hadn't found out yet—then she was going to be heavily pregnant by then.

"We're not going to be having a big wedding," Andi said. "Just a few of our favourite people, and we already have a venue."

"Well, that's the plan. We haven't told our families yet." James coloured faintly. "I don't think my future father-in-law is going to be very pleased."

Andi snorted. "He can get over himself. He gets on with Shane's boyfriend, and he's a hairdresser."

James didn't look convinced, and David didn't blame him. He'd never met Mr Kershaw, but given the picture Andi had on the kitchen wall which showed herself and her older sister as teenagers flanking their father, all three in military combats and holding Army-grade rifles, grinning widely under camouflage paint at some barracks somewhere in Cornwall, he figured James had the right to be a bit nervous about the whole thing.

"So, is it James and Andi Laker, James and Andi Laker-Kershaw..." Vicky prompted.

"Actually, I'm taking Andi's name," James said.

"That should please the father-in-law," David suggested.

"What about you?" Vicky asked.

David was brought up short. "What?"

"You and Ryan. Aren't you getting married?"

"No," he said.

"Really?"

"Really. He's crap at being married."

Andi smirked. "Mm, marrying a divorcee, not a great idea."

"Marrying a guy who cheats on his wife, worse idea," James said.

David flared up at once. "That wasn't what happened."

"Sorry, it's just—it was fast, you have to admi—"

"Marianne had moved out the week before I met Ryan," David said tersely. "He didn't cheat on either of us, and he never has."

"Okay, okay. It's just—"

"It's just nothing," David snapped.

"Wait," Vicky said. "Everybody shut up. I just realised something."

David deflated, eyeing her sceptically.

Then she said, "Oh, God, I'm old!"

"What?" Andi said.

"I'm at that age!"

"What age?" David asked.

"All my friends are getting married and having babies!"

Silence.

Then the room erupted with laughter, and David sat back, one hand on the bump, finally relaxed.

Maybe he could do this after all.

Chapter Twenty-Six

THE GOOD MOOD came crashing down within a week of Ava going back to school.

Her first week back fell on Marianne's turn to have her, so David hadn't paid it any attention—until she called Ryan on Tuesday afternoon, and he hung up with a face like thunder.

"What's wrong?" David asked. He'd taken the afternoon off for an appointment with Nadia and had been taking out his stress on beating the dough for biscuits ever since.

"Ava got sent to the headmistress's office this morning."

David blinked. "You what? She's five."

"She shouted at her teacher and pushed her."

"The hell? Why?"

"Because she's apparently telling everyone her stepdad is pregnant, and the teacher took it upon herself to tell them that men can't get pregnant. And when Ava insisted that you are, Miss Whatshername told her off for telling lies."

David set down his mug with a heavy thud.

"Marianne's still there," Ryan said. "I'm going to call a taxi and go—"

"I'll drive."

Ryan raised his eyebrows. "You sure?"

"Yes," David said tightly. "Let's see them deny this when it's stood right in front of them."

He washed the sticky clumps of dough off his hands and went to change as Ryan covered the mess on the counter with some foil. By the time David got back, wearing the only pair of jeans that fit anymore and a thin cotton T-shirt that did absolutely nothing to hide Sam's existence, Ryan was waiting by the door, still visibly fuming.

"If the first thing out of that teacher's mouth isn't an apology to Ava, then—"

David tuned out the grumbling. Driving was getting difficult, what with Sam barely fitting behind the wheel anymore thanks to David's short legs and the need to pull the seat so far forward to reach the pedals. In another month, he'd have to disconnect the battery altogether and leave the car to sit and gather moss on the driveway.

It was almost four o'clock, so the school was quiet, and David pulled into the staff parking area without a hint of shame. He followed Ryan at a sedate pace, planting a hand in the middle of his own back in one part obnoxious display of his state for the headmistress and this idiot of a teacher, and in one part because the ache from hefting Sam around all day was starting to get to him.

Marianne was sitting outside the office with a young teaching assistant and Ava, who'd clearly been crying. She reached for her dad with a hiccup, and Ryan let her climb up on the chair for a cuddle for once.

"It's all right, sweetie," he soothed, stroking her frizzy hair.

"I wasn't lying!" she wailed. "I wasn't, I wasn't, I wasn't—"

"I know," he said calmly. "I know, honey. You're not in trouble. We'll get this all sorted out."

"What happened?" David asked, easing himself down into the chair next to Marianne.

She had her court face on, and her voice was clipped and cold. "Show and tell after lunch. Ava brought that picture of Sam's scan and was telling them all about getting a baby brother or sister. Then Miss Dalton asked if her mother or her stepmother was pregnant, and she said her stepfather. And it all went downhill from there."

"And then she accused Ava of lying?"

"Basically. At which point, Ava threw a tantrum."

The office door opened. David had never met any of Ava's teachers or the head—his total involvement with the school up to this point had been to drop her off and pick her up again. He wasn't even listed as an emergency contact.

But from the startled look from the dumpy little woman who opened the door, he was suddenly grateful for it.

"Oh," she said, then visibly gathered herself. "Do—do come in."

There was another woman in the office. Tall and thin with long red hair, David vaguely recognised her from seeing her in the playground when he went to collect Ava after school. She gave him an equally startled look, and a dull flush crept up her face.

"Ava, why don't you stay here with Katie?" Ryan said, easing her down and passing her off to the teaching assistant. "If you do your homework book with Katie then you don't have to do it again at home."

"M'kay..."

Ryan kept a lid on it until the office door closed behind him, then his face twisted into a furious scowl and he snapped, "What the hell are you lot playing at?"

"Mr Walsh—" the head began, and he jabbed a finger in her direction.

"No. Can it. I got a phone call half an hour ago that my daughter has been scolded for being excited about having a new baby sibling, called a liar for telling the absolute truth, and dragged to the head's office because her teacher is apparently more interested in shouting at her than getting her own facts right! And now my partner has felt the need to come down here and prove it, which you have no right to ask of him!"

David raised his chin in a direct if silent challenge as both teachers glanced uneasily at his bump again.

"Ava has done nothing wrong, so I'd like to know what you're going to do to fix this!"

He wasn't quite shouting, but David got the sense that it was only due to Ava being right outside. He shifted on his feet, rubbing at the bottom of the bump as a twinge rippled up his side.

"Would you—would you like a seat, Mr..."

The headmistress trailed off, and David raised a sardonic eyebrow.

"There are several to choose from. I'll sit down if I want to. And I would thank you," he added, throwing a dirty look at Miss Dalton, "to stop staring like you've never seen a pregnant person before."

He felt more than a little like he was a specimen on display at a zoo. She was openly gawping, and her only response to his words was to close her mouth.

"This is an unusual situation," the headmistress said. "Ava was very belligerent when she insisted—"

"Maybe because she was being called a liar when she knows full well she's not lying?" Ryan snapped.

"Mr Walsh—"

"I don't want your excuses. You've wrongly accused my daughter of lying, got angry with her when she's rightfully got upset, and showed you're too busy wanting to be right instead of wanting to be correct."

"I apologise if Ava is—"

"That Ava is," David interrupted.

The headmistress paused. Then very slowly said, "That Ava is upset."

"Why did Miss Dalton accuse her of lying instead of exploring how her stepfather could be pregnant and explaining the situation properly?"

Miss Dalton went pink. "Men can't be—"

David cleared his throat and glanced obviously down at his bump.

The teacher's jaw tightened. "Men can't be pregnant," she repeated, and Marianne huffed.

"Right, that's it, this woman has no business teaching my daughter," she snapped. "There's a pregnant man standing right in front of you, and you're still coming out with ignorant garbage. I want Ava moved to another class."

The headmistress coughed. "Now, let's just discus—"

"There's nothing to discuss. I don't want my daughter being called a liar and taught by this ignorant woman," Marianne snapped, waving a hand dismissively at Miss Dalton. "You're going to move Ava to another class, you're going to re-educate the children in both classes about gender identity, and—"

"It will be very confusing for them—"

"That's your job, isn't it? To teach? So they aren't confused?"

David rolled his eyes, tiring of the spectacle.

"When you're all quite done deciding whether I'm a man or not," he said, deliberately pitching his voice to its deepest level, "I will be outside with my stepdaughter. And can I invite you to consider, Mrs Higginbottom, that this baby will in five short years be at your school, as well, and very likely telling stories about their two fathers? I can assure you that we'll be taking a very poor view of it if you try lying to our child, and making up a mother they don't have."

He turned on his heel and—well, waddled out rather than marched, but slamming the door behind him made up for the flounce that was less dramatic than he'd hoped for. Ava was sitting reading with the assistant, but slid down and clamoured to be picked up and cuddled instead, still looking about as happy as a wet weekend.

"I can't really pick you up anymore, honey," he said, sitting down and letting her scramble onto what was left of his lap.

"Is Daddy angry?"

"He's angry with Miss Dalton, not with you."

"I wasn't lying."

"I know."

"Am I in trouble?"

"No."

Relaxing a little, she twisted to grab the edge of her book and drag it over. She flipped back to the page she'd been on and began to tell him a story about a deaf girl with a cat. He listened with half an ear, interjecting only to correct her persistence in mistaking 'she'd' for 'shed.' In truth, he didn't much care what solution Ryan and Marianne came up with between them, but he found himself looking forward. They probably could put Sam in a different junior school. Ava was here due to Marianne's address, not Ryan's. There was a slightly closer school to the bungalow.

He'd never given it any thought, and he frowned down at Ava, leaning against the bump as if she were reading to Sam too. They had to plan for so much more than just having a baby. They had to plan schools, nurseries, babysitting. He'd have to go on parental leave, and then back to work at some point. Ryan would have to adjust his shift patterns or come off them entirely. Christ, David didn't even know how the birth certificate would work. There was no mother. He'd obtained a GRC the moment he could—he was legally a man. He had a male birth certificate now. How on earth would Sam's birth certificate work?

He grimaced and filed it all away in the ever-growing pile of things he just didn't want to think about.

The hubbub of voices behind the door rose into an angry shout from an angry man, and he hastily plastered a pleasant smile on his face when Ava looked up.

"Carry on," he said, tapping the page. "What did the kitten do next?"

Christ, what a mess.

Chapter Twenty-Seven

"ARE YOU SURE?" David asked.

Ryan was in a foul mood, and they'd ended up with Ava for the night after she'd been too upset to go home with her mum, thinking her father was mad at her. And David got ready for the work the next morning with the distinct impression Ryan would like to go up to the school and personally strangle Miss Dalton.

"I'm sure," he said. "She's not going to school today. I'm watching her this morning, and then Marianne's going to pick her up before I go in for the late shift. Go to work. We'll be fine."

David hummed and bent awkwardly to kiss him. "All right. Call me if you need anything."

Ryan patted his bum, mustering up a smirk, but it failed to reach his eyes. David played along and pulled a face anyway, then headed out to the car.

He didn't want to go to work.

The dysphoria was getting...bad. He'd forgotten what it could feel like. That strange distance between himself and his reflection. That odd sensation of his skin not being his own. The revulsion when he caught sight of certain things, like the shape of his bum or the weight of his belly. And the worst of it wasn't even the way he felt, but the way his hormones no longer let him cope with those feelings.

The fact was, hormone therapy changed things. Pre-T, David could cry at the drop of a hat. His response to stress had been tears and getting upset. Things got to him. And that had permeated everything, from soppy films to Ben's funeral. He'd been emotional, reactive, prone to pulling back and expressing inwardly and in private.

But testosterone had changed everything.

Part of it was how he felt better and happier, David knew. But part of it was the hormone itself. The things it did to the brain and body, the way it shaped the literal responses in the human mind and interrupted the cycles that had happened before. It wasn't just that he was better psychologically. He'd changed physically as well.

He'd started T on his nineteenth birthday. And he hadn't cried again until he was twenty-two years old.

He just—hadn't.

He'd been plenty upset enough to cry, in those three years. He sometimes found himself wanting to cry, to open the floodgates and release all the emotion in the best way he had growing up. He had to learn new coping mechanisms and install new release valves in his psyche. His emotional responses changed. Where once he'd have cried in arguments with boyfriends, he found himself entering his mid-twenties and shouting right back. He'd dropped a glass of Coke at fifteen and watched it shatter all over the floor, and cried in bitter frustration. When he'd done it at twenty-five, he'd sworn at the fragments and stamped around the kitchen cleaning up like he was mad at gravity for existing.

On testosterone, David was assertive. Self-confident. Solid. Things didn't get under his skin so much, and when they did, his response wasn't to shrink back and try to scratch them out, but to reach out with both hands and grab them in a chokehold.

So the worst part of the dysphoria wasn't the shape of his bum or the startled looks in public. It was the way his lip shook when he noticed, and his mind cringed when he saw them.

It was the way he reacted.

It was like being an alien in his own head, and David hated it. He hated it, and he hated hating it. A constant spiral of hurt and pain, and all of it internal. The bigger the bump grew, the longer it went on; the further testosterone sank into his past, the worse it got.

And the worse he felt, the less he wanted to go anywhere. The worse it got, the more he wanted to stay at home, in his jogging bottoms with the elastic waistband and one of Ryan's borrowed T-shirts, and not face the outside world. If he could shut out the rest of the universe being shocked and appalled by him, then he could limit the number of times in a day his lip might wobble, and the number of times he'd notice just how little he felt like David anymore.

So when he arrived at work, and the first thing that greeted him when he walked through the door was Paul going, "Christ, David, are you okay? You're looking a bit hefty, aren't you?"

Hefty.

David stopped dead in the middle of the reception. A couple of early clients stared curiously at him.

"Hefty," he echoed. "Where's Sonia?"

"Er. I didn't mean anything by it, mate—"

"Where's Sonia?"

"In the shelter office, I think. Are you—"

David turned on his heel and walked back out. He crossed the little yard in long strides, briefcase still in his hand. He bashed through the office door without knocking and shut it sharply behind him.

"David! Are you—"

"I'm going on leave."

Sonia blinked up at him, wide-eyed. "You—I'm sorry?"

"I'm going on leave. Starting today. For—" He gestured at the bump. "This."

"Is everything all right?" she asked delicately.

"No," he said. "And I don't want to discuss it."

"We can't just move your leave like—"

"Let me put it this way, Sonia—I'm going home now, and I'm not coming back until well after the baby is born."

Her jaw sagged. "David! Your appointments, your—"

"I'm sorry if it leaves you in the lurch, but I can't do this anymore," he said. "Put it as unpaid leave until the end of October if you have to. I really don't care. But I'm not coming in."

She stood up from her chair, all five foot nothing of quivering, indignant boss.

"You can't just turn around and stop coming in like this," she squeaked. "It's a breach of your contract."

"Then sack me."

He spat it out like a challenge, and she stopped, pursing her lips.

David liked working for the surgery. It was close to home, he had his regulars, it was good, steady work. But ultimately, it wasn't the only work. He was highly qualified. Well-experienced. He'd find somewhere else. Maybe even get the chance to go back and specialise like he'd originally intended, or move over into medical research like Andi.

There were other options.

Options outside of turning up every day to be stared at, snidely insulted and probed for answers, and feeling worse and worse every time he walked out the door.

"Your choice," he told Sonia and walked away.

"SONIA LEFT A message," Ryan called from the doorway as David got out of the car, "and said you're not sacked, but she wants to talk to you. What the hell is going on?"

Ryan didn't look angry though. Worried, maybe. His jaw was tight, but his mouth turned down in that little quirk that made David's throat ache.

"Paul made another snide comment, and I walked out," he said, slamming the car door. "I can't do it anymore. I said I'm not going back until after the baby's born, and if she wants to sack me for not giving her enough notice, then she can sack me."

Ryan raised his eyebrows.

"And don't have a go about the bills and shit, because I know." David stalked past Ryan into the hall and threw his bag down in a corner. "I'm going for a fucking shower."

The bathroom was still wet from his morning one, and—like he had not two hours earlier—he cried under the spray. He leaned his forehead against the tiles and kept his eyes screwed shut. He was tired. Tired of work, tired of Sam, tired of being pregnant, tired of being able to be pregnant. He was tired of being a trans man instead of just a man. Tired of being David now, instead of David always.

And most of all, tired of crying when he ought to be punching things. Maybe he ought to invite Jay over and give him another beating. That would make him feel better.

When the water ran cold, he wasn't done crying, and he stepped out feeling only halfway relieved. The heating rail wasn't on, so the towels were cold. And Sam starting kicking when he tried to sit down on the closed toilet and finish venting, making it too uncomfortable to hunch over properly and get a good sob out.

God, David hated this.

"Hey," Ryan called from the living room when he cracked the door open. "C'mere."

"I need to get dressed," David croaked.

"No you don't. Come on, come here."

"I'm not in the mood for—"

He stopped in the doorway. Ryan craned his neck, smiled, and patted his lap.

"Come on," he said.

Ryan had set up a...nest. The spare duvet was draped over the rest of the sofa. He was in his spot, supported by the footstool and all the cushions in the room. The laptop was balanced on his shins and hooked up to the speakers. A stack of David's favourite films was on the arm by Ryan's elbow, and a six-pack of ginger beer was ready and waiting.

David's lip wobbled.

"Oh, hell, come on, come here..."

It wasn't graceful. He climbed into Ryan's lap, far too heavy and far too big. Sam wriggled enthusiastically when Ryan began to massage the bump with one hand, and David stretched out his legs along the sofa to relieve the pressure, sighing when Ryan pulled him down onto his chest and wrapped them up in the duvet.

"Have a cry, have a kip, do whatever," he whispered. "Don't worry about work or the bloody bills. We've got savings. We've got family. We'll be fine. You'll be fine."

David's throat closed up. His face twisted. Without any voluntary action on his part at all, the tears came again, and he buried his face in Ryan's neck, for once unashamed of the display, for once unwilling to keep himself apart.

Ryan held him, and it felt like he was only thing holding David together.

Chapter Twenty-Eight

ON THE SIXTH of October, David started counting down the days.

Thirty left.

Then twenty-nine.

Then twenty-eight.

He could hear that heartbeat in his dreams. He wasn't sleeping properly. He'd wake up every hour to Sam's heartbeat, thundering like the drums of war, and his blunt fingernails buried in his forearm. Twice, he scratched so much he started bleeding, and Ryan threatened to buy him a pair of mittens. And after the GP had blinked stupidly at him and said, "I don't know how sleeping aids might affect a trans patient," David had got up, gone home, and not left the house again.

At all.

He only left to take the bins out for the lorry every Tuesday morning. Other than that, he refused to walk out of the door. He ordered the shopping to be delivered. He sent Ryan to collect Ava from school on his own. He didn't go to the park on Sunday mornings to lob chunks of bread at ducks. Nothing.

He was on eggshells as it was, and even Pamela next door scowling at him was threatening to push him over the edge.

Apparently, Sam knew nothing of their father's problems. They squirmed and kicked away, especially if he lay down. A hot bath felt like his stomach had distended and was going to pop free from him like a bubble—it made his skin crawl, and he'd gotten out as fast as he could. Bed was pointless; he'd not sleep. Even the sofa nest, never deconstructed again after that disastrous last day at work, required him to be sitting up to get any rest out of it.

Twenty-seven.

Twenty-six.

Ryan was counting too, albeit David only knew it by the crosses on the calendar. They didn't talk about it. David knew full well that he would be cruel and harsh if Ryan tried to share his enthusiasm, and Ryan seemed to know David would only feel worse about his own upset if they did try to talk. So they both more or less kept quiet, and David silently reached out whenever he could, mentally noting each and every time.

"I'll make it up to you," he kept promising, and Ryan kept chuckling.

"Get better," he said every time, "and that'll be plenty."

The only bright side was Ava. Mum's trick from when David had been a baby, of persuading the older children the new baby was theirs as well, had worked. Ryan and Marianne both seemed to have picked it up, and all of Ava's library books involved siblings. Ryan would put *Frozen* in for her at least once in every week they had her, much as both he and David hated the film, and David caught her putting her toys in the crib more than once.

"They're for Sam," she said. "She can borrow my dolls until Christmas. Then she has to have her own dolls."

"What makes you think Sam is a girl?" David asked.

Ava regarded him with a little frown. Eventually, she said, "Well, I suppose Sam can borrow my dolls if she's a boy. Maybe."

"I think Sam would like that. But maybe if we put your dolls in your playbox with the other dolls? Then you and Sam can choose which dolls to play with together after Sam gets here, hm?"

David knew what he was doing. As long as he was putting on a smile for Ava and pretending along with her that it was all very exciting, he couldn't really wallow in how bad he felt. He'd always been that way, and it worked again now. But the minute she left, it hit him even harder just how awful he felt.

And worse, the growing fear that it was going to continue. The fear that he wouldn't love Sam when they finally arrived. That the months of hell, especially the last two, were going to permanently damage his ability to love his own baby.

Twenty-five.

Twenty-four.

With twenty-three days to go, and so low that he had a panic attack just walking round to the doctor's surgery to refill his prescriptions, David went from counting days to counting hours—and Ryan snapped.

"You need to see someone," he said.

They were lying in bed together. Ryan was...clingy. David knew full well why, and he'd probably be the same in Ryan's shoes, but it didn't mean that it didn't grate against his already exposed nerves sometimes.

"I'm worried about you."

"So am I," David muttered, "but who am I supposed to see? If you know of any counsellors specialising in the issues a pregnant man might be facing, feel free to ring them up for me."

"Surely anyone's better than—"

"Finish that sentence and I'll gut you."

Ryan obediently fell silent.

"I'd rather deal with it myself."

"Can you?"

David swallowed.

"I know you're struggling," Ryan continued, "and I know I can't do enough. I don't understand. I can't. And you're scaring me the last few weeks. You know I'm getting scared to go to work and leave you at home on your own?"

David swallowed thickly. The truth was a vile, slimy thing slithering around in his brain, and when he opened his mouth, it poured out onto sheets like something physical.

"I don't know that I made the right choice to keep it."

Ryan's hands stilled on his feet.

Then, slowly, they pulled away. David closed his eyes, feeling tears burn for the thousandth time behind his eyes.

Then the chair creaked, and Ryan's arm fell over his shoulder. His lips brushed David's cheek, and the hug was as close as they could be without David climbing into the chair to join him.

"I'm glad you told me."

David sniffed, the tears winning the battle.

"Fuck, why do you have to be so fucking nice?" he croaked.

Ryan chuckled. "Sorry." Another kiss landed on his ear. "I know it's hard. Truth is, David, I don't know I'd make the same call if I'd seen this coming. You're—you're worse than I thought. I thought I could help more than I can. So—yeah, I don't know I'd make the same one either. But here we are, here's Sam, and I'm still really excited about them and about the fifth. I'm just scared about you."

David nodded weakly.

"M'sorry," he mumbled. "I don't want to get rid of our baby, but—"

But.

But it hadn't been a baby then. It had been a theory. A hypothetical situation.

"It's okay."

David wriggled into the awkward hold a little deeper, burying his nose in Ryan's T-shirt and inhaling deeply. When Ryan spoke, his voice was low and sombre. Not the calm reassurance David was used to, but something a little hoarser. A little darker. A little more...personal.

"Ava wasn't our only child."

David turned his head to the side. "What?"

"Me and Marianne. Ava wasn't our only child. Technically."

"Technically?"

Ryan nodded. His jaw brushed the side of David's head as he did, and the muscles were clenched.

"What happened?"

"We terminated it."

It sounded so cold and clinical—so much more David than Ryan—that David frowned.

"What really happened?"

"We'd only been together maybe six months. She found out she was pregnant. I was excited; she was a bit more...not. But then not a month later, I was diagnosed with the HIV."

Usually, Ryan said it like a word. 'Hiv.' He didn't spell out the acronym, but rather talked about it like it was a cold or the measles. He had 'hiv.' He took 'hiv drugs.' But for once, he said HIV properly, H-I-V, and David untangled himself enough to hold his hand.

"It was—I can't describe to you what it felt like. What...what it was like."

David squeezed.

"But Marianne got tested too. She'd—she'd got it. And so did the baby."

"I'm sorry."

"So was I. I was in bits. I had this—that. You know the stigma. I thought the same way. Dirty disease from dirty sex. I must have got it off some bloke before I'd met her. I thought it was my punishment for being a—you know. I thought it was what I deserved, passing on that filth to my girlfriend and my unborn baby. So we got rid of it. Never even found out if it was a boy or a girl. Never had the chance. Just boom, gone. We never talked about it again. Any of it."

"Christ, Ryan..."

"And then life just went on," Ryan said. "I started to wonder if we'd been right. If I'd been right. If having HIV was actually my fault, if it was a dirty disease. If it actually said anything about me beyond I'd been dumb enough to forget the condom on a one-night stand. Who hasn't done that? Hell, who hasn't done that with a girl, never mind a guy? Maybe it didn't mean I was a filthy faggot after all."

He spat the words with more venom than David had ever heard from him. David said nothing.

"We got married, we got it all under control, we managed to have Ava without passing it on. And nothing was happening. You know? We were healthy. Okay, we had to take drugs every day, but we were fine. We didn't fall over dead every time we got a cold. Marianne got promoted twice. I won a marathon race. Even after I had the accident, it didn't matter. The nurses wore gloves all the time, but I wasn't—worse, you know? It didn't seem to matter."

There was a long silence. When Ryan spoke again, his voice was hoarse.

"Then our marriage broke down and I bought this place and I started to try dating again. First guy I went out with, I told him on the spot. You know what he said?"

"What?"

"'Well yeah, I assumed you did. You're black. Doesn't matter to me.'"

David closed his eyes. *Fucking hell.*

"I blew my lid. Nearly got arrested. I just went batshit, and then the next morning, I took a look at myself in the mirror and wondered if I'd not said something similar once."

"Eh?"

"The way I reacted when I was diagnosed. It was all...I was a stereotype. I was black and I'd shagged a bloke, so maybe I deserved it. What did I expect, trying to be black and bi? That was what was in my head. That was how I was thinking. I thought it meant I was something disgusting and getting HIV was the proof of it and I'd never get the stain off. That was what had sunk in."

"That's what you had to wring out," David murmured.

"Yeah."

"And then what?"

"And then you. I told myself that day I wasn't going to have any of that crap. I was like...I'm not taking this shit anymore. From me or from anyone else. It wasn't my fault and it didn't make me anything. Long as I take my drugs properly, I have thirty, forty, fifty years left where I'm fine, and I'm not infectious so whatever. New guy doesn't like it, he can take a hike. New guy thinks 'of course you do, you're from Africa,' then he can take the hike off a cliff."

David quirked a smile.

"Then you didn't take the hike. Any hike."

David squeezed. Ryan squeezed back.

"I never thanked you for that," he said softly.

"Never knew I needed thanking," David said.

"What would you have done, if Sam had HIV from me?"

"Not much."

"What if you caught it?"

"I don't know. Complain to GlaxoSmithKline?"

Ryan laughed wetly.

"I don't want the baby to get it. I mean, a life on pills, it's not exactly fun. And I don't want it to suffer the stigma, especially if it's a boy. It's worse for boys. But—I look back, and I wish me and Marianne knew better. I wish we hadn't—you know. I wish we hadn't thought it was the end of the world and worth—worth that."

"Yeah," David said quietly.

Ryan tugged. David shuffled a little closer on the bed, until their shoulders touched, and laid their joined hands on the bump. Sam kicked jubilantly, the ripple of wrongness at the sensation muted under the weight of their fingers.

"Sam's not the first time for me either," David whispered.

He'd never told a soul, and the truth eased out into the room like the creaking from a door that had never been opened before.

"I was sixteen. Out at home. Desperately trying to keep it secret at school, because I knew they'd kill me if they figured me out. So I got drunk at a party and slept with a couple of random boys to prove I was a proper girl."

"Shit—"

"Didn't take me long to figure out what happened. I wasn't on anything. I was just sixteen and in the closet to everyone outside my mum's locked flat. No doctor was about to start giving me hormones, not some closeted mixed-race kid in the middle of Salford. So when the monthly Carrie act stopped, I knew at once."

"So you...got rid of it?"

"Yes."

"Just like that?"

David snorted. "Yes. I was sixteen. Mum was determined I was going to go to university. My oldest brother was dead, and it was already pretty clear if the other one didn't kick his junk habit, then he'd be next. I didn't know who the father was, and even if I did, it was a one-night stand at a stupid party. We were barely holding onto the flat because of all the money my brother kept stealing off Mum to buy the junk, and I was shredding my arms to ribbons every month when my chest starting aching and the Carrie act began. There was no way I could have had a baby. I didn't tell Mum, I didn't tell my friends, I didn't tell anybody. I just got rid of it, and I never talked about it again. Until now."

"And now?"

David coughed a bitter laugh.

"I kept this baby because of you," he said. "Because I'm thirty-two, and I have a good job and a share in a mortgage and a long-term partner and a stepkid. If I were thirty-two, and we'd just had sex on that first coffee date and never seen each other again? I would have done exactly the same thing."

He tightened his grip and turned his head to look Ryan in the eye.

"I don't regret that decision," he said, "and I never will."

Chapter Twenty-Nine

HE HAD HIS last appointment with Nadia in the middle of October.

She had insisted, rather than David. The last couple of measurements suggested Sam hadn't turned into the right position to allow a natural birth. David had been pushing for a caesarean, anyway, but Nadia said she couldn't really do much more than put a preference on his notes.

"It does depend on the duty surgeon," she'd said. "There's no physical reason you can't deliver naturally."

"Yeah, just every other reason," David said, but she couldn't make promises, and he'd had to accept that.

He was planning on screaming the place down to have one anyway.

It had to be up at the hospital, in case he needed a scan, and they ended up taking Ava with them. Ryan had accidentally dropped it in front of her, and she immediately clamoured to come with them instead of going to swimming club.

"I want to see Sam!" she'd bellowed when Ryan tried to dissuade her, and a short spell in the naughty corner for shouting hadn't done a thing to change her mind.

And so it was that David found himself, two weeks to go, in the same old waiting room full of staring would-be mums and bewildered nurses. Thankfully, Nadia came to collect them within only a few minutes, and the sonographer in the exam room was Grace again.

"And who's this?" Nadia asked brightly when Ava pulled herself up onto a spare chair.

"M'Ava."

"Oh, well, it's lovely to meet you, sweetie. I'm Nadia. Are you going to be a big sister soon, Ava?"

"Uh-huh. Are you a big sister?"

"I'm a little sister," Nadia said. "It's just as good. My wife hasn't got any brothers or sisters at all though! Isn't that lonely?"

Ava seemed to agree, for the first time that David had heard, and they chattered away about the virtues of older versus younger siblings as Nadia rattled away on the computer.

"Right," she said. "Let's see how big we're talking and then have a look at position. Shirt up, please, David. How have you been?"

"Struggling a bit," David admitted under Ryan's watchful eye. "It's been—hard."

She nodded, her expression not flickering. "That's not uncommon at this stage. Your body's exhausted, you just want it to be over, you start counting down. And little one isn't feeling very little anymore, are they?"

"Yeah, no kidding," David muttered. He was only aware he still had feet because Ryan kept massaging them.

"Well—" She whipped the tape measure away, squinting at the number. "It looks like we've had a little turn about. Has Sam been moving a lot?"

"Yeah."

"Anything sudden or painful?"

"No, just kicking a lot."

"Same places?"

"More towards the back now. Kidneys and so on."

"That's good. I think he's turned his back on me ready for the big day, but we'll have a quick look just to make sure. Pop up on the bed for Grace, darling—oh, wait, let me crank it right down first, that'll make it easier..."

He let Ryan arrange his clothes. The sight of the bared bump was nightmare fuel by now, the stretched skin appalling, the rippling movement whenever Sam lashed out like some nightmare creature made out of pure dysphoria. But he hadn't watched Nadia do a single one of her examinations, and she talked a mile a minute at Ryan and Ava without hesitation. It helped. And David suspected she knew it.

"Do you want to see a picture of the new baby, Ava?"

"Yes," she said. "Daddy says it might be boy or a girl. Can't you see on the picture?"

"We can," Nadia said, "but some people like it to be a big surprise."

"Do you know what it is?"

"I don't!" Nadia said. "Another lady took those pictures."

The gel was cold but oddly relieving on David's abused skin. He sighed and closed his hands around Ryan's, holding his T-shirt up and out of the way.

"Okay?" Ryan asked.

"Mm."

"David? Is there any pain?" Grace asked.

"No."

"All right, you let me know if anything hurts."

The pressure of the wand was really uncomfortable now, and David hadn't anticipated a third scan until Nadia had pulled a face at his last appointment. It had all been blood tests and diet sheets and embarrassing questions about his sex life and if he was constipated, right alongside conversational queries about nursery colour schemes and a list of things to put in his baby bag for hospital.

He recited that list as the pressure increased, and Sam objected, punching when the probe pushed against David's hip.

"Oops! Sorry," Grace said. She was squinting at the screen. "I'm sorry, Ava, Sam's obviously wide awake, so there's not a nice pretty picture for you. You'll just have to wait for a couple of weeks."

Ava grumbled, but when Nadia offered to let her hear the heartbeat again, David shook his head.

"Sorry," he said. "That—that makes me feel really—"

Bad. Awful. Guilty.

"It's a bit odd," he said eventually.

Ryan gave him a funny look, but Nadia just nodded.

"Sorry, sweetie. Maybe if you're really good, Sam will come early?"

Ava plainly didn't believe a word of the attempted emotional bribery, but didn't kick up a fuss. David suspected Ryan had given her a talking-to about being good at the appointment, as she was unusually placid given how hyped up she'd been.

"Everything looks good," Grace said, switching off the monitor and handing over a wad of tissues. "Baby's turned to face your spine, so it's in a better position for delivery."

"Small enough for a natural one?"

"Just about."

David didn't like that 'just.'

"You're looking on track for your due date," Nadia said. "Is there anything you want to bring up?"

"No," David said.

Ryan coughed.

David glanced at Grace, showing Ava the wand, then sighed.

"Can we—just you and me?"

"Of course."

Ryan threw him a sour look but took Ava back to the waiting room, and Nadia took David to another room, clearly just for talks by the lack of equipment.

"I didn't want to say anything in front of Ava, but I'm really struggling with this," David admitted. "I feel—awful. Bad. Mentally."

A sympathetic look crossed her face. "Can you break that down for me a little?"

"I—I can barely leave the house. I nearly got myself sacked from my job, and I didn't care. I—I've caught myself thinking that I made the wrong choice by not getting an abortion. And what kind of a father does that ma—"

"A perfectly normal one."

He stopped.

"Lots of people feel like this at the end," Nadia said. "This is very hard. And it's not you—it's your hormonal system going crazy, getting ready for the delivery. It's your body being tired and aching all the time, and running all its resources into the little one. It's perfectly normal to feel like that. You're not a bad parent because of those feelings."

David bit his lip, glancing down at the bump.

"I promise," Nadia said softly. "It'll change when it's over."

He swallowed.

"You swear?"

"I swear, David. You very obviously love this baby. You've done everything, even though it's taking a toll. You've stuck to your diet sheets, you've taking your supplements, you've kept coming to your appointments even though you've admitted it's hard for you to come into a medical facility. It's okay to struggle."

"It's not the same as the way women do it though."

"No, you have added complications," Nadia admitted. "But that doesn't make you any worse of a parent than them. If anything, you're overcoming even more to have Sam. You're going to be fine. It might not feel like it right now, but you are. You can do this."

He laid his fingers over the bump, so carefully that Sam wouldn't notice. It was still. Alien. It didn't feel like a part of him. It felt like he was somebody else, somebody he wasn't supposed to be, with this sticking out of him.

But it would be over soon.

And he'd done all he could.

"Have you ever had a male patient before?" he asked.

"Nope."

"Well, you're doing pretty good."

She smiled. It was wide and bright, and David felt his spirits lifting just at the sight of it. Her breezy confidence and sweet acceptance was infectious, and he felt a little better just at having vented, even though she wouldn't really understand any more than Ryan did.

"Thank you," she said. "That means a lot. And I mean it when I say if there's anything I can do to help more, I'll do it."

He swallowed and nodded jerkily.

He'd heard that a lot over the years from various nurses, doctors, and hospital staff.

But for the first time, a tiny part of him started to believe it.

Chapter Thirty

THE FIFTH OF November arrived with frost, clear blue skies, and absolutely no labour pains whatsoever.

"Maybe it'll start this afternoon?" Ryan suggested over breakfast.

"Is Sam not coming today?" Ava asked, apparently not as busy drowning her toast soldiers in runny egg as David had supposed.

"Not showing any signs of it, no," David replied.

"Does that mean we can go to the fireworks?" she asked hopefully.

Ryan and David exchanged glances over the top of her head.

"Er," Ryan said. "Thing is, honey, when the baby decides to arrive, I'm going to have to take David to hospital right away, and it can take a long time to leave the firework display."

She stuck out her bottom lip. "But—"

"I'm sorry, sweetie. How about we call Mummy and ask if—"

"No! You promised I could come with you when Sam comes!"

"Yes, I did, but I don't think it's a good idea to take David to the fireworks display. And we can't leave him here by himself."

She scowled and beheaded one of her soldiers for its apparent crimes.

"How about we go to the display at the lake instead of the park?" David suggested. "It's smaller, but we can go and have dinner in the pub on the waterfront and watch from there, can't we? Where it's nice and warm, and we can have a nice dinner."

"Pizza!" Ava cheered.

Ryan groaned and gave him a sour look.

"Does that sound like a good idea?"

"Yes!"

"Are you sure?" Ryan asked in a low voice. "If Sam comes—"

"If it starts, we'll have plenty of time from there. There'll be plenty of taxis out and about. And if the worst comes to the worst, we can ring Marianne. She only lives fifteen minutes away."

Ryan looked torn. David could imagine the debate. David volunteering to leave the house, have dinner in public, and enjoy himself? Big tick. Doing so on the same day the baby was due? Big cross.

"How about I give James and Andi a ring, and ask them to come with us?" he suggested. "If they bring their car, then we're fine if Sam decides to put in an appearance, aren't we?"

Ryan sighed. "Fine. Which chair?"

"Oh, the good chair will fit fine. Andi has a Chelsea tractor."

"Andi has a tractor?" Ava echoed in glee.

That did it. Convinced Andi had a magic tractor and they were going have pizza on their way to the fireworks, Ava was a rubber ball bouncing off the walls for the rest of the day. Ryan had to take her out to the park twice, and David was unable to get a nap even when Sam napped in the middle of the afternoon, thanks to Ava shrieking around the kitchen like a banshee.

Still, it was...nice, actually.

He was scared about the impending birth, but looking forward to it all the same. David had no illusions that he'd come out the other side without significant trauma, and he'd probably have to look into finding a trans-friendly counsellor in the Leeds area after all. But at least he wouldn't be pregnant anymore.

And quite frankly, if Ryan thought he was ever getting any front door sex again, then he was in for a rude shock.

Ava was a good distraction from the lack of any movement. Or labour related movement, anyway. Sam was still playing their favourite game of kick-the-kidney whenever David tried to sit in a position not one hundred percent comfortable for the passenger, so he wasn't especially worried. Just—irritable. Watching his watch. Waiting for that first twinge.

At this point, he'd take a thirty-six hour labour if it would just start already.

By the time the dark rolled in and he heard the smooth swish of Andi's car pulling up in the road outside, there wasn't so much as a flicker of progress, and he put on his coat with a sigh.

"No joy," he said to Ryan, who frowned. "Come on. Maybe one noisy rocket will startle Sam out of there."

Ava cheered, dashing to the shoe rack to pull on one red trainer and one sparkly pink wellie boot. Ryan managed to cajole her into swapping the trainer for another wellie boot but gave up on the issue of them matching.

She'd never met James and Andi, though, and went a bit shy until Andi charmed her in the car with how fireworks were made. Ryan kept giving him anxious looks, and David leaned his head back against the rest, stroking the bump with one palm.

Nearly over.

Nearly there.

James had booked a table after David texted him with the suggestion, and when Andi ran out of explanations of how to make fireworks, kept Ava entertained with stories about who invented them. Andi was wearing an engagement ring, and her slim frame was even worse than David's at hiding the truth. She was all angles, so the soft swell, however tiny it was still, was already showing.

"Got a due date yet?" Ryan asked, gesturing at it.

"Not yet," she said. "First scan next week."

"Bet it's due on your wedding day," David said.

"Bring it on." She laughed. "Any tips?"

"Yeah, get another wedding day."

"And don't go to see the fireworks on your due date," Ryan grumbled.

"I wouldn't have the strength!"

"It's that or wallow in misery," David said, and her smile dipped a little.

"I suppose."

He didn't feel like eating much, and busied himself by stealing off Ryan's plate, and occasionally Ava's when he wanted to wind her up. The pub was packed, far too busy for people to pay attention to them, and as Ryan always got the gap where a chair could most easily be removed to allow his own to replace it, David was boxed in beside the window. Nobody could see, and Sam was apparently fast asleep. In his heavy woollen jumper and debating names with Andi—or rather, deliberately suggesting terrible ones to make her laugh—he felt almost normal.

Almost.

Ryan was twitchy, and James kept glancing nervously at him every time David so much as shifted in his seat. He still felt almost foggy, and deeply reluctant to get up and go to the toilet. In the end, he managed to persuade Ryan to come with him and used the disabled toilet instead of the men's room. He had always vilified the use of a disabled toilet as even remotely appropriate, but the sting of his own hypocrisy was nothing compared to the relief of not having to walk into the men's toilet in a pub with nine months of baby very obviously stuck out in front of him.

"You know what the best part of this is going to be?" David asked as he washed his hands.

Ryan just raised his eyebrows.

"Getting to forget I'm trans again."

"You can even do that?"

"For a while there, before all this? Yeah, I kind of did."

Ryan chuckled. "Well, maybe you'll get lucky again. We'll be too busy trying to juggle two jobs and two kids for years for that to get a look-in."

"If only it worked like that."

"Hey."

Ryan caught his arm as David reached for the lock.

"How are you doing? Seriously?"

David thought about it.

His back hurt. His mind was in ribbons. He wanted to sleep forever, but couldn't get so much as half an hour before the nightmares started. He was veering between happiness it was almost over, and terror at what was about to happen.

And he didn't know if he'd even make it through that.

"I have no idea," he said, and Ryan squeezed his wrist.

"Talk to me," he said. "Whatever happens, whatever's going through your head. Talk to me. Even if I can't do jack shit about it."

David smiled faintly.

"I'll try."

He clicked the lock over and followed Ryan out. The first fireworks had started to lift over the lake, the shimmer of thousands of colours exploding over the still water. Ava was pressed up against the window, standing on David's chair, so he took hers beside James instead, and propped his chin on his hand to watch the display.

He'd never really seen the allure of fireworks. The noise was pointless, the colours pretty but fleeting, and usually at Bonfire Night displays, he couldn't get close enough to watch the fire and enjoy that anyway. But in the warm glow of the pub, helping himself to stray chips off Ryan's mostly abandoned plate, David found a new appreciation growing in the back of his mind. Maybe the boom and crackle would wake Sam from their slumber. Maybe the flash of colour would set something off in his body and get everything going. Maybe it would be a nice last memory before the labour wiped out the rest of the night in a haze of pain and trauma, and he would restart in the morning, holding his baby in his arms and finally feeling like himself again.

But as the last firework faded into the smoky sky, David pushed a hand under his bump, and carried the full weight of the baby on the palm of his hand.

Nothing.

Chapter Thirty-One

HE WAITED TEN days before making the call.

"Good morning, maternity. How can I help?"

"Can I speak to Nadia Akbar, please?"

"Can I ask who's calling?"

"It's David Neal."

"And is your wife a patient?"

He couldn't be bothered to get angry. "Yes."

"One moment, please."

Hold music—something boring and copyright-free—flooded the line. David put a hand in the small of his back and waited. Marianne had suggested walking around to try to trigger labour. So far, it was just giving him swollen ankles.

"Nadia Akbar."

"Nadia, it's David Neal."

"David! How nice to hear from you. How's everything going?"

"It's not," he said. "Sam was due on the fifth and now it's the fifteenth."

She hummed. "Well, ten days isn't too late. Has the bump dropped significantly lower?"

"No."

"Is the baby still moving?"

"Yeah."

"Has the movement changed at all? Different target, different strength..."

"Not really," he said.

She made another light humming noise, and he heard her start clicking away in the background.

"Right," she said after an eternity of typing. "I've booked you in to see me, but it'll have to be at the hospital, I'm afraid. We'll have another quick scan and a chat with one of the consultants. That's on the seventeenth, so hopefully in the next forty-eight hours the little one will get the idea and kick-start everything. Ten days isn't exceptionally late, and you've been fighting fit up until now, so try not to worry too much. Sam might just be feeling a bit lazy."

"Okay. Thanks."

He supposed going into hospital would be bearable if they were going to induce him or something. He dropped the phone on the counter and placed both hands in his back. He'd take anything at this point to get it over with. The sheer weight was painful. Sitting down would drive Sam's feet up into his lungs so he couldn't breathe, and standing up made him feel like his stomach was going to be ripped off from the front. Lying on his side was all right, but it was getting harder and harder to get back up again.

"Ryan!"

"What?"

"I'm never doing this again!"

"Uh, yeah, kind of figured," came the bemused reply.

David paced out into the living room to find Ryan repacking the hospital bag for the tenth time.

"It's definitely your baby."

"Well, good, or we need to talk."

"I meant because of this laziness."

"It's not lazy, it's energy efficient."

David snorted. Sam wriggled, but stilled again shortly.

"I need it out."

"It's obviously comfy," Ryan said.

"It can't be comfy. It's cramped as hell in there."

"Maybe it's just like a giant hug, and it takes after me and likes a good cuddle." Ryan looked up from his packing and grinned. "I can't wait now."

"What?"

"For it to arrive!" he said. "To find out if its middle name is Lionel or Mary. Speaking of which, I thought your mum was going to come?"

"Not until I ring her. I texted her before we went to the fireworks and said nothing was happening so not to set off until we called her."

"Ah, I see. Did you win the argument about having her at the birth?"

"Yeah. Barely. And mostly thanks to Jacob."

Ryan whistled. "I like this new boyfriend."

David grunted. He wasn't in the mood to join in the joviality.

"You want to try some of Marianne's ideas?"

"What?"

"About triggering labour."

"I googled them. It's all old wives' tales."

"Can't hurt."

"Raspberry tea is disgusting. I'm not drinking that without a peer review of its efficiency."

Ryan rolled his eyes. "All right, all right. Hot bath?"

"No chance, or I'll have the baby in the bath."

"Be easier to clean up," Ryan said and patted his lap. "Come here."

"No. Your chair can't take all that weight."

"The disclaimer specifically says it can take up to—"

"In one person. Not two people sprawled all over it, both of whom have serious difficulty getting up right now."

Ryan laughed. "Christ, you're prickly."

"And you're on oxycodone or something because you are far too happy about this," David grumbled. He stretched, trying to ease the pain out of his back, but it didn't work. "Can't we just go up to the hospital and get me induced or something?"

"I've no idea, but if Sam isn't ready, then Sam isn't ready," Ryan said. "It'll happen when it happens."

"Easy for you to say."

"Sit down and put something on the TV and relax," Ryan scolded. "I'll make lunch. And I'll ring Marianne and ask if she can't keep Ava this we—"

"No."

"What? David. Come on, it'll be easier if—"

"I said no. Ava's worried enough about the baby as it is. Foisting her off on Marianne is only going to make it worse. You can ring Marianne to come and get her when I go into labour, not before."

Ryan eyed him sceptically. "You sure?"

"Yes, I'm sure. Other people have their kids right up until the last minute, so can we."

"Sure," Ryan said. "But other people aren't you."

The remark stung. David pursed his lips.

"I'm sor—"

"No, you're right. Other people can obviously cope better than I can."

It was childish and petty, and he knew it. But somehow, it didn't stop it from spilling out.

"I know I'm the last person who should be having a baby, Ryan. No need to rub that in my face."

"Stop it."

Ryan's voice was sharp, and it brought David up even shorter.

"That's not what I mean, and you know it. There's nothing wrong with this being hard, for fuck's sake."

David wanted to snap back. Hell, he wanted to slap him. He was fed up with being pregnant, fed up with being a freak, fed up with being out. He wanted to go right back into the closet he'd carefully built and maintained for himself and forget—along with everybody else—the way he'd originally been built. More than a little part of him wanted to take back the decision he'd made at the abortion clinic.

And the rest of him felt guilty at the urge.

But a row wouldn't help, so he turned on his heel and stalked out of the room. He heard Ryan sigh, but thankfully didn't hear him follow. David slammed the door of their bedroom and crashed down onto the bed in a fit of pique. Sam, annoyed at being disturbed, punched a kidney out of spite.

"You lay off as well," David snapped, rapping the top of the bump sharply with two knuckles. "The sooner you come out of there, the fucking better."

IT WAS DARK when he woke up.

He felt foggy, like he'd slept for hours, and the heavy drag of exhaustion hadn't eased at all. For a moment, he wondered why he'd woken up at all.

Then the cramp tightened around his bladder, and David groaned. Great. Yet another bathroom trip.

Heaving himself off the bed alone took incredible effort. His limbs shivered, and the cramp spread over his guts in protest. Brilliant. Getting the runs with a ten-day late baby. Just what he needed.

The rest of the house was dark and quiet too, but he could hear the TV faintly behind the living room door. He decided to go and apologise after going to the toilet, and maybe suggest a takeaway. He didn't feel especially hungry, but it would be a good idea to eat anyway. God knew when Sam would put in a show.

The toilet didn't really help with the cramping sensation, so he headed to the kitchen to make a hot water bottle. His back was hurting too, more than before. He must have slept funny.

Armed, he snuck into the living room to find Ryan had dozed off in front of the TV. The rubber band in his hair had snapped, and his dreadlocks spilled down to frame his snoring face. David found a blanket and tucked himself up next to him, drawing a limp arm over his own shoulders before settling in for a hug and finding a film to watch instead of a shit football match.

Ryan stirred sleepily when a helicopter exploded on the screen, and the arm tightened around David's shoulders. A kiss framed by stubble scratched at his temple.

"I'm sorry for—"

"S'fine," Ryan mumbled.

"But—"

"Shut up."

David shut up, sagging into the hug as it tightened. A wave of that cramped pain tightened around his back and belly, and he sighed, wriggling free.

"Sorry. Gut is playing up."

"Oh. Okay. You okay?"

"Yeah. You want to call for something to eat?"

"There's eggs. I can make a cheese omelette if that'll help settle you down?"

"Maybe."

Another trip to the bathroom brought no relief, and David grumbled irritably as he pulled up his jogging bottoms. The bump was gargantuan, and when he rested his hand on the top of it, tight.

He frowned.

Wait.

His muscles tightened painfully in his back, like period pain, and then the sensation began to ripple outwards, around his sides, over the bump, and sinking into his bowels like claws. It felt like a bad curry. He felt like he needed to take a crap.

Only he didn't need to. At all.

And under his fingers, the bump had gone from a soft kind of solidity to hard as a rock.

Oh.

Shuffling back into the bedroom, he took his phone off the charger and swiped open the browser.

What does early labour feel like? he tapped into Google as he headed for the kitchen. He couldn't remember ever actually asking Nadia that. Or anybody else, for that matter.

"That was fast," Ryan said as David walked into the kitchen. "You want cheesy omelette, or you want to just stick to a couple of boiled eggs? Can make some toast, if you—"

The results popped up, and David grimaced.

"Never mind," he said. "I need to ring Nadia."

Ryan's head snapped up.

"I think it's started."

Chapter Thirty-Two

"WHAT ABOUT NOW?"

David sighed. "No," he said absently, sending the text.

He'd rung the hospital and talked to the duty midwife. She'd said stay put.

"You're in the very early stages," she'd said. "If you come in now, they'll only send you home anyway."

If anything, it was worse than not being in labour at all. He knew the clock was ticking now. Ryan was twitchy as all hell and getting annoying with the hovering. David would have liked to just call a taxi and get on the road—but he didn't really fancy being obviously heavily pregnant and in labour for hours in a hospital cafe with everyone staring at him.

Christ, he hoped Nadia would be able to deliver it.

"How do you—"

"Ryan. I feel fine. Back off."

It came out a little sharp, and he sighed, tipping his head back against the rest.

"Sorry," he muttered.

"It's fine. Here. Let me get the kit out and give you a proper foot massage."

"Thank you."

He was sitting in the armchair. Its ramrod straight back oddly helped with the cramps that came and went in waves, and he had the distinct impression that if he lay down, he'd never get back up again. He had a splitting headache as well but didn't dare take anything for it.

"Hurry up," he told the bump as it tightened once more. He didn't know if this counted as early stage contractions yet or not, but he hoped so. He'd call them again in an hour.

"Okay," Ryan said when he returned with a bowl of hot water and the massage kit. It had originally been for him, a Christmas present from David for the bad pain days, but David had no objection to being on the receiving end for once. "Get that compress on your eyes, and put your feet up in my lap."

David obeyed, sighing as a warm compress smelling of eucalyptus oil plunged him into darkness. He lifted his feet, relaxing as they were laid on a soft towel over Ryan's knees.

"Anything hurt?"

"Ankles are aching."

"Right you are."

The smell of tea tree and mint was sharp and soothing, and David sighed breathily as damp, hot fingers rubbed at the tender swelling that almost obscured the bones entirely. Ryan had magic hands. He'd learned from his physio, Nathan, and usually it was more akin to a sports massage than anything else. Last time David had got a proper massage off Ryan, it had been after dislocating his shoulder in judo over a year ago.

He tried to relax, going through his breathing exercises and feeling the tension leak away—with the exception, of course, of the baby-related tension. His shoulders eased. The sharp stabbing in his head dulled to a throb, and the throbbing in his ankles dulled to an ache. Ryan hummed to himself, a familiar upbeat tune. David let out a long, cathartic breath.

"I'm glad it's nearly over," he murmured.

"Me too."

"I'm sorry I've been so difficult the last couple of months."

"It's understandable."

"I'm still sorry."

"I'm sorry it's so hard on you," Ryan returned. "And whatever you want to do afterwards to get yourself back to normal, I'm with you one hundred percent. I miss you."

David's throat felt thick. "Mm."

"It's not your fault."

"No, I know. Still doesn't feel great."

"Nope. If it helps, you're not as bad as Marianne was."

"Seriously?"

"Yep. She threw a lamp at me the day before she went into labour and turfed me out of the house."

"Oh. I'm a bit less sorry, then."

"Better." Ryan squeezed an ankle and David groaned. "I know this is a way off, but are you going to have it all removed?"

"I don't know. The dysphoria might go away when this is done. But I need the hormones back. I'm going to work on the endocrinologist first. I can't wait a year."

"Plus your beard's looking a bit shit."

David laughed. "That too."

"Do you want to try and have a nap?"

"Mm, yeah, maybe."

"I'll keep going. Even do your toenails if you conk out properly."

"If you paint them, I'll kill you."

"Yeah, yeah, whatever..."

David drifted, focusing on the heavenly sensation of Ryan's hands squeezing and soothing, squeezing and soothing, over and over again.

Then he drifted away entirely.

DAVID WAS BROUGHT back to earth by a bone-shuddering pain.

Doubling up, he howled as the pain ripped through his abdomen, worse than the worst drunk curry he'd ever had. It passed like a tide going out, every muscle collapsing again in a great ripple, and he thumped back into the armchair with a groan.

"Ryan!"

He heard something bang in the kitchen, and then the run of the wheels bumping over the lip between the tiles and the wood.

"Call a taxi," David said as the second wave of pain crashed over him. He creased in half and would have ended up bent double if not for the bump. It was like concrete and felt impossibly heavier than it had before. "This is—yeah. Baby's coming."

"Shit," Ryan called. "Right, I'll get the taxi and your bag. You just—breathe. Need anything?"

"A midwife!"

"Yeah, yeah, I got it—"

The chair was soaked when he managed to lever himself out of it, but David honestly couldn't tell if he'd pissed himself or the waters had broken. He dropped his jogging bottoms and limped into the bedroom to find another pair and change his boxers. He may as well at least start out dry.

He'd just managed to change when the third wave hit and he fumbled blindly for Ryan's watch on the side table as he breathed through it. The moment it passed, he clicked the stopwatch function and watched the seconds begin to spiral.

"Taxi's on its way!" Ryan called from the hall. "Just going to ring the hospital. You okay?"

"Yeah," David said, shuffling into the hall. He leaned up against the wall, holding a hand under the bump. It had dropped. A lot. "Sam's definitely coming."

"Just sit—hello, hi, my name's Ryan Walsh, my partner went into labour this morning and it's gotten a lot further along now."

David rolled his head back against the wall, exhaling in a long breath. *Nearly there. Nearly over.*

"Nadia Akbar. Yes. Thanks." Ryan glanced up at him. "Okay?"

"Mm."

"Is the pain bad?"

"Not at the minute," David said. "Contractions are shit though."

Oddly, the pain didn't bother him. He could focus on the pain. When it hurt, he was too busy breathing through it to get upset about why it was happening. Pain helped.

The contraction hit, and he clicked off the stopwatch. When it had passed and he could open his eyes again to reset the watch, he grimaced at the display.

"Four minutes thirty seconds," he said to Ryan, who relayed it to whoever he'd managed to get hold of at the hospital. He had no idea what that meant.

It was another four cycles before the taxi turned up, and the poor bastard looked immediately perplexed as to whether to help Ryan get in first or David. David tried to keep his mouth shut and avoid any awkward questions—or worse—if the cabbie clocked his gender, but all too soon another contraction was tearing through him in the back seat, and he couldn't keep the groan behind his teeth.

"Dewsbury or Pinders?" the cabbie asked, flinging himself into the front.

"Dewsbury," Ryan said.

"On it. Hang on, missus."

David flipped him off, and didn't feel a shred of shame.

To give the guy his due, though, he could drive like a stuntman in the movies. David clung to the door and kept his eyes closed out of a lack of desire to see imminent death rather than the pain, and he got the distinct impression Ryan was holding his hand so tight out of terror rather than a desire to help. David didn't know the journey to Dewsbury Hospital was possible in under half an hour from their house—and certainly not in mid-afternoon traffic.

There was nobody to meet them, but the cabbie sprinted inside, one hand comically clapped down over his hat to keep it on, and came dashing back out within a couple of minutes, followed by a far more relaxed orderly pushing an empty wheelchair.

"In you get," he said, and David grimaced as he was roughly manhandled into the chair.

"I'll follow," Ryan said, waving off the orderly. "Driver can sort me out. Come on, pal, just get her unfolded. Yep, that catch there—"

David leaned back in the chair as the contraction passed, raking a breath in through his nose. He kept his eyes shut. He still had the watch and knew he had less than three minutes before the next one now.

"First, second, fifth?" the orderly asked, but David just grunted. He was in no mood for small talk.

"Ah, David Neal, isn't it?" Gloves snapped. "Come on, then, dear, let's find you a nice spot, eh?"

He relaxed as the nurses began to flock. He was transferred from the wheelchair into a bed, and grimaced through the examination.

"Five centimetres," one nurse said. "You've got a little wait yet—"

"Caesarean. They agreed a caesarean."

"All right, dear, let us find your notes. A midwife is on her way."

David nodded, grimacing as another rush of pain swept over him. By the time he opened his eyes again, Ryan had found him, and David reached for his hand.

"Five centimetres."

"What does that mean?" Ryan asked.

"No idea," David replied and laughed giddily. "They're finding my notes and a midwife."

"Least you had a good nap before it all kicked off, eh?"

It was just as well. David hadn't been under any illusions that labour was fast, but now that he'd arrived at the hospital, Sam seemed to decide they weren't so keen on being born after all. The contractions stuck at every three minutes for almost forty minutes and slowed right back to every five before beginning to speed up again.

And then, somewhere about ten o'clock in the evening, the duty midwife frowned at the foetal heartbeat monitor and called for a nurse.

"Fetch Dr Yunis, please."

The nurse scuttled off. David frowned at the ceiling.

"What's wrong?" he asked.

"Your heartbeat is far too fast," she said gently. "And it's beginning to upset the baby a wee bit. I'd just like a second opinion."

"Is the baby safe?"

"It's not in any danger zones just yet," she said, which wasn't the most reassuring thing in the world.

There was a clatter of flat shoes at the door, and a familiar face breezed into view.

"I can take this one from here, Helen."

"Nadia," Ryan said, and David groaned with relief.

"Hello, David. I'm sorry; I was on another delivery when you arrived. Two babies today, let's have a hat trick by the end of my shift, eh?" she said cheerily.

"Mother's distress is becoming significant, starting to affect the foetal heartbeat," the midwife said quietly, and Nadia nodded.

"Okay, David, let's get you on some of the hard stuff, shall we, and see if we can't bring your numbers down out of the rafters, darling."

He'd been on gas and air for an hour, but it wasn't so much as taking the edge off. Whatever the nurse gave him didn't do much, either, and the constant flow of people, as well as the unending agony, wasn't helping.

"Don't think I can," he ground out, and Nadia squeezed his knee.

"I'm sure you can, love," she said. "Ah, Dr Yunis, thank you. Have a look and see what you think. I would have preferred to let labour continue naturally for another half hour, but look at the blood pressure—"

Dr Yunis—an exceptionally tall man with glasses perched precariously on the end of a long, thin nose, peered at Nadia's monitor, then picked up David's notes and leafed through them.

"Yes," he said in a heavy Pakistani accent. "Move to theatre, please. Standard requirements. I will perform."

And with that, he was gone again.

"What's that mean?" David demanded.

"Caesarean," Nadia said breezily. "Sam's getting a little bit upset in there, and your blood pressure is dropping."

"Dropping?" Ryan echoed.

"It could be a number of things," she said, "and it's probably nothing to panic about, but I think Helen was right on this one. We're going to get you all prepared and into theatre. You'll be awake, David, but you won't feel anything but some tugging."

"Ryan can come?"

"Of course, he can, sweetie. Ryan, you'll need some scrubs. Lizzy! Lizzy, could you help Ryan wash up and get into some scrubs, please? Theatre delivery."

David zoned out a little as they began to move him and prepare. He clung to the gas and air pump like it was his lifeline. Even if the stuff wasn't helping, the physical act of using it oddly did, and he squeezed so hard he almost broke it when they turned him for the epidural. When he felt the cold chill of an anaesthetic seeping into his skin, he closed his eyes and reached for Ryan's hand.

"Right here."

"They starting?"

"Yep," Ryan said.

"How's—"

"Everything's fine. Promise."

There was a sharp jerk on his stomach, and he grimaced.

"Just relax for us, David."

"You're doing great," Ryan said, stroking a knuckle over his cheekbone. He was pressed close, like he didn't want to see what was happening over the curtain they'd set up. "You're doing really, really great..."

The ceiling was rippling, like a stone thrown into water. David blinked hazily and distantly heard something blare.

"David? David, you still with us?"

He squeezed Ryan's hand tightly and nodded, but he felt woozy and sick.

"We're almost there, love. Have a chat with Ryan if you can."

"Can't," he mumbled. "Feel crap."

"Well, you don't look a million dollars, but I wasn't going to say anything," Ryan quipped.

"Is it over?"

"Almost over. Can you feel anything?"

"Tugging..."

He felt like he was drifting. Like he was floating on a haze of pain and drugs. Like the prickle of dysphoria, ever-present, had swelled into a great wrenching tear and ripped him free of himself.

And then he heard it.

The consultant's deep voice saying, "Here we are." The splutter of something trying to breathe. The wet sound of flesh separating from flesh. And then the shrill, high scream of a newborn baby, absolutely furious at its undignified entrance into the world.

Ryan's hand was tight on his own, and lips brushed his forehead.

"You did it," he murmured. "You bloody went and did it."

"Congratulations, both of you. One big, beautiful baby. Emphasis on the word big."

It was here.

It was over.

Done.

So David loosened his grip, and slipped away.

Chapter Thirty-Three

HE WAS WARM.

The pillow under his head was soft and smelled of Ryan. Thick cotton. Smooth, almost velvety surface.

Blinking hazily—the telltale yellow halos smearing everything that spoke of some incredibly strong drugs—David realised his pillow had been wrapped in Ryan's hoodie, and his nose was tucked against an empty sleeve.

He blinked again, feeling exhausted and grimy, and the halos wobbled but didn't dissipate.

It was very quiet. He could hear hustle and bustle somewhere very far away, and somebody was humming quietly. The sound was deep and familiar. Soothing.

Ryan. Ryan was here.

David sighed and closed his eyes again, taking stock. He struggled to remember. The gas and air not working. The tugging on his abdomen when the surgeon had gone in. And then—nothing.

He opened his eyes again and stared dully down his body. He was half sitting against the back of the bed, and the enormous bump had deflated somewhat. He looked fat and flabby, loose under the thin sheets. He could feel something around his hips and thighs, like a large sanitary pad or an incontinence nappy. A dull throbbing ache permeated everything between his ribs and knees, yet it felt so very far away.

God, the drugs were good.

"Hey."

Fingers rubbed gently over his wrist. He closed his own clumsily and caught Ryan's hand. His movements felt sluggish, and overwhelmingly, he just wanted to sleep.

"Hey, sweetheart."

Ryan never called him sweetheart. David didn't like it. Would never like it.

"Don't."

"Sorry." A chair creaked. "How are you feeling?"

"Tired..."

"You want to wake up a bit and say hi to Sam?"

He ought to want to hold the baby. He ought to want to see it, cuddle it, find out all about it. But—

The exhaustion dragged on him, and he mumbled a no. He wanted to sleep. If he could sleep forever, and wake up only when everything had passed, then he would be happy. He would be better then, when it was all over.

After all, it didn't end at birth. He'd look wrong for months. His stomach and hips might never recover. He'd bleed for weeks, like the longest Carrie act of his life. It would still be months, maybe even a year, before the endocrinologist would let him go back on the testosterone and do away with this feeling once and for all.

He just wanted to sleep until that day came.

So he relaxed his grip on Ryan's hand and let himself drift free again. Ryan was here. The baby was here. So David didn't need to be.

David could be anywhere else.

David—

HE BLINKED.

His eyelids felt crusty. Ryan's hoodie was still under his cheek. He could feel someone tugging on the IV in his hand, and he blinked hazily at the nurse bending over him.

"Good evening, dear," she said, smiling. "Don't you worry. You had a bit of a bleed, but you're all patched up now. Get some rest."

He heard a familiar creak, and a warm hand rubbed up his arm. He felt cool.

"Hey."

"M'cold."

"You want an extra blanket?"

"Mm."

"No problem..."

Cotton smoothed over him. It smelled of home. He sighed, curling his fingers into the blanket, and realised it was the throw off their sofa.

"What time is it?"

A knuckle gently grazed his temple. "Late. Just go back to sleep. You had a bad time of it."

"You..."

"I'm staying right here. They've agreed to let me stay the night with you and Sam."

"S'm..."

"He's fine."

He. A boy. Some painful part of David he didn't want to admit was there relaxed. He knew better. Sam might turn out to be a girl anyway, might turn out to be both or neither or anything in between, but—but some horrible, awful part of David was relieved, and quietly hoped they'd assigned him the right label.

After everything, after all of it, they had a son.

"Son..."

He could hear the smile in Ryan's voice and nudged his face into the kiss that was pressed to his forehead.

"Yeah. Our son. Go to sleep."

He squeezed a fistful of the blanket and let the drugs take him under once more.

SOMETHING BANGED IN the corridor, and David started awake. He yawned and dug through the dregs of his memory. He felt like he'd slept for hours, but was vaguely aware of the consultant stopping by, and a nurse changing his sanitary pad and giving his lower half a sponge bath. He felt no rush of embarrassment, so the drugs were still working nicely.

"Hey."

He turned his head and frowned sleepily at Ryan. He was unshaven and looked tired, but was beaming widely. A thumb brushed David's jaw, and he twisted to kiss it.

"You finally properly awake?"

"I think so," David mumbled, extracting an arm from the tangle of blanket and scrubbing sleep out of his eyes. "What happened?"

"You needed two blood transfusions. And you were panicking so much that the consultant was worried you were going to give yourself cardiac arrest, so he got you more or less stoned on the hardest thing he could find." Ryan hesitated and then added, "You've been out of it for a while."

"How long is a while?"

"About twenty-four hours."

"Christ..."

"It's fine," Ryan said, still smiling. "You'll be fine. They said once the drugs have worn off, you can come home."

"Where's Ava?"

"With her mum. I rang Marianne and told her you'd started but not to tell Ava until Sam got here and you were ready to see her."

"What 'bout Mum..."

"Haven't called her yet. I, um. You're fine. But you were a bit rough, and...I got a bit upset. Wasn't exactly thinking of ringing your mum."

David smiled faintly, closing his eyes when Ryan touched his jaw again.

"Hey. You did great," Ryan whispered.

"Don't exactly feel it right now," David admitted.

"No, but it's still true. You want to hold him?"

David frowned, his gaze finally sliding past Ryan to the hospital cot beside his chair. All he could see was a bundle of white blankets, perfectly still inside.

"Okay."

Ryan beamed, darting in for a quick kiss before turning and reaching into the cot. The bundle wriggled and mewled in his hands, and he cradled it against his chest, peering down into the folds with the most gut-wrenchingly besotted look David had ever seen. His heart twisted in his chest, and he reached out, wanting to have his own look. Wanting that rush of affection and love to wipe out everything else, and reorient himself around the baby.

"Say hi to your dad, Sam."

He was heavy. David couldn't remember holding a baby before, but his hands and arms knew what to do even if he didn't. The weight settled against his chest, and a tiny fist thumped him in a very familiar manner. He tugged back the blanket to see what he'd done more clearly, and waited.

Nothing happened.

Sam had taken Ryan's darker colouring, but David's sharper features. He yawned in the same way David did. His nose was the same. He was going to be big like Ryan, going by the hands and feet that were already large by comparison to the rest of him. He was entirely bald, so it remained to be seen whether he'd inherit David's fluffy frizz or Ryan's dense curls.

He was their baby. Visibly theirs.

And yet nothing happened.

There was no rush of love. There was no emotional wave. There was nothing. David could have been holding a bag of flour.

His chest seized tight as he realised his worst fear had come true.

The baby was here—and David didn't love him.

Chapter Thirty-Four

"IT'S PERFECTLY NORMAL."

David snorted.

"It is," Nadia said. "Plenty of new parents go through this. It's a very difficult process, your hormones are all over the place, and sometimes, building that bond with your baby takes time."

David's hospital bag was packed and ready at the end of the bed. He was sitting in the visitor's chair, waiting for the taxi to come. Ryan had, on his demand, gone to wait in the corridor with Sam, nestled in a new Moses basket Mum had brought and bundled up against the storm raging outside.

But David didn't want to go home.

"You probably have more than a touch of PTSD," she continued. "You may well develop postnatal depression. You've been through a lot, David. It's understandable if your brain can't just switch that off and flood you with all the happy hormones right now."

"He's my son. I'm supposed to love him."

"And you do. There's just so much going on in there right now that it's not immediately apparent to you," she chided. "Here's my recommendation. For the first couple of weeks, just take it easy at home. Restrict your visitors. I know everyone will want to come and see the new baby, but just take the first couple of weeks to find your feet as a family unit. Just you, your partner, and your little ones. Give yourself plenty of time and space to bond with him. I know it might feel a little scary to pick him up when you're not responding to him much emotionally, but give him regular cuddles, feed him, get used to him. Lots of new parents find it comes along a few days after the birth, once the shock's worn off."

He swallowed uneasily, staring at the ward door. Ryan was waiting out there. With their son.

The son David didn't love.

"What if it doesn't?"

"You've worked long and hard for this baby," she said gently. "I don't think that's going to happen."

"What if a couple of weeks doesn't work?"

"I'll give you some contacts for a counsellor, and you'll be coming back in to see me regularly with Sam anyway, to monitor his progress over the first few weeks. Talk to your partner, talk to your doctor, talk to anyone who will listen. Don't bottle this up," Nadia said. "Just let everything you're feeling out, even if it's ugly. If you try and hem it all in, then it'll make everything worse."

"Okay."

"Pregnancy worries never end with the pregnancy," she said. "You just need your body and brain to catch up to the worst part being over, and then they'll let you get on with adoring your little boy. Just relax and let that happen."

He nodded jerkily and stood up, reaching for the bag. He didn't hurt nearly as much as he thought he would, but the flabby weight hanging around his thighs, hips and stomach was painful to look at, and the shift of his bum like he'd turned into his mother sent prickles of unease up his spine.

"Call me if you need anything at all," Nadia said.

He nodded and stepped out into the corridor.

Ryan was waiting by the lifts, the basket in his lap. He had one hand tucked into it, stroking Sam's cheek with one finger. The baby was determinedly asleep, tiny hands encased in mittens thrown up by his face.

"Ready to go?" David asked.

"Yep. Taxi's about ten minutes out thanks to the weather, but we can wait down by the main entrance. Here."

Ryan held up the basket, and David took the handle. He swallowed uneasily at the nothingness that happened when he stared at his son's face, then squared his shoulders and pressed the button for the lift.

"What did Nadia say?"

David took a deep breath. "I—I don't feel anything when I hold him, Ryan."

Ryan reached out and squeezed his knee.

"I should get this huge rush of love, like you do, but...I don't."

"You will," Ryan said. "You love Ava to bits. We talked about adopting, and you were all for it. This is just—shock."

"I hope so."

"It is," Ryan said as the lift doors opened. "Trust me. Trust her. She knows what she's talking about."

David smiled thinly, but he didn't feel any of Ryan's confidence. He just felt tired. He wanted to go home, give the baby to Ryan, and go to bed for the next thousand years. Maybe he could re-emerge when his body had healed and Sam was two and already walking and talking.

The storm was turning into a hurricane, and when they finally got home, it was as black as night outside. David stood stupidly in the hall with the basket, staring down at it like he'd never seen a baby before, and Ryan tutted.

"Go and get yourself washed and changed and pampered, and I'll pop our little bundle of joy on the sofa and take lots of pictures to send round everyone," he said. "Leave the door unlocked."

"What?"

"Just in case. Please."

David blinked slowly and nodded. "Sorry. I think—I feel tired."

"Not exactly a surprise," Ryan said. "Holler if you need any help."

In truth, David wanted to sleep more than he wanted a shower, but the smell of hospital stuck to him, and his skin felt grimy. But the idea of changing the dressing, of washing all the loose folds that Sam had left behind, rankled. He ended up giving himself a quick rub down at the sink with an exfoliating sponge, then finding some clean clothes. Joggers. A T-shirt from Ryan's side of the middle drawer. They smelled of fabric softener and were too large, and David eyed his reflection in the mirror critically.

Christ, he was a mess.

And not just physically. He could fix the body. Going back to judo after Christmas would wipe out the chaos Sam had left behind.

But his mind?

David wasn't so sure about that.

He wanted to leave Ryan with Sam, and go about his day as if nothing had happened. But Nadia's advice was sitting heavy in the pit of his stomach, so he shuffled into the kitchen to make himself a cup of tea and get some mild inoffensive biscuits to settle his still-upset stomach before heading back into the living room.

"Feeling better?" Ryan asked.

The empty basket was sitting in the middle of the coffee table, and Ryan had levered himself from his chair onto the sofa. Sam was in his lap, half-asleep, judging by the jerky little movements of his limbs, and Ryan—far from taking pictures—was tweaking tiny fingers in his hands in fascination.

"You've already had a baby," David said a little stupidly.

"What?"

"You're looking at him like you've never seen a baby before."

"I've never seen *this* baby before," Ryan countered and held up his phone. "Take a picture for me?"

David nodded, beating a retreat to the bookshelf to take it as Ryan gathered Sam up into his arms for a proper cuddle. That tiny mouth yawned widely, and he settled without complaint.

"He's gorgeous," Ryan murmured, beaming down at him.

David's stomach clenched, and he took the picture. Christ, Ryan was wearing all his love on his face. He was utterly enraptured, and David wanted to feel it. *Why didn't he feel it?*

"Here," he said, putting the phone on the arm of the sofa and holding out his arms. "Let me hold him."

Ryan's smile was hopeful, and David bit his lip as he passed the baby up. Sam grumbled, blinking sleepily up at him, then sighed and dozed off again peaceably. The weight was comfortable. The warmth was nice. It was a bit like holding an affectionate cat—heavy and hot, solid when he looked delicate.

But still nothing happened.

"Give it time," Ryan murmured, touching the outside of his knee lightly. "Don't beat yourself up, eh? Just give it a bit of time."

David nodded jerkily, stroking a thumb over the Babygro. He sank painfully onto the sofa, before turning sideways and lying down against the arm, hefting Sam higher up on his chest.

"Film?" he suggested weakly, and Ryan patted his lap.

"Pop your feet here, and we'll see what's on, eh?"

David nodded. Maybe it would work. Maybe being home and everything being over would help. He just had to trust Nadia and Ryan were right.

"If I go to sleep—"

"It'll be good for you," Ryan said, stroking his ankles. "Doze off whenever you want. Sam's going to be awake and asleep whenever he feels like it, you might as well join in."

David nodded.

"And I heard you and Nadia talking."

"Oh, fuck."

"Hey, it's all right," Ryan said, still in that gentle voice.

David wanted to snap at him. It wasn't bloody all right. He'd rather a row than that endless patience sometimes. "It's not."

"It is," Ryan countered. "I'll send some pictures round and tell everyone we need a week or two to ourselves with the baby. We can't do much about having Ava next week, but we can put everyone else off for a while."

David felt awful at the prospect. Mum was so excited about her new grandbaby. She'd be crestfallen at having to wait. Their friends could wait, and Marianne probably wouldn't be that interested anyway, but Mum...

"I'll ring your mum in person," Ryan murmured. "She'll understand."

David knew she would. She'd complain, but she'd understand. And that only made him feel worse.

"Have a kip," Ryan said, squeezing his foot. "Have a nap with our son, and by the time you wake up, everything will start looking better."

Chapter Thirty-Five

IT DIDN'T.

David lay wide awake that night, staring at the ceiling and feeling the lumpy clots of blood sinking into the sanitary pad between his legs. Every slide of slimy liquid made the bile jump up the inside of his throat and burn the back of his mouth. When Sam began to cry at two in the morning, David felt like he was changing a doll rather than his own son, and stood over the crib for nearly an hour afterwards, staring at the sleeping baby.

And it happened again at four, and again at six, and then David stayed up and faced the new day, exhausted and hollow.

He felt empty.

David felt as though he'd been presented with one of Ava's dolls instead of a baby, albeit one that moved when he handled it. He felt blank when picking Sam up, and comforting him when he cried was hard. The temptation to pass him to Ryan was almost overpowering, but Ryan would frown and Nadia's advice would echo in his ears, and David would grit his teeth and get on with it, hoping if he forced himself to knuckle down and look after Sam, it would kick-start everything else.

But it didn't.

That first week was—lonely. He felt locked in and lonely. He didn't want to admit to Ryan the growing fear that nothing was going to change, and David had had a baby he didn't love. He didn't want to see his mum or his friends—the very suggestion of inviting James and Andi over had triggered a panic attack—but he felt isolated and numb.

Numb.

It was as though a glass screen had gone up between him and the rest of the world. He could see it, but he couldn't touch. He could hear it, but he couldn't listen.

Couldn't feel.

It was like being a teenager again, when he'd lashed out in an effort to break through the depression and anxiety. When he'd shredded his own arms to ribbons because it punctured the cling film over his skin and shook the cobwebs out of his head.

As the week drew to a close and the second one beckoned, the calls started coming. James and Andi, checking in. Vicky, wanting a visit. Mum. Always Mum.

But David couldn't answer.

He'd sit, holding the baby and watching his mobile jumping on the coffee table, lit up and singing, and couldn't move.

THEY WENT TO the GP's surgery to see Nadia at the end of that awful first week. David insisted on a taxi from door to door, refusing to go out and not even wanting to push the pram. The Moses basket was dug back out of the cupboard, and Sam stared curiously at the ribbon sewn to the edge of the wicker the whole way there, fascinated.

"He's going to be a chewer," Ryan predicted, but David wasn't really listening.

"Do you mind—" he began as the taxi pulled up, but cut off the thought. It wasn't until they were out, had had the typical rude stare from the receptionist, and found a seat, that he tried again. "Do you mind if—if I just go with Sam on my own?"

Ryan frowned. "What? Why?"

"I—I think I need a private word with Nadia."

Ryan licked his lips. "David—"

"Not about Sam. About me."

Ryan sighed and squeezed his wrist. "I—fine. Okay. If—if it'll help. But you tell me everything you talked about, okay? About you and Sam."

David nodded dully. He knew he'd have to. He just didn't quite want to air it all right in front of Ryan, even if Ryan was already aware of it all. It just seemed too—too—

"One day, you'll stop thinking that your personal affairs aren't my business," Ryan grumbled, and David jumped.

Personal.

It did feel personal. Too personal, but not in the way Ryan was thinking. It felt like giving him a window into what David had been like as a teenager. Those long years of hazy fog punctured only by bursts of violent pain as he'd tried—desperately tried—to not be David. As he'd forced everything into being a girl, only to discover he had no choice.

And, back then, in the middle of Salford at a rough inner-city school where tranny meant a Ford Transit van because actual, living, breathing human beings who were trans was just unthinkably funny and something stupid off the telly—

Back then, David had known he had no choice but to not be himself.

Back then, being where he was now had been up there with fairy stories. Dragons. Witches. Knights riding in on white wheelchairs to save the day.

David had spent nearly a decade resolutely blocking out and forgetting what it had been like to grow up then and there, and he didn't want to give himself the window into that past, never mind Ryan. He knew how Ryan would react. He'd be scared, he'd be upset, he'd want David to talk about it. And maybe talking worked for guys like Ryan—big men who'd never had their masculinity questioned, even when they weren't straight, even with mobility issues, even if people on dating sites assumed they weren't into sex anymore because, hey, couldn't feel it, right?

Even then, Ryan had shoulders like a front row forward, and even when people curled their lip and sneered, they weren't seriously thinking he wasn't a man. Not particularly masculine, maybe. A broken specimen, maybe. But still a man.

He could afford to talk about it.

But it didn't always work for guys like David. If he talked about it, it only got worse. If he talked about it, he'd never stop.

And when he ran out of words, and felt no different, he'd try something else. David knew that. He knew that about himself.

"It's not that it's personal," he said quietly. "It's that—the way I feel right now? It's taking me back to being a teenager."

Ryan opened his mouth, but then slowly closed it again.

"I tried talking about it," David said, "but it didn't help. It made things worse. And I don't want to think about it any more than I have to, much less talk about the past."

Ryan sighed and looped an arm over his shoulders. He dragged, and David allowed the hug for once, despite the public setting.

"I get it," he said, his voice heavy and meaningful. "I know how that feels. Different things, maybe, but I do know how that feels."

"I know," David whispered.

"Sam Walsh!"

Nadia's sunny smile was at the door to the offices, and David wriggled out of the hug and picked up the basket like it was a box. To his relief, Ryan didn't move, and David followed Nadia into her little exam room on his own.

"Ryan not joining us?" she asked.

"No."

"How have you all been?" she asked as he set the basket down.

David shrugged. "He's feeding well. Getting bigger by the minute, I think. Oh, uh, Ryan did mention wanting to get one last HIV test, just in case."

She nodded, already snapping gloves on, but her gaze stayed resolutely on him.

"And what about you?"

He shrugged, sinking into a chair.

"Tired."

She hummed a little sceptically. Sam squeaked as she lifted him out of the basket, flailing chubby arms.

"Hello, gorgeous," she crooned, and David grimaced. Even the midwife sounded more emotionally invested in the baby than he did. "Let's get you weighed and measured, eh, then I'm going to prod you with a couple of pointy needles. You're not going to like me very much in a minute, I'm afraid."

David watched as she bustled about with Sam, who was distinctly unconvinced. He grunted when she passed him back to David, whined at the heel prick test, and positively howled when she took the blood sample.

"I'm sorry, chook," she said, grasping his other hand between finger and thumb and waving it. He jerked it free, wailing. David sighed, standing up, and began to pace with Sam on his shoulder. "You're very natural with him."

David shrugged.

"I take it you don't agree?"

"I still don't feel anything for him," David said. "It's like looking after a doll. I'm just empty all the time. I can't sleep—and that's without the crying at night—and I feel wrong all the time. I just feel wrong. I know you said give it time and I'll get over it, but when the hell does that begin?"

It just boiled over in a frustrated torrent, and he sighed through his nose. Sam picked up on his tone and began to cry harder, so David gritted his teeth, slowed his pace, and tried to do his breathing exercises. Nadia hummed, taking her seat at the desk and propping her chin on her hand to watch him.

"Have you talked to your GP?"

David snorted. "No."

"Don't get on?"

"Every doctor in here thinks everything can be caused by HRT," he retorted. "I once came in to get some antibiotics for an ear infection, and they tried to stop my hormones."

Nadia's face didn't so much as twitch. It looked as carefully constructed as Ava's paper-mache projects from school.

"I wouldn't trust any of them to doctor their way out of a paper bag."

"So you don't trust them?"

"That's the polite way of putting it."

She clicked her tongue. "What about a different surgery? You know you don't have to register to the closest one, don't you?"

"There's not another one for miles around. And the next one over is being shut down."

"I see. You could try a locum doctor at the walk-in clinic?" she offered. "I think you need to be referred for some help in any case."

"Like what?" he asked warily.

"In the long term, some counselling," she said. "In the short term, medication can help with the sleeping problems. Perhaps some antidepressants in the longer terms, or antianxiety medication to help you find—"

"I don't want to go on happy pills or talk to some counsellor," he said. "I've tried happy pills. I tried them for years. They're shit, they make me shit—"

"A counsellor, then?"

He snorted. Sam had quieted to a grumpy grizzling, and David stopped to tuck him back into the Moses basket.

"Are we done here?" he snapped.

He knew he was being an arse, but somehow it didn't stop him. He'd send a card or something at some point. Right now, he just wanted to leave. He didn't want to be in the GP surgery, talking about treatments that had never worked before and weren't going to start working now. When she nodded, David stood up with the basket handle gripped in a shaking fist.

"I know you're trying to help," he said, "but what's talking about it with someone who's never seen a pregnant man in their life going to do to help me? What's adding pills to the stack I already take going to do to stop this? I'm sorry, Nadia. I know you're trying. But I don't think you can help me with this one."

The thought occurred, as he headed for the door, that it was entirely possible nobody could.

And what kind of thought was that?

Chapter Thirty-Six

DAVID PRIDED HIMSELF on not showing the cracks in his armour.

It had always been his defence. The one thing he could rely on. No matter how bad he felt, nobody else could really tell. Nobody else knew the secrets he carried around inside. Nobody had any idea what was really going on under the surface unless David wanted them to know, and it was something he'd refined and perfected for most of his life.

But the cracks started to show the following week when the world invited itself to dinner.

Ryan had wisely left him alone after the appointment with Nadia, quietly offering a foot massage when they got home and ordering takeaway from David's favourite place. Saturday had been quiet—that sensation of being crowded in surrounding him again like a smothering blanket, itchy and uncomfortable.

But on Sunday afternoon, the blanket was torn away by the familiar hammering on the front door.

"Oh, Christ," David said and covered his face in both hands. "You have to be kidding me."

Ryan, who hadn't grown up hearing that thundering on his bedroom door whenever he'd done something stupid, eyed him blankly.

"What? It's probably Mormons or something."

"That's not Mormons," David said. And as if their God had heard him, his phone started ringing.

With the opening screech from 'Day Oh.' So chosen because it thoroughly pissed off the only person who triggered that ringtone on his entire contact list.

"Oh," Ryan said and pushed back from the table. "You want me to—"

"No," David said tiredly, switching off the burner. "It'll only make it worse."

Sure enough, Mum was on the other side of the door. She was wearing a sedate black coat over a colour explosion of a blouse, and a headwrap that was either a tie-dye job or the result of washing a bright orange headwrap in with a stack of blue bed sheets. She was alone, at least, the fancy cane she'd won in a charity raffle years ago testimony as to how she'd arrived. She didn't need a cane. She just used one whenever she used public transport to whack people's ankles and make them move out of the way.

She whacked his ankle too, and David yelped.

"Mum!"

"You were supposed to call!" she huffed. "Where's my new grandbaby, eh? Come on, boy, don't just stand there!"

He was hustled out of the way. Her only acknowledgement that he'd given birth to said grandbaby instead of adopting it was that she dropped her things all over the floor rather than on him like she usually did, and marched off towards the kitchen.

David sighed, pinching the bridge of his nose.

He loved his mum. He did. He just—really wasn't ready for her to show up in full force right now.

Thankfully, her immediate attention was completely on Sam. He'd already been fed and changed for the morning, and was asleep in his basket on the table while Ryan did the bills for the month. At least Mum wasn't so nuts as to disturb a sleeping newborn, but she sat and took pictures with her phone, nursing the coffee Ryan made for her and crooning at every twitch from those tiny fingers.

"He looks just like you did," she told David, who raised his eyebrows.

"Really? I thought he looked more like Ryan than me."

"Ooh, no, you looked just the same. Is he regular? I take it he's on formula. None of this supermarket rubbish, I hope—and don't you listen to them midwives, busybodies; rub a little gin on his gums if he's not going off to sleep..."

She prattled away, the noise grating on David's nerves, and his jaw clenched involuntarily when she broke off a lecture on how best to position Sam to sleep for the night to demand after the delivery.

"What?"

"I said, how was the birth?"

"Awful," he said, and Ryan glanced up from the bills.

"Natural though," she said in a confident manner.

"Caesarean."

"Why?" she huffed. "You've got my hips, you know, you could have easily—"

"No, I couldn't, and it wasn't about my hips," he snapped.

"It's all about the hips, if your—"

"I had to have a caesarean because I was having panic attacks when stoned out of my mind," he interrupted. "I was going to give myself a heart attack. And Sam was nowhere near actually being born at that point."

"There's no need for that tone—"

"I'm going for a nap." He pushed himself up from the table, feeling short of breath. His chest was tight. Ryan shot him a look but reached out a hand to his mum.

"Don't," Ryan said, and David felt a rush of oddly angry gratitude as he stalked out of the kitchen, towards the bedroom.

But he didn't go into theirs.

Instead, he ducked sideways into Sam's and closed the door behind him.

Then, slowly, he leaned up against it, slid down to the carpet, and stretched out his legs.

And breathed.

For several minutes, he just sat there and breathed. The room tilted violently around him, even sitting down with his eyes closed, so he tried to blot out everything and simply breathe through it. He didn't mean to snap at her. She just had a habit of talking before she thought, and forgetting how things weren't the same for him. He knew she meant well.

But—

But.

Usually, David could be pragmatic about that sort of thing, but ever since that phone call in the car on the way to collect Ava from—

Oh, shit, Ava. He groaned when he remembered it was their Sunday. Marianne would be bringing her over in time for lunch any minute now, and it would be the first time they'd see Sam. He wanted to call it off. He wanted to retreat and just leave Ryan to the wolves.

But he couldn't—because David had a very sharp fear that if he did, he'd never come back.

He ground the heel of his palm into his eye and took a hitching breath. He couldn't begrudge Mum her time with her new grandson, nor Ava the chance to see her baby brother. But David needed to not be here. He felt panicky just at having them in the house. Now, the cracks were on show, he wasn't sure he could paper them over for Ava anymore and prevent her seeing. He wasn't sure he could roll his eyes and tolerate Mum's missteps right now. The power of even the slightest wrong turn to hurt was magnified a thousandfold, and suddenly he was afraid. Afraid of a remark equating him to anything feminine, scared of a deadname slipping out at the wrong moment, terrified of even a normal question being asked too bluntly.

He was made of glass, and it had finally shattered.

So when he heard Mum starting to bustle about and make lunch, he didn't move. When he heard Sam start to cry for his own lunch, David did nothing. And when he heard a car in the road, followed by the persistent ringing of a doorbell being aggressively punched by an overeager five-year-old, he put his hands over his ears and pretended it wasn't there.

The shriek permeated the shield anyway. "Can I see the baby now!" delivered at top volume and with no pauses between any of the words. He screwed up his face as she thundered past, and ignored the low rumble of adult voices.

Then flinched when someone knocked on the door.

"David?"

To his surprise, it wasn't Ryan. Or worse, Mum.

It was Marianne.

"Can I come in? I've got a few things for Sam."

Sighing, he shuffled sideways. She cracked open the door—then slipped in, a box under one arm, and closed it.

"Hey."

He stared tiredly at her as she slid down next to him, abandoning the box on the floor. A couple of soft toys were poking out of the top.

"Some of Ava's old things," she said. "How are you doing?"

"Crap."

"You don't seem like yourself."

He shrugged.

"Postnatal?"

"What?"

"Postnatal depression?"

He blinked, and Marianne smiled wanly.

"Happened to me," she said. "Baby blues magnified a hundredfold. Felt awful for a good three months. Every time Ava cried, I wanted to join in. It's a horrible feeling. And the guilt makes it worse."

"The guilt?"

"Yeah." She pulled a face. "You have a new baby, you're meant to be over the moon and just swimming in love all the time, but all you want to do is cry and sleep. You don't even want to pick her up—well, him—and sometimes you don't even know if you love her—him."

David winced.

"Yeah. Bit of that. Bit of some other stuff too."

Her palm rubbed the cotton over his knee as if trying to erase a stain.

"You seen a doctor?"

"Wouldn't go near a doctor if you paid me," he admitted.

"Yeah, Ryan's a bit like that since the accident. Can't say I blame him. Some of them, urgh."

"All of them."

She shrugged but didn't actually voice any disagreement.

"I just feel stuck," David blurted out. "Talking never helped me. It never has. I need to do something practical. Pragmatic. And I don't want to be stuck on happy pills when what I need is to stop feeling—"

Like a mother who'd given birth.

Like something other than just David.

"Like this."

"Like what?"

He groaned.

"Sorry..."

"Like I'm like you."

It came out harsh and aggressive, a spitting of four words, yet Marianne cocked her head and gave him a look like she'd heard what he meant rather than what he'd said.

"Oh," she said. "Well—you used to be, didn't you?"

He shot her a filthy look.

"When you were young."

"Yes. I did. When I was young. And it was—"

"So what changed it?"

He gestured at his stubble with an incredulous look, and she chuckled.

"Sorry, stupid comment. I meant, was there a tipping point? Or—or some thing, one little thing, that made a huge difference. Something you could maybe do again now?"

There'd been a lot of things. Leaving Salford. Being in the men's group at judo. Shaving his head every six weeks but not his face, to get the scruffy look going. The first time he'd started sweating through his shirt when all of his female colleagues had been complaining it was cold, way back when he'd been just another pockmarked face behind the tills at Tesco paying his way through university.

The first hormone shot.

Christ, that very first shot. It had been like something healed, right then and there, right inside his chest. There'd not even been any side effects for two months, either incidental ones or the ones he was after, but he'd felt so instantly better—

"HRT."

"Are you not on it now?"

"No. Taken off after the car accident to let my liver heal. Was going to go back on but then they found Sam on my blood tests."

Marianne's hand tightened.

"Then do something pragmatic. If your HRT would help, tell the specialist where to stick it. If you're this ill without it, how could having it early possibly be worse?"

David rubbed a hand down the length of his face, and knocked his head back against the door.

"It's different for you," she said. "So why are you asking for this part to be the same?"

David frowned at the ceiling.

He had been, hadn't he? Talking treatments and antidepressants. He'd been listening to the solutions for women. And not listening to himself properly, when he already knew what his solution would be until everything settled down of its own accord.

"Last time I was this bad, it was the HRT that made me better," he croaked.

"Exactly," Marianne said. "So maybe it'll do it again."

He squeezed back.

"I need to make a phone call."

Chapter Thirty-Seven

DAVID'S ENDOCRINOLOGIST WORKED out of York.

That was just the way of the NHS when it came to men like David. If he were diabetic, he'd have been able to pick from a number of specialists all around the area. Wakefield, Leeds, Dewsbury, Barnsley—even Doncaster, if he really wanted. He would have had choices.

But there was only one endocrinologist in the whole of Yorkshire prepared to see men like David. David didn't believe a word of his bullshit that he was the only one with the specialist training, seeing as how he hadn't performed a single test to ensure David was fit to take HRT in the first place all those years ago, and had seen him exactly twice since then, both times instigated by David. And so there were no options left.

David went to York.

Alone.

Ryan didn't like it. At all. They'd had a blazing row the night before, which ended when David threw a glass at the kitchen wall and shouted that if it wasn't York—to sit in a diabetes clinic for hours until he guilted the consultant into seeing him—then it was Leeds, to take a dip in the River Aire. They'd both slept badly after that, and Ryan had seen him off at the door with a sour face.

"Call me when you're done," he said. "And text back for once in your fucking life."

David just got in the taxi without a word.

The anger gave way to guilt at Wakefield Westgate and simmered into regret by the time he reached the hospital. He didn't actually have an appointment. The persistent phone calls that had gone from negotiated persuasion to outright begging resulted in an awkward suggestion of 'coming along and seeing if I have a free spot.' So David had plenty of time to put his feet up in the tiny waiting area of the diabetes and endocrinology unit, and stare at his phone.

He shouldn't have lost his temper.

Ryan had the more explosive temper of the two of them. Or at least the more consistently explosive one. David tended to shut down and walk away. Always had. They rarely had proper blowout arguments because of that. When they rowed, and David got too close to losing his rag, he just walked off. He kept his real temper tantrums for other people.

But maybe, right now, just walking off wasn't the best thing he could do.

David: *I'm sorry.*

He sighed as he sent it. He wanted this to be over. He wanted to be better. He wanted to be himself again.

Ryan (& ICE): *I'm sorry for shouting. But you can't say shit like going to Leeds to jump in the river.*

David: *I know. I just lost my temper.*

Ryan (& ICE): *Are you really that bad?*

David paused. His fingers tightened around the phone case. What if the so-called specialist stuck to his twelve-month guns? What if he said no?

David: *I don't know.*

Ryan (& ICE): *Shit.*

Ryan (& ICE): *We need to sort something out.*

Ryan (& ICE): *You can't just bottle it all up and hope it goes away.*

David: *I know. I've been here before, remember?*

Ryan (& ICE): *That was different. This is different.*

David: *If the doctor says I can have at least gel then things will get better.*

Ryan (& ICE): *How sure are you of that?*

David: *Of what?*

Ryan (& ICE): *That things will get better.*

David: *It did last time.*

David: *And it will.*

David: *It won't be permanent if he at least lets me have the gel. That's what's really scaring me. The idea that maybe I fucked myself up permanently by doing this.*

David: *If I can just get some proof that I'll get better again then maybe it'll help with Sam too.*

David: *I'm good at waiting when I know there's an end somewhere.*

Ryan (& ICE): *I fucking hate this. If he doesn't let you have the gel I'm going to come up there and run him over.*

David: *Good luck, it'll smash up your chair.*

Ryan (& ICE): *I'll get the big fucker out of the summerhouse. The winter one.*

David: *Oh right, going to put snow chains on and then run him over?*

Ryan (& ICE): *That's the idea ;)*

David smiled thinly. The flash of humour was weak and wobbly at best, but at least it was something.

Ryan (& ICE): *I love you.*

His vision fogged.

Ryan (& ICE): *That's all last night was. I love you and I'm terrified. I love every single thing about Sam, and I'm so glad he's here, and I will never breathe a word of this to him as long as I live, but honestly? If I'd known you were going to be this bad, I would have said no. I need you more.*

David swallowed thickly.

Ryan (& ICE): *I have three things I absolutely need in this world, and they're you and Ava and Sam. And one of those three things is drowning and I can't pull him out. So I'm scared. And I'm sorry that I lashed out last night instead of tried to talk about it properly.*

David: *I'm sorry too x*

David scrubbed a hand over his eyes, swearing quietly to himself.

David: *Love you.*

He was poised to say something else—though he wasn't entirely sure what, exactly—when the door opened and an elderly gentleman came shuffling out, being loudly scolded by his wife. As Arthur (as he was apparently named, although pronounced 'Arfah' in a strong southern squawk) tottered off towards the main corridor, Dr Swift pushed his glasses up his nose and blinked at David.

Who was the only patient in the waiting area.

"Time to see me yet?" David asked a little tartly, scrubbing away the last of the tears.

"Oh. Yes. David Neal, wasn't it?" He plainly had no memory of David. "Yes, come in. Yes. You, ah. You were calling last week, weren't you?"

"Persistently," David agreed as he followed Dr Swift into his office.

Dr Swift was someone David needed, not someone he liked or trusted. David was unashamed to say he'd told bald-faced lies to get around Dr Swift's peculiar gatekeeping habits about issuing HRT to his patients. He had no idea why Swift—who regarded anyone trying to transition with deep suspicion and was well known for inappropriate questioning of mental state and decision-making abilities—had bothered to agree to treat trans people in the first place

But if he didn't want to go to London to see someone privately, and pay through the nose for the privilege, then he didn't have much choice.

So David wrenched his face into a polite smile and sat opposite the consultant as if he had all the time in the world.

"You, ah. You had a baby recently, didn't you?"

David struggled to keep a wayward eyebrow from rising in a sardonic manner. "Yes."

"And, ah. How was that?"

"Traumatic. It was awful. It's still awful. I'm really struggling, I'm really sensitive to hormone fluctuations, and I know you said wait a year after the baby's born, and—"

He glanced down at his phone, still clutched in his hand.

"—and last night I broke down in tears in front of my partner and said I was either going to come to York today and at least get some gel or something, or I was going to go to Leeds and jump in the River Aire."

There was a short silence.

Then Dr Swift blinked and began to slowly tap away on the computer.

"I, ah. I see. Uh."

He adjusted his collar. His face was going pink. David watched as, in the cool examination room, a single bead of sweat developed on the doctor's receding hairline and slowly crept down towards his not-so-receding eyebrows.

"HRT literally saved my life," David said. "And I can't wait a year. I can't. So I don't care if it's the same dose as I used to have, I don't care if it's lowered or more infrequent, I don't even care if you want to dial it right down to a low dose and some blockers. I just—I need something. And I can tell you right now that if I walk out of here today without a prescription, then—then there won't be another appointment."

He leaned forward.

Stared.

Used every trick in the emotional manipulation handbook, learned over years and years of battling doctor after doctor to gain every single inch of progress he'd ever made.

"And it'll be on you."

DAVID: *DONE.*

Ryan (& ICE): *How did it go? You on your way home? Which train?*

David: *Walking to the station now. Not sure which one yet, didn't check the times. Plus I need to find a pharmacy.*

Ryan (& ICE): *Success?*

David: *Success :)*

Ryan (& ICE): *Thank god.*

Ryan (& ICE): *Now come home xxx*

Chapter Thirty-Eight

THE FIRST DAY David put the gel on, he cried for the entire half hour it took to sink into his skin and disappear.

Just—stood in the bathroom and cried.

Because crying hadn't been his release since before he'd start T, it only made him feel worse. He finally emerged to find Ryan had set up the living room again, and forced him to stay right there by depositing a drowsy Sam on him.

"Just have a lie-down and cuddle him," Ryan said. "You could do with a kip too, frankly."

His gruff affection grated against David's jagged edges, and he was only prevented from snapping at him by the sleepy snuffles of the baby against his chest.

But the next day, he didn't cry.

And the next, he woke up at nine in the morning, not four, and realised he'd not only not had any nightmares, but he'd slept the whole night through.

He found Ryan on the sofa that morning, in his jogging bottoms and a ratty old T-shirt. He had Sam asleep on one arm, and a book in the other, but he looked up with a smile when David emerged.

"Hey. Feeling a bit better?"

"I slept," David said.

"Like the dead. Didn't so much as twitch when Sam started howling for his four o'clock feed."

The baby was like clockwork. And definitely Ryan's son. He'd got through his first box of formula in the space of a week, despite it promising a fortnight's worth of feedings. And they'd already had to upgrade him to clothes for three-month-olds.

"Did you take him with you when you took Ava to school?"

"Marianne took her to school," Ryan said. "We still have her for the week, but Marianne's offered to ferry her to and fro until you're feeling a bit more like yourself."

David grimaced. "Christ."

"It's fine," Ryan said. "She understands. Well, as much as she can anyway."

David cracked a very faint smile, sinking onto the sofa beside Ryan and leaning into his side. He peered at Sam, but the baby was resolutely asleep and didn't so much as grumble.

"He's going to be impossible to get down for a nap if you keep holding him."

"That's why I'm holding him. He was impossible. I think he wanted you; I wasn't good enough."

A spark of something warm flickered in David's stomach at that, and he blinked.

"What?"

"Surprised?" Ryan asked, setting the book down.

"Well...yeah, a little bit."

"Don't get an ego. He probably just likes the way you pace up and down the nursery with him," Ryan joked, and then his face softened. "He does prefer you when it's bedtime. He likes going places. I can't cuddle him and move around much, so you're clearly preferable."

David tucked his head against Ryan's neck.

"Yeah, well, he's smart," he mumbled through a hoarse throat. "Everyone knows I'm superior to you."

"Yeah, yeah, and everybody else. Smug git."

David chuckled.

"This is nice." Ryan slid an arm carefully around David's back. Sam grumbled at the way his chest moved but didn't wake up. "You feeling a bit brighter today?"

"Little bit."

"Sam's got that hospital appointment tomorrow. You up to it?"

"I think so," David said.

"I didn't think the gel would work that fast," Ryan said in an awed tone, and David snorted.

"I wish. It's psychological."

He knew it was all in his head. The gel was as low a dose as possible without being totally useless. It was a far cry from the massive dose he'd been getting via a needle for the last few years, and the effect wouldn't be nearly as powerful. No leg jitters, no restless energy, and probably no shift from shy upset to assertive belligerence as an emotional response. In medical terms, David knew full well the gel would do very little to counteract the wash of female hormones in his system after giving birth.

But psychologically, it helped. It unquestionably helped. The simple fact that the endocrinologist had listened and changed his mind, rather than dogmatically insisting David wait until Sam was a year old. The tiny act of taking back control of his body in applying the gel every morning. The shift of being able to think of his injections as 'when' instead of 'if.'

He no longer felt quite so stuck, no longer felt quite like it was a permanent derailment.

It was temporary. He would recover. He would be able to return to those years upon years without so much as a glimmer of dysphoria. He would be just David again, just a man.

It might take a while to get there, but for the first time since finding out he was pregnant, David finally believed it would happen.

And it bled over into everything else. He took a deep breath when Sam woke up and cried for a bottle, and relaxed when there was still no emotional response to him. He held him, fed him, burped him, returned to the sofa to watch a crap action film with Ryan, and shuffled up and down by the window until Sam went to sleep and David could put him down in the nursery. He did it all without that gnawing sensation of something being wrong.

He'd get there.

And when he voiced it to Ryan, he was offered a wide smile that made his heart stutter in his chest for a split second.

"There you are," Ryan said, and patted his lap. "Come on. Sit down here while we have an hour before he wakes up again and demands to be held."

David raised his eyebrows.

"Come on, you tart. Sit!"

"My name," he said in a snotty tone, "is David."

Then for the first time in weeks, he smiled, and felt it reach his eyes.

"DAVID?"

Ryan's knuckles were rapping on the bathroom door.

"Just a minute," David called.

"Ava wants to go and see the lights," Ryan said. "Why don't we all go?"

David paused in the act of pulling up his trousers.

The only reason he'd physically left the house since Sam had been born was to see medical staff. That was it. In the four weeks since delivery day, he'd been out of the house exactly three times, and no more. No lunches out, no walks round the park, no picking Ava up from school, nothing. They weren't even going on their traditional Christmas lunch down the pub this year. They were staying home with Sam and having Ava on Boxing Day, as it wasn't their turn.

A prickle of anxiety inched up his spine like cold fingers.

"David?"

He jumped, and zipped up.

"Sorry. Hang on."

He unlocked the door before turning to wash his hands, and Ryan cracked it open. His face was carefully blank when David glanced over his shoulder, and David had the distinct sense there was a right and a wrong answer to Ryan's suggestion.

"It's traditional," he said. "And it's snowing. Sam might like the snow."

"Your chair won't," David said.

"It's not that bad if we go now."

Go out. David swallowed. Just go for a walk. It wasn't far. 'The lights' was a street of houses about a half mile away that always had a ridiculously lavish Christmas display. The neighbours either all loved it and joined in, or it was some weird middle-class passive-aggressive thing. David usually walked round for his pre-Christmas shot just to go past the lights and have a look at what insanity they'd shoved up on their roofs this time.

Ava loved it.

And he could push the pram.

They'd never taken the pram out. It sat in the hall, unused. Ryan couldn't push himself and the pram at the same time, and David had only been out with the baby in a taxi, directly there and back.

Ryan was just looking at him—

"Okay."

Ryan smiled. David's heart hiccuped. When Ryan beckoned, he leaned down almost drunkenly, and felt the kiss from very far away.

"Come on, then. Little Miss is already hyped up."

"Let me—let me get changed."

He changed slowly. His heavy jeans for winter weather barely fit, his stomach twinging uncomfortably as he buttoned them. His jumpers felt soft and neglected from weeks of being unwanted. He tucked his nose into the collar of a particularly fluffy monstrosity and selected it for the smell of home. His hair needed shaving again, and properly. Ryan had been doing it with the clippers, but maybe it was time David went to the barber. Could get a hot towel shave too. Really do himself over.

Slowly, the grip around his spine relaxed.

His boots were in the back of the cupboard, and he had to get Ryan to do the laces, still unable to quite bend all the way. Ava laughed at him, hanging off the living room door and cackling like a banshee, and David found himself grumbling back at her, snottily saying he could at least do up his shirt with all the right buttons unlike her attempts with her school dress every summer.

"Want to pop Sam in the pram?" Ryan asked, patting the booted foot until David put it down again. "I'll wrestle this one into her coat."

"Don't need a coat!" she sang as David ducked past her into the living room.

Sam was stretched out on the sofa, boxed in by cushions and staring in endless fascination at the lights on the Christmas tree. He was four weeks old, and the size of the average four-month-old.

"Monster baby," David commented as he awkwardly stooped to lift him. Sam's gaze jerked away from the lights, and he crowed happily at the sight of his father.

And David—stopped.

Just stopped, holding his son's head in the palm of his hand.

"Hello," he whispered.

Two huge brown eyes stared balefully up at him, the familiar mouth twisted up in a grumpy expression as David failed to complete the lifting motion and turn it into Sam's favourite activity, a cuddle—

Something stopped in his chest.

David blinked.

Then the spell was broken by the loud wail, all four limbs curling up over Sam's torso before he began to flail, and David jumped. He let out a breath and cradled him to his chest.

"Okay," he said on autopilot, patting an empty nappy and deciding it was just the absent cuddle that had caused the explosion. "All right, let's—let's have none of that, shall we? We're going to see the snow and the Christmas lights. You'll like Christmas lights..."

The weight on his shoulder felt different somehow. He pressed his nose into the soft cotton-clad shoulder without quite knowing why, and inhaled deeply. As he shuffled into the hall, the crying slowly dialling down again, David was struck with the strangest sensation of handling an entirely different baby than the one he'd brought home from the hospital.

Things felt...different.

He frowned at the pram and Ryan persuading Ava into her coat, rocking on the spot automatically. He felt hyperaware. The crackle of his skin against Sam's. The heavy weight. The anticipation of his squirms and wriggles as David bounced him gently.

His heart was beating impossibly hard in his chest, yet he felt grounded and secure. There was no catching in his lungs or spots in his vision. And he found himself turning his back on the commotion and walking back into the living room, rather than putting the baby down in the pram and being done with it.

Instead, he sank down into the softness of the sofa and stared down at his son in disbelief.

His son.

Brown eyes regarded him keenly. A tiny fist curled into the sleeve of his jumper. A tiny dusting of hair was growing through, deep brown like David's rather than jet black like Ryan's. He'd have frizz, not curls. Like his dad. David sank a little further into the cushions—and smiled.

Smiled when he felt something warm creeping outwards from his rapidly beating heart. It was like being flooded with hot water, deep under his skin. The smile stretched wider as he slowly stroked his thumb over Sam's hip, and patted the empty nappy lightly with his fingers.

Oh, God.

The tears blurred his vision, and he sniffed noisily, unable to detach a hand from the baby long enough to wipe at his face. Christ, it had happened. Nadia had been right. The first sob hurt, like unlocking thirty-two years of pain via his chest. It grated like a key in a rusty lock, and he bowed his head over the blissfully unaware baby as the second followed.

When the first warm touch smoothed over his skin, he didn't even question it. He just leaned, baby and all, into Ryan's hold, and cried.

"There you go," Ryan murmured, lips brushing against his scalp. "About time."

It was like a boil being lanced. Fear, anger, hatred, loathing, pain, doubt—they drained out of him, leaking down his face in ugly rivers, and he did nothing to stop it. He just rested his head against the cushions, against Ryan, and let it all crash over him in a great wave.

And afterwards, as the storm passed, a gentler tide crept in to smooth down the edges. Relief. Happiness. Joy. A sense of having reached the end of a very long journey, or seeing the light at the end of a tunnel that had been going on for his entire life.

Sam chirped, squirmed, and began to hiccup.

David blinked through the fog and lifted Sam up to his shoulder. He pressed his nose to the baby's head, closing his eyes against more tears, and leaned further into Ryan's arms as their son snuffled sleepily between them, warm and heavy and content. Hands locked around his waist, securing him in Ryan's hold. One arm around his back, one around his front, and his entire heart and soul caught between them. And their baby on his shoulder, nuzzling his head against David's as he hiccuped peaceably.

Perfect.

"He's perfect," David croaked.

"Yes."

"This is perfect."

"Yes."

It wasn't the end. It was the beginning. It was starting all over again and would unfold in ways David couldn't even imagine. But—

"We got this."

Ryan squeezed. The baby squeaked. And the kiss that made its way past Sam to David's ear was twisted by a smile.

"Yeah. You got this."

Epilogue

"THANK YOU," DAVID said. "Yes. I'll check my diary and make an appointment. Yes. Thank you. Goodbye."

He hung up, rolling his eyes before sending a text to Ryan, and then tossed the phone over onto the empty passenger seat and put the car into gear.

David: Kitchen fitter cancelled. Bollocks to this, we're going to Wickes.

Thankfully, the phone call had happened just around the corner from his usual parking spot. He was running late. He'd thought medical research would be less prone to late finishes than veterinary surgery, but he'd been very wrong. Sliding the car into a free space, he bent forward to peer out of the windscreen down the road. It was the first time they'd tried this, and David couldn't deny he wasn't exactly sold on the wisdom of the idea—even though it had been his idea in the first place. He raked a deep breath in, held it for a count of ten, and let it out slowly.

All right.

It would be fine.

He straightened up, squared his shoulders, and got out.

David never bothered trying to park right near the school. It was always a melee of mums and Mitsubishis, and he was terrified of someone's kid running into the road right under his bumper. It was cool outside, threatening rain. The short walk helped him clear the unease out of his head and refocus. Everything would be fine, all happy and normal, no problems whatsoever, nothing. Ava was sensible. Sam was a good kid.

It'd be fine.

He could see the sea of white mums at the very end of the road—but then a smile broke out over his face as he saw two familiar figures sitting on the wall outside the newsagents, two sets of eyes scanning the road for him. Waiting exactly where he'd told them to wait. Ava's first day of secondary school hadn't gone to her head after all.

He waved, and the eyes lit up.

"Daddy!"

Ava's hand lashed out before Sam could so much as jump down off the wall, and caught his hood in a fist.

"The road!" she scolded, and David jogged across it to catch Sam up in his arms and toss him above his head.

"So, how was your first day, little man?"

"Awesome! I made a picture and I got my own hook and Josh is in my class and—"

He rambled on and on, a mile a minute, chattering away like he would explode if he couldn't relay the entire day's incredible events in a single breath. He clung when David tried to set him down, whining, and David raised his eyebrows.

"Only babies need carrying during the daytime," David said. "You're not a baby anymore, are you?"

It had been an infallible obedience tool ever since his school uniform had arrived. He let go with a sulky expression, identical to the one his sister used to deliver in response to the same remark, and jammed his sticky hand into David's.

"How about you, Ava?"

She shrugged. "It was okay."

Everything was okay now. Ava was 'nearly twelve!' and ever since leaving primary school at the beginning of the summer, had been shrugging and saying things were okay to cover the entire range between awful and amazing.

"Can we have pizza?" Sam asked as they crossed the road and turned the corner to head for the car. In time, David would work them up to Ava collecting Sam and bringing him all the way to the car on her own. But for the first few weeks, the newsagents it was.

"We'll ask Daddy."

"Daddy never says yes to pizza," Sam said mournfully, in the same tone of voice one might use to say someone had died.

"Daddy doesn't eat pizza," David corrected. "That doesn't mean we can't have pizza sometimes."

"Can today be sometimes?"

"That's what we'll ask Daddy."

He was in a good mood, and David let it wash over him. Sam had been demanding to go to school since he was two and a half, desperate to join in on Ava's fun. He'd played more dress-up with her school skirts than with actual dress-up costumes. At least his first day seemed to have lived up to expectations.

As he scrambled up into the back, lost the argument about the booster seat, and insisted on doing his own seatbelt, Ava waited patiently by the car with a hopeful look on her face.

"So," she said when David turned to her. "I did what you asked."

"You did."

"He didn't run off or get squashed or anything."

"That's good."

"So...are you going to talk to Dad about cadets?"

Ava wanted to join the army cadets. Marianne wasn't keen—the military was well below her ambitions for her only child. Ryan was even less keen—the military was full of racists, in his mind, and he didn't want his little angel exposed to that. But Ava had her heart set, and there'd been many bawling arguments over the last six months about letting her join when she turned twelve.

So David had come up with a plan.

"If she can prove that she's responsible this summer, then why not let her?" he'd suggested. "If she's old enough to do all her chores and walk Sam back from school, then she's old enough to try cadets."

Ryan still hadn't liked it, but he'd agreed.

David cocked his head.

"Please?" she whined. "I'll wait with Sam every Monday and Wednesday! And I've been good with my new phone!"

David eyed the back seat. Sam had buckled himself in, fished one of his comic books out of the back pocket of the passenger seat, and was giving one of the villains a sufficiently evil-looking moustache. It looked suspiciously liked Pamela's next door.

"Come on, Dad! Please!"

David raised his eyebrows.

"You *have* been good," he agreed. "And you did a good job with Sam this evening..."

Her face turned mutinous—then lit up when he snapped off a salute.

"We agreed last night. We're going to pop over next week to see them."

"Really?"

"Yep. So if you keep proving you're mature enough to give it a go, you can start after you turn twelve."

She shrieked and launched, seizing him around the middle to hug him tightly, and David laughed. Warmth burned through his blood, and he squeezed her back tightly before letting go.

"Come on, kid. You can sit up front today. And—" He leaned close to whisper in her ear. "—we'll blame Sam for making us get pizza."

Ryan would be home by the time they got there. David would drive the whole way to the background noise of a five-year-old telling him about how rainbows were made, and an eleven-year-old insisting she would simply die if she didn't have the same bag as all her friends. There would be a fifty-five-year-old on the radio chirping about hits as if he were young, and David could hand both kids off to Ryan just long enough to order pizzas without being caught, then feign total innocence and pretend Sam must have gotten into the Just Eat app on Ryan's phone again.

"Dad, you're not listening!"

"Daddy, Daddy, look at this, look!"

He smiled.

Then told them both to knock it off.

Because he was a father, and that was his job.

About the Author

Matthew J. Metzger is an ace, trans author posing as a functional human being in the wilds of Yorkshire, England. Although mainly a writer of contemporary, working-class romance, he also strays into fantasy when the mood strikes. Whatever the genre, the focus is inevitably on queer characters and their relationships, be they familial, platonic, sexual, or romantic.

When not crunching numbers at his day job, or writing books by night, Matthew can be found tweeting from the gym, being used as a pillow by his cat, or trying to keep his website in some semblance of order.

Email: mattmetzger@hotmail.co.uk

Facebook: www.facebook.com/mattjmetzger

Twitter: @MatthewJMetzger

Website: www.matthewjmetzger.com

Other books by this author

Walking on Water
Big Man
Life Underwater

Coming Soon from
Matthew J. Metzger

Tea

John only went into the cafe to have a brew and wait out the storm. He didn't expect to find love at the same time.

And it really is love at first sight. Chris is like nobody John's ever known, and John is caught from the start. All he wants, from that very first touch, is to never let go. But John is badly burned from his last relationship and in no fit state to try again. When Chris asks him out, he ought to say no.

But what if he says yes instead?

Also Available from NineStar Press

Connect with NineStar Press

Website: NineStarPress.com

Facebook: NineStarPress

Facebook Reader Group: NineStarNiche

Twitter: @ninestarpress

Tumblr: NineStarPress

9 781949 909180